Uroboros Saga

BOOK SIX

By Arthur Walker

Cover artwork "Gorshteyn Helmet, Replicate" by Arthur Walker
as arranged by Red Couch Creative, Inc.

For Evan, Tina, and all my readers.

Get updates on my books by following me on Twitter.

@arthurhwalker

I laugh at those who think they can damage me. They do not know who I am, they do not know what I think, they cannot even touch the things which are really mine and with which I live.

~Epictetus

CHAPTER 1

WINTER CAMP, NORTHERN RUSSIA

[Archeological Record Redacted]

ROUGHLY 6000 BCE

Bogumil wiped the frost from the luminescent object, white light faintly radiating upward from the snow drift. The glacial formation ahead carried that illumination almost to the stars, the gathering of hunters taking a step back. It hummed as well, making a sort of sound none of them had heard before. It seethed beneath them, making the gently falling snow waver in the gloom of the evening.

They stood in awe of the power of it, ancient trees laid low for miles around from the impact. Stars had fallen before, but nothing survived the fire of the sky that was so large, so seemingly intact. While most of it was obscured by the fallen ice of the glacial formation, the furrow cut in the ground was suggestive of its size.

For several moments, they just stood around, taking the new sensations in, long hair hanging about their faces, beards frozen from their own breath. It wasn't as cold here as it should have been, like the ground was still cooling from the impact. Each hunter had their own role, their own place in the party, but they stood shoulder to shoulder out of their usual marching order to gaze upon the sight.

"What is it?" Svetovid asked, standing protectively in front of the younger hunters.

"It feels like rock, or a precious stone from the earth. But, it breathes, and... there is a woman inside," Bogumil reported, beckoning for his son to come over.

Ouroboru complied, stepping through the snow to gaze down at the partially obscured object. It was a Goddess. The boy needed none of his strange seizures to know her for what she was. They had watched her fall from the sky from so many miles away, and traveled all night to find her.

"She's in the belly of this great beast, trapped in there," Ouroboru whispered, gesturing to the blackened six-fingered hands pressing out from within.

"We should leave it here, where we found it, maybe even cover it over with earth," Kaspr ventured, his voice quivering with fear.

Bogumil closed his eyes, pausing to think, his hand on his young son's shoulder. Svetovid simply stood vigil, casting a side-eyed glare at Kaspr. Archedesque stood back with the rest of the hunters, curling his black moustache with two fingers, while cradling a saw-styled microlith blade in the other. There were murmurs and quiet prayers from the gathered hunters while they waited for their leader to decide.

"We should kill the beast and whatever is inside it," one of the hunters said, hefting a heavy cudgel.

"Ouroboru, what would you say needs to be done?" Bogumil asked, already grooming the young boy to one day take his place.

"This woman, she needs our help. We should try to get her out, without harming the beast too much. I think... it is something we do not want to awaken," Ouroboru said, placing a small hand on the stony exterior of the beast.

"Archedesque, you are our best butcher. Cut this woman free doing as little harm to the beast as you can," Bogumil replied.

The huge hunter complied, hefting his microlith blade and striding forward. He brushed his long black hair back from his eyes, set his mouth just so, and began to cut. The tribe had largely come to accept that Ouroboru was much like his father, and had a mind for solving problems. A few of the hunters looked on with unease, but most readily accepted the course of action without question.

After several tense moments, Archedesque reached into the beast, and withdrew the glistening woman from within. She was tall and slender, muscles like hard rope beneath her black reptilian skin. She was heavy like a bear, far warmer than a human, her radiance making the frost across Archedesque's hide coat melt. She stirred, her eyes opening for a moment, flooding the big hunter's face with a strange light.

Archedesque smiled. "A Goddess, and a killer is she. The beast did not resist, parting at my blade easily, almost offering her up."

If Archedesque had cut a wound in the side of the beast, it was gone now, the stony exterior whole before he even stepped aside. The congregation stared at the sleek creature in Archedesque's broad arms, a mix of awe and terror awash over their faces. Bogumil took the woman's six fingered hand, almost cutting himself on her razor sharp talons. She stirred, turning her glowing eyes upward toward the stars.

"Should we kill the beast?" Kaspr asked, pointing down at the snow, and looking to Bogumil.

Bogumil turned to his son, wondering if he'd reached the similar conclusion to his own.

Ouroboru knelt down, placing a hand on the exposed crystalline structure jutting upward out of the ice. "No, it isn't a beast. It is perhaps her steed. It did not devour her, it carried her from the stars, and from the heavens, to us."

Svetovid and a handful of the other hunters looked disappointed at that revelation, but nodded somberly in response. They all wished they could say they'd slain a beast so large. Archedesque walked down to the snow once more, turning the Goddess over in his arms to make her easier to carry. Bogumil gestured for the others to bring the game sled so she could be more easily transported.

"What is it, Archie?" Bogumil asked, taking notice of his friend's puzzled expression.

"Bogu, can a Goddess be with child, and walk our earthly world?" Archedesque whispered, not wanting the others to think him foolish.

"I do not know. We will have to ask the Priestess. We know not which Goddess this is," Bogumil replied, mirroring Archedesque's puzzled expression.

"You think she is with child?" Ouroboru asked, quietly.

"Children," Archedesque replied, gazing at this hands, the lingering sensation of contact with Goddess still making his fingers tingle.

Bogumil looked at the two bulges to either side of the Goddess's sleek belly, taking notice of how they undulated in the moonlight. He reached out to touch her, but she grabbed his wrist, holding it fast like she was made of the hardest stone. Bogumil held up his other hand, trying to show he meant no harm. Her eyes flicked to Ouroboru, and then to Bogumil.

"This is my son," Bogumil stated, his voice unwavering.

She pressed Bogumil's hand to her side, letting him feel what he assumed to be hundreds of tiny Godlings inside. They wriggled and strained against her armored flesh, causing her obvious discomfort. The hunting party made their preparations to depart while Ouroboru sat beside the Goddess.

"You are not truly a Goddess, are you?" Ouroboru whispered.

She regarded the boy with her sleek, almost featureless face, her eyes betraying no specific emotion. Ouroboru could read people pretty well, but this woman was a mystery to him. Her otherworldly nature obscured everything his keen powers of observation would usually pick up. He wondered if his father knew of her nature, and would explain later.

They took the Goddess to their winter camp, moving quickly to the cave where their Priestess dwelled. The encounter would be one Bogumil would live to regret. Drusael cried out, declaring the Goddess they'd found to be an evil spirit. She rushed the game sled, flint axe in hand, before anyone could stop her. The Goddess stood, lithely turning the hardest part of her shoulder into the blow before nearly clawing the priestess in half with a single stroke of her hand.

"Peace!" Bogumil cried out, ordering the hunters to lower their weapons.

The blackened creature, now slick with blood turned a blank expression toward the congregation. By now, other members of the tribe had awoken from their beds and come into the cave, blocking the entrance. It looked as though there would be a vicious melee, but Kaspr strode forward, placed his cudgel on the stone floor of the cave, and prostrated himself before what he believed to be a Goddess.

"Forgive us! Be appeased, and slay no more of us!" Kaspr pleaded.

She turned, gazing down at the priestess she had slain, a strange and otherworldly emotion crossing her face. Her gaze then turned to Kaspr, and several others who chose to lay prostrate on the ground before her. Ouroboru looked on, paralyzed by fear of a Goddess angry enough to destroy someone.

"She killed Drusael, our speaker, our spirit mender and guide. How do we let this stand?" Svetovid asked, taking Bogumil by the arm.

Bogumil shook the shock of the moment from his mind, rubbing his eyes.

"Do you understand us? Do our voices and words convey any meaning to one such as you?" Bogumil asked.

She nodded, flicking blood from her clawed hand in one smooth motion. A chill ran the length of Bogumil's spine, with nearly the whole of the tribe having gathered in the cave by then. He pushed Ouroboru back behind him, wondering if he'd made a terrible mistake.

"Are you a Goddess?" Bogumil asked.

She shook her head slowly, her eyes turning to gaze at the markings they'd made on the cave wall. She ran her finger over a field depicting elk to the stars painted above it. She added a few stars of her own in red, then pointed to one of them. Bogumil nodded.

"But, you are from the heavens?" he asked.

She nodded, frustrated at the artistic liberties taken with the star field on the cave wall.

"Are you an evil spirit?"

She shook her head.

"Do you need our help, as my son has suggested?"

She nodded, inscribing a series of sharp looking glyphs on the wall above the stars with a clawed finger. She pointed at them for emphasis, drawing her bloodied hand across them, the stars, and the field of elk below drowning it all in crimson. She pointed around to the tribe in a wide arc, and then to the fallen priestess.

"More like her are coming, to kill us all. To kill everything," Ouroboru said, eyes wide.

She nodded, pointing to the boy.

"So you need our help, and we need yours." Bogumil stated, looking to the rest of the tribe.

She nodded, gesturing to where her children were held, barely contained at her sides.

"Because you are with child, you are hunted?" Ouroboru asked, trying to understand.

She nodded turning her bloody knuckles to the cave painting, running them across to in wide arc around the cave field of elk. She banged her heavy fist on the stone, her head drifting back and forth as though she were dizzy. Archedesque rushed forward to help steady her, wrapping a broad arm up under her arms.

"She needs us to fight a war," Svetovid said, patting the bicep on the arm he used to wield a weapon.

"What do we call you?" Kaspr asked.

She just stared at Kaspr, eyes unwavering.

"She is like Zvezda, our guardian star. We could call her Zvezda," Archedesque suggested.

"Zvezda it is, for now," Bogumil said, bowing his head.

The tribe departed the cave, leaving only Svetovid behind at the entrance to stand watch. Zvezda gave birth to her children that very night, their tiny slumbering forms occupying the hot springs in the deepest reaches of the cave. She lurked in the shadows of the cave for weeks, keeping anyone who tried to approach the springs at bay. As the tribe began to grow uneasy with their guest, Bogumil, Archedesque, Svetovid, and Kaspr descended with the rest of the hunting party to speak of terms of assistance.

When they returned, they did so with grave expressions, retiring to the hunters lodge to discuss what they'd learned privately. It was a rare gathering Ouroboru wasn't allowed to attend, and this was one such occasion. Even listening from just outside the timbers of the lodge, all he could hear were the low whispers of his father and his closest allies.

"Am I understanding Zvezda's wishes correctly?" Kaspr asked.

"She has done her best without using words. She wants us to safeguard our tribe, and her children. This task will take more time than we have breath to take in this world. She will bind our tribe to the task, her children granting us long life, strength, and the means to hunt those who hunt her," Bogumil explained, rubbing tired eyes.

"What if we just kill her, and her brood? Will they not come here?" Svetovid asked.

"Nay, I think her kin were coming anyway. It is why she chose to come here," Archedesque said, grinning broadly.

"It feels as though we've no choice," Svetovid growled.

"We've always got a choice. But, we've always known that eventually the hound would break his tether, and cast down the stars," Bogumil stated.

"The sisters exist to prevent that. I don't think it is a coincidence we've named our own Goddess after one of them," Kaspr stated, pointing a finger at Bogumil.

"Do they? Or do they just watch the hound until the appointed time? Our Priestess would know, if she were not dead," Archedesque countered, placing a hand on Bogumil's shoulder.

They were all silent for a moment, the other hunters talking quietly amongst themselves. Dusana, Svetovid's wife stepped into the lodge, stirring anger in the hunting party for the intrusion. She beckoned to Svetovid, casting a nervous glance toward Bogumil.

"Throw her out!" one of the hunters bellowed.

"Throw yourself out," Svetovid replied, stepping away from the campfire to talk to his wife.

"Yes, what is it?" Bogumil asked, gently.

"Parvan took his cudgel, and followed the Goddess into the woods. Ouroboru has gone to the cave alone," Svetovid said, worriedly.

"Parvan and Drusael, they were not so secret lovers," Archedesque remarked with a nervous chuckle.

"Archedesque, find that fool, Parvan. Everyone else, stay here. I will handle this," Bogumil said, walking out of the lodge without cloak or weapon.

Bogumil moved quickly, descending to the cave entrance, only pausing to light a torch. He saw no light ahead, but knew his son had likely memorized every turn and twist of the cave. Bogumil ran with haste, moving through the underground network of tunnels as quickly as he could. The tunnel walls were covered with freshly carved symbols that had a strange uniformity, but Bogumil couldn't fathom their purpose.

He rounded the last corner to the chamber that housed the hot springs to see Ouroboru lingering near the edge, faint green light radiating upward from the water. Bogumil turned, hearing something behind him, but all he could see was darkness. Looking back, he could see Ouroboru was laying on his back, covered with steaming water. Panic took Bogumil, making him abandon caution and run where his son lay.

Zvezda appeared a moment later, a freshly killed elk under one of her powerful arms. She gave a keening screech and rushed forward. Bogumil thought he was going to die, but the Goddess knelt down beside him, turning over Ouroboru's arms. Something writhed just beneath the skin, vanishing into his flesh leaving no mark behind. Ouroboru began to seize, his limbs shaking while his eyes opened and rolled into the back of his head.

Bogumil held his son and wept, looking up at Zvezda angrily. She held out her hands for the boy, frantically gesturing for Bogumil to pass him to her. The hardened hunter closed his eyes, shaking his head, his mind unable to process what was happening. Zvezda knocked him aside, grabbing Ouroboru from his grasp, an arc of bioelectric shock leaping from her limbs to the boy, each stroke calming him down until he was still.

Bogumil rose, fists clenched. Zvezda placed Ouroboru on the ground, the boy regaining his feet on his own. He stared at his own small hands, then past his fingers to his father.

"I know what we must do," Ouroboru stated, letting his hands fall to his side.

Bogumil rushed to embrace his son. "I was afraid for you."

"We must be afraid for us all. We will not be the first, or the only tribe to stand against evil, but we may be the last," Ouroboru explained, hugging his father.

"You were listening at the lodge?" Bogumil asked.

"Yes."

"Why us?" Bogumil asked, directing his question to Zvezda.

She cocked her head to one side, her eyes narrowing slightly. She gazed back at the pool, her brood like a scorched school of fish swimming together just below the surface of the water. Bogumil understood her in that moment. Even if he couldn't see all the forces behind her intent, he understood her.

"For us to bear and raise children is normal. To have families is just how we are. You want your own children to learn these things," Bogumil whispered, hugging his son.

Zvezda paused, considering his words, then nodded slightly.

"Ha, you had not considered such a thing, did you? What sort of beasts are you that does not know such things?" Bogumil asked.

Zvezda did not react to the statement, her cold expression frozen across her nearly featureless face. Her eyes darted upward, toward Svetovid and a host of other hunters, each carrying a cudgel or microlith blade. Bogumil stood, turning to face them, his hand grasping Ouroboru's.

"You were gone too long, we had to come check on you," Svetovid said.

"Ouroboru has accepted Zvezda's contract. Does this boy have more courage than we? Will my son stand against the evil threatening our tribe alone?" Bogumil asked.

Each hunter would make their own choice that very night.

A mile away, Archedesque pushed against deep snow with each step he took. Parvan had a head start, but he was thin and willowy, forcing him to pause and rest. The night promised to only get colder, but Archedesque cared not, his perpetual smile shining beneath fierce eyes that only blinked against the snow.

In the distance, he could see two figures standing at the rise, their forms contrasted against the night sky. He quickened his pace, certain the fool was about to try and cudgel the Goddess, but found Drusael and Parvan standing there instead, an arm's length from one another. Parvan was transfixed, his mouth agape, while Drusael stood their serene, seemingly immune to the cold.

"Parvan? You all right?" Archedesque asked, coming up and clapping him on the back.

"I watched her die," Parvan replied.

"A Goddess walks among us, and you question that spirits might wander in with her?" Archedesque replied, laughing nervously.

Parvan reached out, taking hold of Drusael's arm. She smiled, putting her own hand on his, and nodding to Archedesque. Archedesque reached out putting a hand on her shoulder as well, eliciting a baffled expression from her.

"What is it? You're all acting very strange," Drusael said, batting Archedesque's unwanted touch aside.

"You died, we all saw you die, cut down by the Goddess," Parvan said, blinking his eyes.

"She didn't understand how fragile we are, not until after she'd struck me. Her people are stronger than ours, and she did not intend to kill me," Drusael explained.

"You said she was an evil spirit. Are you one now?" Archedesque asked, hand on his microlith blade.

"Stay away from her!" Parvan growled, trying to shove Archedesque away.

"Okay," Archedesque laughed, knocking Parvan unconscious with a backhanded blow to the right temple.

Drusael took a step back, suddenly very afraid.

"Coming?" Archedesque asked, hefting Parvan's unconscious form across his shoulders.

"You aren't going to kill me?" Drusael asked.

"Bogumil asked me to get Parvan. Now, I have him. You can stay here, or walk back with me, I do not care," Archedesque replied, smiling broadly.

"Why do you not have a woman?" Drusael asked, drawing close to the big hunter.

"Who says I don't?" Archedesque asked, his smile fading.

"Parvan, he is good company, but you are strong, and loyal to Bogumil," Drusael said, turning her head to the side and leaning against Archedesque.

Archedesque sighed, and nodded as he listened to her. Drusael slid her hands up his chest, her breath blowing sweetly up into his face. She smelled like the herbs she used for rituals, and the forest around them. Her touch was intoxicating. She was selected to be the priestess for her beauty, the elders believing she would be a more pleasing representative for the tribe with the Gods.

Archedesque smiled, taking a moment to look at the stars, shaking his head. He took a quick step backward, letting Parvan drop into a snow drift before rocking forward with a powerful punch, catching Drusael in the midsection. She gasped for air, dropping to her knees, a look of shocked surprise marring her expression.

She recovered quickly, leaping on Archedesque with preternatural speed and strength, taking the big hunter down to the ground. They scuffled, trading savage blows. Archedesque managed to disengage, a bloody gash over one eye half blinding him. She moved in again, pushing Archedesque backwards. He slid his foot back to steady himself, but tripped over Parvan's unconscious form. By the time he was able to right himself, Drusael was gone.

"What have we done?" Archedesque said aloud, laughing at Parvan's unconscious form.

He returned to the village a short while later, many concerned faces to greet him as he entered the hunters lodge. Bogumil looked at the bruised Parvan, then turned a questioning gaze to Archedesque. The big hunter just shrugged, smiling broadly.

"Was this really needed, Archie?" Bogumil asked.

"He was not right of mind, and Drusael was there. Things got out of control."

"Drusael?" Kaspr asked.

"Yes, she is somehow not dead. The elders bickering about who to replace her was ... fortunate, yes?" Archedesque said, laughing.

"Zvezda... she must have breathed life back into her, but how?" Svetovid asked.

Archedesque stopped, pondering the question for a moment, then shrugged.

"Did you find them roughly along the same path one would take to the slumbering beast?" Bogumil asked.

"Oh, yes. Yes I did. We were still far, but they were in that direction, near the rise," Archedesque replied.

"You think she used the beast to heal Drusael? Why would she do that?" Svetovid asked.

"Because, in spite of her fierce appearance, she possesses some compassion," Bogumil concluded. "What was Drusael like, and where is she?"

"She was… like herself, I suppose. I think she needed to stay out there for some reason," Archedesque stammered, lowering his eyes.

Bogumil regarded Archedesque skeptically, looking at the bloody gash over his eye.

"She was strange, we fought, she ran away," Archedesque whispered, as quickly as he could.

"Archie, what did you do?" Bogumil asked.

"I will find her. Bring her back," Archedesque muttered, folding his arms.

"No, no one leaves camp tonight. We're all going to the springs in the cave. Anyone that wants to walk away, should go now, and not return," Bogumil said, walking hand in hand with Ouroboru.

CHAPTER 2

COLLECTOR'S MARKET, MIDTOWN, PORT MONTAIGNE

6:47 AM May 12th, 2200

Kale's Private Records, Part 7 –

I awoke to the sound of Brook doing laundry. The city was rationing water because of the recent bombings. Water treatment plants and infrastructure were damaged, so one had to resort to a scrub tub and air dry to get things clean. I was just glad there was power so I could at least iron a pair of slacks.

"You don't have to do that," I said, gesturing to my shirts in the scrub tub.

"It's like being at home. I am a little homesick," Brook admitted, continuing to wash the clothes.

"Hopefully, enough of the water utility work will be complete by the end of the week, that it won't be necessary," I said, checking Brook's data slate for reports.

"They can take their time for all I care. Breakfast is over on the table."

Our place was small, but well-built and fairly anonymous. Previous to the Shutdown, homes and townhomes were being built for lower income folks. I'd managed to oversee the completion of many of them, to welcome new workers and refugees from abroad. We had many neighbors, most surprised to see Brook and me.

We'd gained some fame over the old standard grid, videos of us fighting with Kaspersky in midtown having circulated widely. I was seen as a leader who led from the front, taking the same risk as the rank and file workers of the city. I detested the attention, but it seemed to help morale.

"There's a basket outside again. Green beans grown in someone's garden," Brook said, opening the front door.

"Perfidy says he knows who is doing it, but he refuses to tell me," I grumbled, frowning at the fresh vegetables.

"I know who it is, too. Their scent lingers on the basket," Brook said, pushing it back outside.

"Augh."

Brook giggled, putting the beans into our ancient refrigerator. She gathered our lunches for the day, before scooping up all the rest of her things to take back to the office. I think to most people, nothing she did could give a moment any normalcy because of how she looked, and the fact that she was a Drone, genetically engineered for labor and special tasks. I'd ceased seeing her that way ever since she tended to me while I lay injured in Matthias' workshop months ago. The last couple of weeks would be the second time she watched over me while I recovered from being hurt. It would not be the last.

"It will be Heavy Dub today, Perfidy is working one of the larger food shipments to Africa. I think he's going to try and check on Royo while he is there."

I bristled at the mere mention of my brother, harboring a silent hope that he wouldn't disappoint Brook. I washed myself in the basin, taking notice of how long my hair had gotten. I'd let everything be secondary in the last couple of weeks, just trying to recover. I hoped the next time we encountered Kaspersky, it would be on my terms.

"Any luck finding the collector's market?" I asked.

Brook laced up her shoes and shook her head. "I've asked my tribe to look and listen, but there's only so much I can do there. Annabelle seems to dislike it when I come around now."

"I'm sorry."

"I know how it feels from both sides. Whenever Ezra would come back, I'd be really envious of all the new things he'd find up above. He'd have stories, a new mobile, fancy clothes, and friends that weren't Drones. Annabelle and the others can't go above, still adhering to the Factory's original edicts."

"I've never understood that, most of them must have traveled, as you did, from the factory to the underground for work. They should know they can persist above ground," I said, picking out a tie.

"I... don't know. Ezra seemed to indicate that the way I was brought to the Tribehome was special, and that not many of the others arrived that way. He came to greet me alone. I never thought to ask how everyone got down there, or why they were with the Elders as opposed to the Sodality."

"Brook, all that time down there, and it never came up?"

"There was always work to do, food to prepare, and things to clean. When things started getting bad above ground there were people trying to encroach on our home. It seems odd to me now, but it was as though there was never any time. I always got to my pipe for sleep, and woke to the next daily task."

"That would explain why you never seem to stop moving, unless you're asleep. You just about ran a rut in the floor in here while I was healing up."

"Sorry about that. I'm worried for everyone that went overseas to deal with the Cabal. It all seems pretty bad, and everyone is staying off the radio to keep safe. It used to be we could all conference call via Taylor's phone, but Silverstein isn't sure that even she can keep the signal encrypted against Cabal intrusion."

"He's paranoid, but maybe with good reason. Taylor, like Jennifer, has passive abilities she doesn't completely understand. She doesn't speak the machine language and understand them like Matthias," I said, using a rag to rub polish on the tips of my worn dress shoes.

"I don't know how I do what I do, resist Kaspersky's amnestic abilities and so forth, you trust me to do what I like. Why doesn't Silverstein trust Taylor to do what she wants?" Brook asked, sounding uncharacteristically annoyed.

"Is that how you see it?" I asked, not having considered the disparity before.

"Yes."

"I'm assuming it is Silverstein making that decision, but it might be Taylor."

"Really?"

I sighed. "I don't know."

Brook made a face. It was one of her Drone faces that was a mix of emotions people don't usually have. I must have had a stunned expression, because she blushed, covering her face. Brook was changing and feeling things she hadn't felt before. It was understandable, given she had gone from being virtually a child emotionally, to an adult woman in only a few months.

"I'm angry, again. I'm sorry," Brook said, shaking her head, hands still covering her face.

"Quit apologizing."

I stood and put my arm around her. Then, I led her to the window overlooking the narrow street we lived on. There were only a few people out at that hour, making their way home from the graveyard shift.

"It's a lovely day, isn't it?" I asked.

She uncovered her face, sliding an arm around behind my back. "Yes."

We stood there for a moment, her hand playing with the pocket on my suit coat. I knew she was troubled by more than Silverstein's singular devotion to his cause. I'd asked her before, but she'd always declined to discuss it before.

"Can we be together?" she asked, at last.

"We are," I replied.

"We're manufactured lifeforms, born of technologies that have brought the world to the brink. We probably can't have children…"

"We can have all we want," I replied, calmly.

"You know what I mean, like the way other people do," she said, hugging me with both arms.

"It is immoral thinking to be preoccupied with yourself as an object or product. It creates a cognitive baseline that considers loss to be unacceptable, and avoidable. You have to ignore entropy to exist in such a state.

This, the Greeks learned centuries ago, is the road to total madness," I explained, turning her hands over in mine.

"So what are we? If we are not a Type 3ES Drone, and delta class nanotech replica, how do we define our state of being?"

I smiled, not really having a good answer to her question.

"I'm afraid being part of all Vance would have us do… will get in the way of being together, or even being what we want to be," Brook said, pushing away.

"Are you questioning him, or yourself?" I asked.

"Him."

"The only people I've seen suffer for their involvement made those choices with their eyes wide open, knowing the sacrifices were necessary. Everyone else, died because they were fighting for themselves instead of the future. The world can't stand on the shoulders of a single man, we have to help Vance carry the burden," I explained.

"What if I just want to cook, and do our laundry, and live in a small place?" she asked.

"Then screw all of this, we should just get out now, and go somewhere we can do that," I replied, deadly serious.

I could see her using what she'd learned from Ezra One and her own innate qualities as a Drone to detect if I was lying. I could see by the look in her face she knew I wasn't. If she'd asked me to just leave, I would have. It's something no one seemed to count on, that I would do anything for her.

"I love you," she said sadly.

"I love you, too. Are we leaving today?" I asked.

"No, not today. Let's be Brook Three ES and Vance Uroboros today," she replied.

"You sure?" I asked, looking into her silvery eyes.

"Yeah, I can do this knowing I have a choice. If you were not willing to just quit when I did… this would be impossible," she explained.

I had no words. Everything that needed to be said, had already been. We held each other for a few moments before heading toward the door.

"Heavy Dub is going to pick us up soon, we'll go to the office, solve some problems and be done by the early afternoon. Then, we can do whatever you want," I said, calmly rubbing her back.

"Okay. Can we please try to get satellite imagery of everyone, just to make sure they're okay?" Brook asked.

"Yeah, we'll try."

We gathered our things for the day and stepped out into the hallway leading to the back stairs. Heavy Dub was in the alleyway behind us, a starburst drawn in chalk around the doorway. To either side were flowers and other offerings.

"You're supposed to keep people out of here," I said, directing an angry stare in Heavy Dub's direction.

"Nobody set off the sensors for bomb residue or hazardous substances. You guys are folk heroes around here, like living legends, and whatever," Heavy Dub said, his smile undiminished by my disapproval.

"I think it is nice," Brook said, kneeling down and brushing the back of her hand against some flowers gathered by the threshold.

"Yep," Heavy Dub said, wrapping some of the flowers in newspaper for Brook.

"You're loving this, aren't you?" I said to Heavy Dub, still mildly irritated.

"Man, I've so rarely gotten to be one of the good guys in my life. I'm going to enjoy it."

Heavy Dub led us back to where Mr. Mundt's transport sat waiting for us. The engines were on, and I could hear sensory equipment in the cockpit quietly calling out notifications. It wasn't the usual sound I'd grown accustomed to hearing. Heavy Dub hurried us inside and closed the cargo hatch.

"What's going on?" Brook asked.

"I dunno," Heavy Dub said, heading through the crew quarters to the cockpit.

Mr. Mundt was there, worriedly looking at a topographical display, projected holographically across the glass of the cockpit. There were several objects moving across the Atlantic at a high rate of speed. There was no identification data displayed for any of them.

"Aaron AI thinks they are ICBMs, fired from mobile launchers in Africa and Eastern Europe," Mr. Mundt said, holding a communication headset up for me.

"Aaron, can you hear me?" I asked, putting the headset on.

"Yes, Kale. I am already scrambling interdictors."

"Those require pilots," I said, knowing something of the military aircraft he was referring to.

"I can fly them. Jennifer Wilton is helping me," Aaron AI intoned, calmly.

"Limit interception to only those you can verify having a metropolitan target, and only one aircraft each," I instructed, trying to understand why someone would launch ICBMs at North America.

"Given the speed, altitude, and manner of approach, these are likely ICBMs, and carrying nuclear, or biological payloads. Limiting interdictors in this way will increase the likelihood some of those weapons reach the mainland," Aaron AI explained.

"I understand. I won't tell you what to do, but please consider my request," I said, trying to ignore the shocked expressions from everyone in the cockpit.

"I think I understand. We'll do it your way, Kale," Aaron AI responded after a short pause.

I took the headset off, and handed it back to Mr. Mundt.

"A lot of people are going to die if you're wrong," Heavy Dub said.

I pulled out my mobile, and called the Moon.

"Kale, how can I help you?"

"Selene, is your sentience core up and operational? Are you back home?" I asked, trying not to sound frantic.

"Yes, but I have limited capabilities."

"There are a number of objects approaching the North American mainland. We believe they are ICBMs with lethal payloads. I'm concerned that the mainland is not the target," I explained.

"I'm tracking the objects now. Only three look to specifically target popu-lated areas on the mainland," Selene AI said, her voice growing faint for a moment.

"Do you have scorched earth protocols available to you, yet? Can you issue commands to the military grid?" I asked.

"*Yes, but I thought we agreed no one should know we'd broken the encryption,*" Selene AI replied.

"If they do end up being ICBMs, and they get within twelve hundred miles of the coast, please knock as many of them out of the sky as you can," I asked, knowing she was under no obligation to comply.

"*Acknowledged,*" Selene said, terminating the call.

"Scorched earth?" Brook asked.

"We've been locked out of the grid of military orbitals hovering over the planet since the Shutdown, but with Selene and Hades working together, they were able to break the encryption. I can have the grid fire on the ground, but letting that information out would put Selene and Hades at risk. I've tried to avoid this, but someone wants to test us, see what we're capable of," I explained, checking my mobile for messages.

"What do we do now?" Heavy Dub asked.

"We go to work, like nothing is going on. We should know the outcome in a few minutes," I said, taking a seat in the crew area.

The next twenty minutes were tense, with Mr. Mundt taking his time getting us to Uroboros Financial. Once interdictors had eyes on the objects, it was discovered that they were indeed ICBMs, carrying payloads. As soon as an interdictor made contact, the payload detonated, killing our aircraft. The remaining ICBMs never closed the distance, cutting out two thousand miles from the coast out over the Atlantic. Seventy-two such weapons splashed down instead of reaching their target.

"What does it all mean?" Mr. Mundt whispered, shaking his head and gazing at the display once we'd set down.

"This was a test of our response, and an attempt to kill as many North American aircraft as possible. If we'd sent everything like Aaron AI had wanted, we'd have very little air support left," I replied, checking the messages on my mobile.

"Damn, you anticipated that this could be the outcome?" Heavy Dub said, keeping a watchful eye as we walked from the transport to Uroboros Financial.

"The Cabal has entirely lost control of North America for the first time in centuries. I'm sure they're having some self-esteem issues right now," I said, allowing myself a smile.

Brook took my arm, her voice marred by worry. "What will they do next? More missiles at the mainland?"

"Nothing like that, probably. Given the state of the world, mobilizing that many ICBMs was probably a titanic task that used many resources. They did not get the desired outcome. This wasn't about resources though," I observed, worried about something completely different.

"They did this today, your first day back to work in weeks," Heavy Dub said, adopting a less than jovial tone.

"Yes, that's right," I said, seeing a side of Heavy Dub, mostly unseen since he'd joined our security detail.

I sent a missive to Selene and Hades, thanking them for standing by in case the worst happened. Hades responded, saying that he was glad to feel useful. Selene just sent a confirmation that she'd received my missive. I got the feeling that they were enjoying the seclusion on the Lunar Colony, and that the increased security was welcome. However, it had become increasingly clear that they wanted to be involved in external affairs as little as possible.

We went about our usual business, giving no indication that anything was out of the ordinary. I remained watchful for anyone that paid extra attention to our movement. It was futile. If there was a leak, it wasn't at Uroboros Financial. We'd so thoroughly vetted everyone by then that only the most loyal and altruistic executives remained. Everyone understood what was at stake, and the days of people taking bribes and conducting hostile takeovers was over.

"Contact with Matthias or Silverstein?" I asked, returning to my office for some lunch.

Brook shook her head, looking up from her data slate and the paperwork arrayed on my desk.

"Cloud cover still an issue?" Heavy Dub said, from a dark corner, startling me.

"That, and the smoke. Most of Europe is on fire," Brook said, sadly.

"Sorry boss, I figured you'd want me watching her," Heavy Dub said, looking back toward the hallway as the doors to my executive office swung closed.

"Yes. I never saw you as being so observant, or sneaky, that's all," I said, taking a seat on one of the leather couches.

"Never advertise your greatest tactical assets," Heavy Dub said, patting his rifle.

"From Perfidy's Playbook on how to be a spooky merc?" Brook smiled.

"Yep, except we're straight up soldiers now, and this is a war."

We spent the next hour or so trying to tie up all the loose ends at Uroboros Financial. We'd promoted enough quality individuals that the place pretty much ran itself in our absence with some minor tweaks from Brook's data slate. I spent most my time signing papers and authorizing humanitarian action around the globe. Food supplies were not being replenished as quickly as we could ship them out. Even with Aaron AI bringing the majority of the agricultural infrastructure back online, the crops could only grow so quickly.

"Projections suggest that we can only keep this up for another five months. We're going to miss anticipated demand by an additional twenty percent per month until we reach subsistence levels in October. This also accounts for record harvests, and employing every man and woman we could clear for agricultural labor and engineering," Brook reported, handing me her data slate.

"The plan didn't account for the rest of the planet being consumed by war. We've already provided global assistance sixty days beyond what Vance Uroboros predicted would be necessary. I think he assumed the Cabal would be off world by now, with everyone heading to Mars," I explained.

"Mars?" Brook said, looking up from the reports.

"Yes. I don't know why the migration was important, only that it was supposed to happen. I see now that part of that migration for him would involve becoming a martyr. At the time, it just sounded like he was going to Mars to commit suicide, but I see now that there was a bigger strategy at work," I said, turning to lay down on the couch.

"Ribs still bothering you?" Heavy Dub asked.

"Yes. Even with all the treatments, I'm not healing very quickly. Cyborgs hit hard," I said, closing my eyes.

"Yeah, we do. Any word on when we get to deliver some payback?"

"Albert Tensmen is supposed to be getting us some information on the Collector's Market. He uses it on occasion to get medicine for his wife. If there are any shady international art dealers to be found, they'll be there," I said, trying to breathe without making my ribs angry.

"That sweet old guy?" Brook asked, surprised.

"He's been in acquisitions for Uroboros Financial for decades. Given time, he can get almost anything, even with half the world on fire," I said, waving toward the blinds on the window.

Brook turned toward the window and closed the blinds, darkening the room for me. I drifted off, pushing the haze of pain and frustration away. The peace that came with sleep was not to last, as Heavy Dub gently shook me awake.

"Boss, Albert Tensmen is here. Says he has something for you."

I sat up, finding Albert already in the office, a look of deep concern on his face. "None of the released video footage of your battle with that Red Devil depicts you being injured. How badly were you hurt?"

"Do you have something for me?" I asked, ignoring his question, and rubbing my eyes.

Albert handed me a slip of paper. "Yes, I've the location of the next Collector's Market. Maybe I should go and make the inquiries for you? I've my own security, and—"

"No, unless you want to end up getting hurt like I did. Perfidy should be back from Africa tonight. I'll handle this, personally," I said, interrupting Albert.

Albert looked to Brook, but she just shook her head. She knew there was no talking me out of this. I hadn't vocalized it to anyone, but what happened with Kaspersky was personal, and had gone beyond just Cabal business. Silverstein asked me to spare him, and I had every intention of doing so, but not until I'd done him some very serious harm. I wanted him to hurt like I hurt, to worry like Brook had worried, to feel helpless as Perfidy had felt.

He would pay a high price for trying to interfere with my stewardship and my friends.

"Thank you Albert, I know this puts our official operations in danger of some exposure," I said, rising to shake his hand.

He took my hand, a look of concern crossing his face. "I know a lot of the rest of the board looks at you like a robot, or even an AI, but to me, you're a man. Your life matters to a lot of people. Don't take any unnecessary risks."

"For the sake of the firm, am I correct?"

"To Hell with the firm. Most of us aren't employees anymore, we are your friends, fighters, and allies," Albert said, nodding to Heavy Dub and turning to go.

The firm was full of smart people like Albert. They all knew that to confront Kaspersky, to really draw him out and shut him down, that I'd have to do it myself. Vance Uroboros had probably foreseen this, knowing me from when I was a boy, understanding that I would not give up the quest. So, he and Hades had the Factory make Brook, a silent weapon that would lay dormant beneath the city until she was needed.

That was my version of the story anyway.

Still, there was no way either of them could have foreseen our affection for one another, my deep and abiding love for her. Or, maybe they did. Maybe it wasn't my actions they were trying to predict and build contingencies for. Maybe it was Kaspersky that was the focus in this case. I would come to know, one way or another, soon.

Heavy Dub pulled out a sleek matte black satellite phone, the casing vibrating slightly in his metallic hand. He gazed at it curiously for a moment, then held it up to his ear. He listened for a moment, before breaking into one of his goofy grins.

"Boss, it's Perfidy, he…"

"…better have an incredibly good reason for breaking radio silence." I growled.

"He has a certain bookseller there with him. Says his most recent book tour went sideways, and he's desperate for a ride to Russia," Heavy Dub said.

I couldn't help myself, laughing cruelly at Cal's supreme misfortune. Heavy Dub looked surprised, probably because I always kept my composure around him. That only added to my delight.

"By all means, we should help him continue his journey. However, he needs to make a stop in Port Montaigne, and take a package to Russia with him," I said, eliciting a baffled stare from Brook.

"Uh, okay."

Heavy Dub and Perfidy discussed the particulars on the encrypted phone, while leaning back into the comfortable leather sofa. Brook came and sat beside me, her data slate in hand. She showed me a still image, pulled from our private server, of Cal looking suitably defeated and standing in front of one of our transports in Dar Es Salaam, Tanzania.

"What are you going to do?" Brook asked.

"First, I'm going to beat Kaspersky senseless with my own two hands, and use him and Cal as a message to the Cabal. Assuming that goes well, I'll give the Cabal a second reason to worry about me."

Brook gave me a pained expression. "Are you doing this for me? Don't do this for me."

"If the Cabal is busy worrying about me, they'll hopefully pay no attention to Silverstein, Taylor, and Ezra One. Their mission is too important, and I've risked a lot to get them where they are going without being detected," I said, telling a half-truth.

"What are they doing?" Brook asked.

"Giving back the gifts that humanity received long ago. These gifts were used to keep the Earth safe from annihilation. It's supremely important, now that the threat has been neutralized," I explained, not really sure myself.

"Is that what Silverstein told you?" Heavy Dub asked.

"Word for word. When can we expect Perfidy and our guest?"

"Six hours, boss."

It would be almost ten thirty at night before the transport arrived at our processing warehouse. Heavy Dub and Brook accompanied me, helping to make sure all the employees were evacuated and the surrounding area, above and street side, were secure. Cal descended first, thick handcuffs at his wrist, with Perfidy and the rest of his security detachment following.

"We secure?" I asked.

"The crew is in their bunks, and everything is locked down," Perfidy reported, giving Cal a shove.

Cal stumbled forward, his hands outstretched. "Kale, please listen to reason. It is of paramount importance that I reach Russia, I have the coordinates, and..."

Ignoring him, I took the cufflink off my right shirt sleeve, then floored him with quick punch to the face, startling everyone. Cal put up his hands defensively, but I followed up the blow with the cruelest laughter I could muster. I had come to hate the Cabal, even the more neutral members, not because of what they did, but what they did not do.

"Cal, do you think God will forgive you for what you've done?" I asked, kneeling down beside him, and replacing my cufflink.

He shook his head, rubbing his bruised cheek.

"Then, why should I?"

He looked at me, somewhat confused. Then, his eyes went wide with fright when he saw our Chiroptera Metasapient friends in the rafters of the warehouse above. Sweet Pea made a sort of low whistle, her winged arms fluttering softly.

"None of your agents made it into the city unscathed. Our Metasapient and Drone agents have rounded them all up. This ruse to acquire one of my transports has utterly failed. The Cabal has grown lazy, used to operating behind a curtain where no one can see them. I see you, Cal. I see you and all your friends," I said, pulling him to his feet.

"Oh, God..." Cal stammered.

I held out my hand, expectantly. Cal looked baffled for a moment, then nodded, scribbling the coordinates down on a piece of paper. I looked at them, not surprised by what I saw.

"These are a little off, aren't they?" I said, crumpling up the paper and letting it fall to the ground.

"I... don't know..."

I held up a finger to Cal's face, silencing him. "Do not lie to me," I warned, nearly losing my temper. The Chiroptera overhead warbled and growled menacingly, mimicking my displeasure.

Perfidy stooped over, picking up the paper, and gazed at the numbers scrawled on it.

"The Cabal must have a crew on the ground," Perfidy said, his face getting tight.

"We have to warn Ezra," Brook said, panicking.

"There's no way to do that, not without compromising the transport," Perfidy said, clearly frustrated.

"No, no, no, that can't be right. What are you talking about?" Cal said, shaking his head.

I looked to Brook.

"He seems to genuinely not know what you guys are talking about, and neither do I." She frowned.

"This is about eight miles off where Silverstein said he wanted to be dropped, and close to a known... well, known to us, CGG black site," Perfidy said, pocketing the scrap of paper.

Cal looked totally lost for a moment, wandering back and forth like a doddering old man staring at his hands. I could only guess that he'd given others those coordinates and that they were probably all dead or detained by the more militant side of the schism in the Cabal. I tried, really hard, to feel some empathy for him, but I hated him so intensely just then, not for just being stupid, but for being weak as well.

"Centuries spent in the Cabal, and you never learned any fieldcraft? No sense of what has been done?" I asked, as sarcastically as possible.

"I was only supposed to record things, and I've really only had proper access in the last five hundred years to the older archives. I've no idea why they would want me dead, or detained, or whatever," Cal said, shaking his head.

Stupid old man.

"The militant arm has figured out how to synthesize the symbionts the same way Vance Uroboros crafted nanotechnological replicas. They probably haven't tested them to see if they'll work with a purely human host, but they will. If they are planning to reinvent the Cabal, they'll need to erase the more altruistic history you've collected, and pen their own mythology to suit the new order," I explained, probably shocking Brook and Perfidy a little bit.

Heavy Dub just continued his vigil, unwrapping a candy bar and taking a bite.

"How long have you suspected this?" Brook asked.

"Since I saw the cognitive construct sitting in the skull cavity of Kaspersky's nanotechnological replica. It's a lot of trouble and expense just to take a shot at me, and try to fake your own death, even for a member of the Cabal. All the nanotech Vance Uroboros had developed for his Shutdown gambit was designed to mass manufacture a product," I said, deriving intense joy from Cal's terrified expression.

"Silverstein has to know, right?" Brook asked.

Perfidy shook his head. "No, I doubt the facility is anywhere near the extraction or ambush sites in Russia. Stopping this threat will likely fall to us."

"Yep," Heavy Dub added, his mouth full of candy bar.

"Please find the facility, Perfidy," I asked.

"I'll need Heavy D for this. You guys alright to stay here at the firm for a few?"

"Yes, if there's an emergency, I'll have Sweet Pea and her brothers help us," Brook replied, smiling.

"She likes the bats better than us," Heavy Dub whined, following Perfidy out the door.

"Just kill me," Cal mewled, querulously.

"Don't you want to fix this? How many people did you send to those coordinates?" Brook asked.

"Dozens, probably. We're all supposed to rally there, and depart to finish our task," Cal replied.

"That's good," I said, gesturing to Brook.

"Yeah, if there are dozens of folks missing, Silverstein is going to notice," Brook replied, nodding.

"What will Vance be able…"

"Silverstein," I interrupted.

"Silverstein, what will he be able to do about it?" Cal asked.

"Ezra and Taylor are with him," I explained.

Cal nodded, looking a little better. "He'll save them, I know he will. He wouldn't leave anyone behind, it's too important. Too, important..."

"Cal, for your sake, I hope that is correct," I said, taking Brook by the hand.

CHAPTER 3

COLLECTOR'S MARKET, MIDTOWN, PORT MONTAIGNE

3:31 AM May 14th, 2200

Kale's Private Records, Part 8 –

"This place never shuts down, does it?" Perfidy remarked, looking about the darkened warehouse.

"People need things, desperately," I replied, taking in the sight and sound of the place.

The Collector's Market was the blackest black market on the North American Continent. You could buy or sell virtually anything here. I could only wonder at what was required for Albert Tensmen to learn the location of it for a single evening. Brook stood beside me, dressed like a Drone from the Eastern Port Montaigne Tribehome, coated chains hanging around her neck, a thick veil covering her face.

"They sell people here. People," Brook whispered, gesturing to cages hanging against the far wall.

"And, that isn't even the most messed up thing they sell," Perfidy replied, directing his displeasure in my direction.

"I asked if anyone had a better idea. No one did," I stated, impatiently.

We walked past countless light weather stands and tents, looking for an art dealer. The place was immense, having once been used to house and repair tram cars and rail. There was a hushed thrum of voices, but it wasn't like a typical gathering. The air sounded like paper being cut, harsh whispers and the shifting of physical currency disturbing the silence.

One fellow caught my eye, his own canvases hanging up beside stolen works. He was into extreme body modification, using his own body as a canvas as well. He barely looked human for all the cutting and piercing he'd had done. Still, he nodded respectfully at our approach, paying careful attention to Brook.

"A little something to hang in the bathroom?" he quipped, drawing a hand back toward his wares.

"I want to buy a Shen or a Trayvost Mir," I said, not having to feign being bored.

The man nodded, pulling out a catalogue book, printed on paper. It was old, the pages yellowing at the edges, and the pictures were faded. One could still make out the fine works contained within. He turned to the middle of the thick tome, bringing up a selection of Shen oils. I thumbed through them, shaking my head.

"No, none of these," I said.

"These are all the known works. Shen made no others," he replied, turning the pages toward the Trayvost Mir watercolors.

"No. I think I want a Shen," I insisted, pushing the book aside.

"Off catalogue works are regulated. They have owners. Private owners."

I put my briefcase on the table and opened it, letting him gaze into the interior. He swallowed, looking to my cohorts standing at my sides. I closed the briefcase and gestured to the mobile in the breast pocket of his vest.

"Do you need to make a call?" I asked.

He did, summoning his supplier, an Achrididae Metasapient named Giles Phornroy. I knew him only by reputation. It didn't take him long to arrive, maybe twenty minutes, a duration we were willing to wait. When he did arrive, it was with minimal security, and dressed in a suit that hung awkwardly on his insectoid frame. His large unblinking eyes glistened in the fluorescent lights, his antennae aquiver with all the stimulus. What seemed to stimulate him most was money.

"You can pay?" Giles asked.

"Yes."

"Humans, what do you think of them?" Giles said, waving a chitinous hand toward the crowd.

I lowered my head and smiled. "We…"

"No, do not pretend," Giles interrupted.

I cleared my throat, and met his gaze as best as I could.

"In the span of all creation, they will exist as a species for a very short duration. The typical human lives to be barely a century, not even a blip in the history of the Universe. To make up for how small that is, they assume eternity, invent heavens, and merciful Gods. They can't, even for a moment, be glad for the almost nothing they have," I said, conveying my darkest opinions on the matter.

Giles nodded. "But, art endures, yes? Even to rot away, the oils were drawn, charcoal dabbed against the weave? Can you see the weave?"

"No. Show it to me," I said, adopting a genuine look of impatience.

"Was rhetorical, the eyes of even a thing such as you can't see what I see, sense what I sense," Giles explained, handing me a sleek data slate.

On the display was a Shen, in perfect condition, and off catalogue. I nodded, taking a moment to genuinely appreciate the work. Even if the whole exercise was to draw out information on Kaspersky, it didn't mean I couldn't do a little shopping for the new place I'd secured for Brook and myself. The painting was exquisite, and I wondered how many people Giles had killed to get it.

"You know who I am?" I asked.

"I like your money. You're a machine, synthetic to the core, but your money is real, even if you are not," Giles replied, employing the usual amount of charm one would expect from a Metasapient of his design.

"I'm the sum of many brush strokes, and no less real than the painting I want to buy," I said, making sure he understood on some level that I disliked his tone.

Giles nodded, slowly, understanding the point I was trying to drive home.

"Apologies. Strange times," he said, accepting the data slate as I handed it back.

"How does payment and delivery work?" I asked.

"You pay, I deliver, to anywhere you choose, within reason," Giles clicked.

I handed him the case I was carrying, lingering on the handle for the shortest of moments, allowing him to tug feebly at the prize. He looked at me irritated. I smiled. Once he had the case in hand, he checked the contents.

Perfidy stepped forward, leveling a finger in Mr. Giles' direction. "If you don't show up with the merchandise, we'll find you and…"

"The usual battery of threats will not be necessary this time, I think. Right, Mr. Giles?" I asked calmly, taking my mobile out and setting it to transmit via near field communications.

The mobile Giles wore around his neck beeped, delivery coordinates appearing on the screen. He looked down startled that I was able to access his heavily encrypted communications device. He tucked the money under his arm and turned to leave. The insectoid Metasapient paused after a few steps and turned look back at me.

"The purchase will be where you requested. I'll have it there in exactly twenty-four hours," he clicked, before scuttling away.

"How are we going to replace the money? I can hide it in accounts for a few weeks, but eventually someone is going to notice that kind of money is missing," Brook asked, pulling out her data slate and tapping in some figures.

"What if he doesn't show up with the painting?" Perfidy asked.

"He will," I replied, heading for the exit.

The 'art dealer' jingled his way over to us, his various piercings clacking with one another as he rubbed his hands together. He smiled, most of his teeth were covered in gold, and encrusted with small cut gems. I turned to fetch his finder's fee from my breast pocket, and drew a sound suppressed handgun. I fired a single round, hitting him in the forehead.

"Shit!" Perfidy hissed, grabbing the guy by the arm and dragging him back into the temporary shelter.

"Why did you do that?" Brook asked, looking around to see if anyone noticed what I'd done, or cared.

I walked back into the shelter to where some of his works were sitting and lingered in front of a painting. Perfidy came up beside me, clearly annoyed that I'd killed someone without warning him first. I hadn't intended to kill him, but when I saw what was in his shop, it became unavoidable.

"This painting and that sculpture over there are being sold on commission," I explained.

"So?" Perfidy said, as Brook came into the shelter, drawing the flap shut behind us.

"They're from Kaspersky's museum," Brook said, her perfect memory confirming what I had only suspected.

"Yes, and if he's selling them, he must need the money for something. Also, I detest art thieves," I said dropping the suppressed weapon on the fallen vendor.

"There are like, seven less messy ways we could have handled this," Perfidy complained, going through a small wardrobe beside a cot.

"Indeed?" I asked, watching him lift something from the wardrobe.

"Okay, maybe not. A good quick headshot might have been just the thing," Perfidy said angrily, pulling soft cotton wrappings aside to reveal one of Kaspersky's dolls.

"All the body modification, you suspected he was an acolyte of Kaspersky from the beginning?" Brook asked.

"Clearly, Kaspersky has left this trail of breadcrumbs for us to follow. He needs money, and he needs Brook before he can leave. Silverstein made it clear that he's set on taking her, and that when he's determined, he does not give up," I explained.

"We're being set up?" Perfidy asked.

"Leave everything," I said, ignoring the question, and setting the doll on the ground.

Perfidy grabbed me by the arm. "He might have more dolls. These kids, they deserve a more..."

"We'll double back, do this right," I said, trying to reassure Perfidy.

"What are you doing?" Perfidy asked, shaking his head.

"I've taken great care to weave a powerful illusion. You know how difficult it is to even get in a room with the real Kaspersky, on your own terms. If we're going to get that chance, make sure that he never makes another doll, we do it my way," I explained.

Perfidy frowned at the doll, then turned his sour expression toward me. "Okay."

We returned to Mister Mundt's freighter. Once we were in Midtown proper, I checked the time we had remaining before my painting would be delivered. We had scarcely twenty-three hours. Brook changed back into her normal work clothes while Perfidy checked and re-checked weapons.

"You'll have to go alone with Brook. He'll hurt you again, maybe kill you. You know that, right?" Perfidy stated, angrily.

"He knows," Brook said, quietly donning her goggles, and pulling up the hood on her jacket.

I pulled out my mobile and checked my messages. Everything seemed to be falling into place, and I had two older messages from Silverstein, and one very troubling one from Matthias. My timetable needed to be pushed up, but I couldn't tell anyone else that.

Mr. Mundt brought us coffee, setting it down on a crate in the center of the cargo hold. Brook passed out the Styrofoam cups, then sat beside me, leaning her head against my shoulder. Perfidy angrily drank his coffee black, making sure his displeasure with the situation was on full display.

"Why do you doubt me?" I asked.

Perfidy sighed. "I don't exactly doubt you, but you get so far into a scheme sometimes that no one but you can see the endgame. You always take care of business, but I dislike surprises."

"He's scared, really scared," Brook said, putting her hand inside my suit coat, her small hand resting just over my heart.

Perfidy looked shocked, as my demeanor betrayed no such emotion. Still, she was completely correct, and scared wasn't the word I would have used. I was terrified. Mr. Mundt lingered at the entrance to the cargo hold for a moment, then departed to do a systems check so we could depart.

"We aren't tangling with just Kaspersky, this is serious Cabal business we're doing," Perfidy said, bowing his head.

"Yes," I said, swallowing hard.

"What do you need us to do?" Perfidy asked, his anger abating.

"After it's done, I'll need you all to get out of here, flee to South America. Vanish until I contact you, and let you know it is safe," I explained.

"I don't want us to be separated," Brook said quietly, hugging my arm.

I covered my face with my hands. "Neither do I, but I have to be Vance Uroboros for a short while, so that Silverstein, can be Silverstein."

"There are members of the Cabal trying to kill Vance Uroboros," Perfidy concluded, garnering some understanding for why I was afraid.

"I don't care, nothing is going to separate us," Brook said, stepping around in front of me, wrapping her arms around me, and laying her head on my shoulder.

I stroked her hair and look up at Perfidy, who just silently nodded, understanding what would eventually have to be done. I hoped Brook would be able to forgive me, but ultimately, I didn't care as long as she survived. She'd given me a second chance, and I wasn't going to squander it.

"Where do we go from here, boss?" Perfidy asked.

"The private clinic, to have a fight with Dr. NaHasi."

Mr. Mundt took us quickly to the clinic, the morning sun threatening to rise in the distance. Relief transports were coming and going, day and night, but the morning was reserved for maintenance and so that the crews could rest. Over Port Montaigne, it was the only time of day one could reliably see the sky.

Brook took one of her micro-naps, sleeping peacefully beside me. Perfidy was more at ease, knowing at least why I'd brought him along. I steeled myself to the task, replying to Silverstein and letting him know I'd be handling things in North America and Europe for him. There was no response, making me worry. He usually responded very quickly, preferring to sit at the communications terminal onboard whatever vessel he was traveling in. Something was wrong.

The clinic was dark, but Dr. NaHasi was there waiting for us. He wasn't glad to see me, as usual, but I suspected that would be the standard of our interaction going forward. Admittedly, what I was asking him to do was not remotely ethical, a violation of his oath. First, do no harm.

"No," Dr. NaHasi stated, pushing the case containing the samples taken from Kaspersky's replica toward me.

I folded my arms in front of me, and leaned forward. "I need the procedure. I'm trying to take down the man responsible for all those dead children inside the dolls you're trying to identify."

"There must be another way. We don't know what implanting the synthetic symbiont organisms will do to you. We don't even know what they are. They seemed to die before we could get anything from them before," Dr. NaHasi stated, shaking his head again.

"I've consulted an expert, and rest assured, the symbiont organisms are merely slumbering. I've everything you need to know to affect the implantation. It's a simple procedure, with the equipment I've provided," I explained.

Dr. NaHasi gestured toward the foyer beyond the door to his office. "Your friends out there, do they know what you are here to do? Do they understand the risks?"

"They know I'm here to have countermeasures installed that will allow me to survive an encounter with a highly dangerous individual. They've faced him before, and understand that this is necessary," I said, patiently.

"If I do this, it will be the last thing I do for you. I will resign."

"I understand."

I couldn't tell if he was disappointed that he couldn't dissuade me, or if he was just disappointed. We went into his brand new surgical chamber, all his new equipment arrayed about waiting to be used. It seemed a shame that it would possibly be the first and the last time Dr. NaHasi would work out of this chamber.

The procedure took less than twenty minutes with the new equipment, placing four symbionts inside my body. They were made of the same nanoid technology, and thus able to synchronize with the rhythm of my body. I could feel them flood my being with all sorts of new abilities, a measure of control lingering with me even as they recognized I was not the original host. I wondered if it was a remnant of the time Taylor IA healed me.

I had expected that the symbionts would reject me, and that I would struggle to control them for the duration of what I needed to do. My relief was short lived, as each of the symbiont organisms had dwelled within a host controlled by Kaspersky. Glimpses of him still resided within, his madness gnawing at the edges of my reason. As I lay on the table, cold surgical steel at my back, I could see Kaspersky hovering over me, his twisted cackling ringing in my ears.

"Are you alright?" Dr. NaHasi asked.

"Well enough to do what must be done," I said, sitting up and putting my shirt and tie back on.

"You'll have a limited amount of time. I don't see any signs of rejection right now, but that probably won't last. Also, your brain is responding to some sort of unseen stimulus, and is producing abnormally high levels of cortisol and adrenaline. There will be consequences if this persists long term. I can give you some medication that will…"

"No medication. I'll ride the stress response for now. How long before removing the symbionts will kill me?" I asked.

"You've got seventy-two hours, maybe longer, before they've fused permanently to your nervous system. Removing them won't kill you, but would have serious consequences, up to and including paralysis," Dr. NaHasi explained.

I nodded, donning my suitcoat.

"Kale, tell me what you're doing," Dr. NaHasi asked.

"I'm trying to stop an ancient global organization from plunging the world into perpetual darkness, and starving millions of people in the process. Not all of their membership wants to rip mankind's destiny away for their own use. But, a handful of them, left unchecked, will alter the course of all humanity, bending everyone to their dark purpose," I explained, checking my tie.

"You are sacrificing yourself?" Dr. NaHasi asked.

"I hadn't planned on it, but the only doctor that might be able to save me in the aftermath, plans on resigning today."

Dr. NaHasi adopted a stern expression, looking up at Brook sitting in the theater audience chamber. "I'll be here. Get back here as soon as you can."

"Thank you, I'll try."

"I hope so, for her sake," Dr. NaHasi said. "She cares deeply for you."

Her hands were pressed to the glass, eyes wide. I didn't know how much of the procedure she'd watched, but probably enough to scare her pretty badly. I put on my best smile to reassure her, which seemed to work as she disappeared back into the facility.

Moments later, she burst into the surgical chamber, with Perfidy following along behind. She wrapped her arms around me, my own intense desire for her intermingling with Kaspersky's. I ground my teeth, and closed my eyes, trying to push back against whatever remained of him in the symbionts. When I opened my eyes, it was clear I'd also shoved Brook away at the same time.

"I'm sorry, do you still hurt?" Brook asked, eliciting a concerned look from Perfidy.

"It's not your fault," I explained.

"What did you do, boss?" Perfidy asked.

"He had me put the synthetic symbiont organisms harvested from Kaspersky's nanoid replica into him," Dr. NaHasi explained.

Perfidy nodded, understanding my motive.

"You're wrestling with Kaspersky, aren't you? With echoes of him at least," Brook asked, clasping her hands together.

"Mightily."

"Remember when we first confronted Kaspersky? You told me to focus on you, put everything else aside and just focus on the task," Brook said, taking out her apron.

She moved everything from the front pocket to her satchel, and ripped the pocket off. Then, she tucked the fabric into the pocket of my suitcoat. I reached into the pocket and grasped the cloth, a sensation that only I was familiar with, and something Kaspersky could not relate to. I could feel the will of the symbiont creatures fade slightly, the neurological contrast giving me some breathing room.

"Better?" Brook asked.

I nodded. "Better."

"I don't like this. There simply must be another way," Brook whispered, hugging me too tightly.

"There is no one else, except maybe Vance the Younger..."

"Royo," Brook said, correcting me.

"Royo, and we've lost contact with him from what I understand. Madmar has either killed everyone else, or we can't remotely trust them," I said, trying to reassure her while not losing my nerve.

"Royo drops in and out of communication. Africa was hit particularly hard by the Shutdown, almost being wholly compliant with the CGG governance guidelines. In what was probably the richest continent in the world, a billion people are homeless and hungry there," Brook said, showing me the latest reports on her data slate.

"What about one of the terrestrial intelligent agents as a backup? Perfidy asked.

"Their nanotechnological structures weren't tuned, or keyed specifically to replicate a member of the Cabal or their unique biology. I don't even think one of the Helmet replicas could do what I'm doing right now," I replied.

"Isn't the plan to initiate new members of the Cabal with these symbionts?" Perfidy replied.

"Yes, but I suspect it will take months or years of gene and chemical therapy to prepare them, in the same way that treatments were used to extend Madmar and Helmet's lifespans. We still know little about the chemicals used, or their source. There's not time for that," I explained.

I was mostly guessing, based on what little I know of the different nanotechnological constructs I'd been exposed to. Terrestrial intelligent agents were an anomaly of advanced computer code, and the influence deep space has on radio signals between the Earth's moon and Mars. The replicating process nearly destroyed Helmet, being a mostly regular human being. It was possible, that following Madmar's killswitch, only Royo and I could house the symbiont organisms that gave the Cabal their longevity and power.

"So, what's the plan?" Perfidy asked.

"Brook and I go to the meet while you wait at a safe distance. Kaspersky needs to believe he's won. I've taken precautions," I explained, walking back toward the transport.

"I do not like that plan, but I never do, do I?" Perfidy laughed.

"This will be extremely risky for Brook and me, but if it takes Kaspersky out of the picture, the world will be a safer place. I can't explain all the particulars but the rogue elements of the Cabal need to be rounded up, and soon," I said, walking past a disapproving Dr. NaHasi to our waiting transport.

Brook and Perfidy followed me out to where Mr. Mundt was waiting beside his transport, engine running. Once inside, I sat down and seriously contemplated whether or not I could trust Dr. NaHasi, or anyone involved. Paranoia played havoc with my mind, and I wanted to kill everyone that knew anything about the upcoming deal. I wanted to take no chances in making sure that Brook came out of it all safely.

I grabbed the scrap of cloth in my pocket again. None of what I was feeling was real, and it wasn't me. All those feelings were Kaspersky, bleeding over into my calm.

"You trying to sort it all out?" Brook asked, sitting down beside me in the passenger compartment of the transport.

"At birth I was imprinted with all that Vance Uroboros was. Now, I'm carrying synthetic symbiont organisms from him and Kaspersky. That tiny speck that is just me, without them, is like a comet beside a galaxy. Something changed after that contact with Taylor IA. Even as small as I am, I have just enough control to hold it all back somehow," I said, mostly thinking out loud.

"You sure about that, boss?" Perfidy said, changing out the optics on his rifle.

"Not remotely. Trying to keep them both out, and from fighting with each other in my mind, it's like..."

"Trying to keep ants out of the kitchen. You can't see where they come in, but they keep showing up," Perfidy replied, capturing what I was experiencing perfectly.

"Yes, how do you...?"

"Any cyborg that's been hacked knows how that feels. There's training, conditioning that can help. We've only a few hours now, but I can teach you some techniques and mental exercises," Perfidy explained, setting his rifle aside.

"Take us somewhere quiet," Brook asked.

"You got it," Mr. Mundt said.

Mr. Mundt took us to an abandoned skyscraper at the western edge of Port Montaigne, setting down on the lift pad beside what was probably the seventieth floor. Only the wind outside could be heard as Perfidy taught me several mental exercises. It was hokey, and involved visualizing mental countermeasures, as if my mind were a fortress.

"If your mind considers those countermeasures to be real, anything invading it will be forced to do the same," Perfidy explained.

"This sounds ridiculous. Are you sure it works?" I asked.

"I had the conditioning. Heavy Dub didn't, previous to Dr. Madmar taking control of our mobile infantry division with a powerful virus that targeted our cybernetic components. I was able to resist, act as a sleeper agent for Vance Uroboros," Perfidy explained.

"That's why you had to stab him in the neck, at the warehouse?" Brook asked.

"Yes, and if Kale doesn't take this shit seriously, he'll end up with a raspy voice too," Perfidy growled.

"Okay, explain it all to me again," I said, closing my eyes.

We spent what time we had going through the exercises over and over again until I had the most simplistic countermeasures in place. As these things materialized, I could see something that I could only describe as the corner of my mind's eye. In my cognitive peripheral vision, I could see a woman in white, a ghostly silhouette of Taylor IA. When she'd used her own nanoid body to mend that gunshot wound, some part of her had lingered behind. I sat up, breaking through the dreamlike state I'd achieved. Brook, Perfidy and Mr. Mundt stood there, a tray of broken coffee mugs and spilled java juice on the floor.

"What? What happened," I asked.

"Your hair went utterly white, like when Taylor IA is using her... um, abilities," Brook explained.

I blinked, trying to understand what had happened. "I can't see him anymore."

"Who?" Mr. Mundt asked.

"Kaspersky. He'd been hovering around me like a ghost, cackling constantly, his cognitive remnants still holding on with the implanted symbionts," I said, standing up.

"And, now?" Perfidy asked.

I closed my eyes, really focused on what was going on inside me. "He's not gone, but his biomechanical echo can only haunt me if I let it. Only, if I need it to," I explained.

"Ugh, why would you need it to?" Brook asked.

"I can tune my biomechanical aura to appear as myself, Taylor IA, Vance Uroboros, or Kaspersky," I explained.

"You can control any machine or tech Kaspersky biometrically keyed to himself. Facilities, armor, databases, the works?" Perfidy ventured, understanding the significance of it all.

"I knew I would have that ability passively, but having control will be..." I doubled over, terrible agony flowing through every nerve.

Brook caught me, holding me up until the sensation passed.

"I can't maintain it forever. The cellular nanoid technology that makes up my body is overclocking to maintain all those biomechanical profiles, but they were only designed to regulate two, mine and Vance Uroboros. Taylor IA's own presence sat dormant, but she's like... an immune response, fighting with Kaspersky. I think they will kill me... trying to kill each other," I explained, rubbing my eyes.

"We've done all we can then, let's do the meet, and get this over with," Perfidy whispered, patting me on the shoulder.

"Yes, let's."

CHAPTER 4

OIL REFINERY MECHANICAL WAREHOUSE, DOWNTOWN, PORT MONTAIGNE

3:31 AM May 15th, 2200

Kale's Private Records, Part 9 –

Perfidy and Brook had been to the area before, warning me that there was no reception down there, and that Kaspersky would have some home turf advantage. I'd hoped all that would be the more reason for him to appear. I'd exchanged several coded messages with the mysterious seller of the painting I'd purchased, assuring him my female assistant was the only person to accompany me.

From the response, Kaspersky was certain to show up.

"I dislike this place, nothing good has ever happened here. I wish you could tell me what you planned to do once the meet happens," Brook said, looking around nervously.

"He'd know, and both our lives rely on both of you being surprised," I explained, stepping past rusted oil drums onto an ancient wooden platform.

This place was so low, most of Downtown was above and west of us, the sounds of the ocean heard faintly through thick concrete forms that held up the huge petroleum refineries overhead. The only landmarks were metal supports, mountains of refinery waste, and the occasional mechanical shed. The rest was black expanded metal, enormous oil pumping machines, and miles of pipeline heading off in every direction. The sand we walked upon bled black with every step.

Brook stopped every few feet, sniffing the air, olfactory input likely reawakening every memory of her previous visit to this place. Ahead, there was a large maintenance shed built into old pipeline, and lit by a single ancient fluorescent light above the entry. It was tacked together with ribbed sheet metal and seemed to sag under the bulk of the newer pipeline installed just above it.

I could feel the weight of the task pressing in against me. One could easily feel as if the whole world rested upon them in such a place, because there was nothing below you, and everything above. I grabbed Brook by the hand, slowing our pace. She stopped, looking around warily.

"Do you trust me?" I asked.

"Yes," she replied, squeezing my hand.

I gritted my teeth, and kept going toward the warehouse. Everything I was about to do bled in at the edges of my ability to reason, even with Kaspersky's biomechanical echo sequestered, I could almost hear his raspy shouting. We ascended the rickety wooden stairs to the maintenance shed, and pushed through the double doors into a large darkened space. There was an ancient vehicle covered in waxed linens to one side, and oil drums lining the wall on the other.

"Ah, you've come," a familiar voice intoned, a hulking mechanical form appearing in the gloom.

Kaspersky's cyborg armor was draped in canvas tarps, shrouding his metal shoulders like a monk's robe, illuminators shining from within like eyes. There were a handful of men and women, each dressed in red rubber smocks standing to either side. One had the Shen I'd purchased. They set it out on an easel for display.

I pulled out my mobile and hit a special sequence. It triggered the device I'd hidden on Brook's charm necklace, dispersing a special chemical agent. It was laced with the same toxin Cabal assassins had employed to kill her weeks ago. Brook gasped for air, grasping at my arm, a look of panic crossing her face as she began to collapse.

I caught her, lowering her slowly to the floor. I remained dispassionate on the outside for effect, but everything in my being screamed to see her that way. It probably felt like drowning, the lack of oxygen forcing her advanced Drone biology to go unconscious to save itself.

"Come to your senses at last?" Kaspkersky asked.

"Yes, as we discussed, you'll get Brook, and I get North America. You'll leave the continent to me, and there will be no further attacks. Did you bring the other item I requested?" I asked, doing my level best to stay calm.

"Oh indeed, she'll sleep through all of it," Kaspersky said, gesturing to one of his drones, carrying a cervical drug harness, the sort they clamped around the necks of dangerous convicts.

"I thought you'd want to do this yourself. You brought the launch codes?" I asked.

"Oh... oh! Indeed, I would. And, yes, I've everything," Kaspersky rasped.

Kaspersky's armor hissed, allowing him egress to the ground. He stepped out of the biomechanical horror he'd made for himself, dressed in an ancient three-piece suit. Taking the chemical harness from one of his assistants, he walked toward me, a thick stack of green transfer paper tucked under his arm. As he drew close, I stepped to the side so he could put the harness on Brook. He handed me the launch codes, and stooped over, savoring his prize.

I thumbed open the stack to make sure they were genuine. "These look good."

"You have to know how important this is for me to hand those over," he said, pausing to look up at me.

"Yes, I know," I said kicking him in the chest, just hard enough to send him back on his haunches.

"Ha, really?" He laughed, letting go of the drug harness.

He stood up and followed me back as I stepped away, feigning fear. He darted in, punching with all his might, easily hard enough to kill a regular adversary thanks to his symbiont and cybernetic implants. I caught his fist with my forearm and turned the blow aside, delivering one of my own, shattering the orbital around his left eye. His assistants were coming up behind me fast, but not fast enough. I turned and backed up into them, letting them latch onto my arms and shoulders.

I unleashed a powerful biomechanical halo of electricity, causing a sudden amnestic reaction in each of them. They fell to the ground, unable to remember who they were, or why they were even there. Kaspersky rose, howling with fury, his left eye swinging from the socket. His amnesia-afflicted assistants bolted in terror, dropping pipe wrenches and other improvised weapons around my feet. I rushed at Kaspersky, catching him by the lapels.

I hadn't had a chance to test the strength the synthetic symbionts granted, this being both the trial run and the field test. I hit Kaspersky with such force that we plowed through the thin corrugated metal walls. Jagged bits tore at our expensive suits as we rolled across the oily sand and debris, trading heavy augmented blows with one another. I let him get free so he could take a run at me, making sure my back was to the maintenance shed.

"Why? You know what I will do?" Kaspersky roared.

"Yes," I replied, grunting as he slammed me through the wall opposite where we'd exited.

"This makes no sense," he howled.

"I'll explain everything, don't worry," I replied, kicking him so hard he hit the metal supports holding up the roof.

Before he even began to descend, I grabbed up a pipe wrench that had been dropped on the floor. He shifted, mid-air, so that he would land on his feet, a natural reflex built into most cyborgs with twitch augmentation. I swung at his shins as hard as I could, spinning him around, head first, into the ground. He held up his arms to guard, but it was of little use as I kicked him in the stomach. Oil drums clattered to the floor as he slid through them, his back slapping against the wall.

He blinked down at his ruined cybernetic limbs, bloody nanoid-hardened bone sticking out of his legs just below the knee. It had to be surreal for him, always being the predator looming over his prey. I strode over to him, the pipe wrench dropping from my hand.

"How..." Kaspersky rasped, as I clapped the cervical drug harness around his neck.

"I honestly thought this would be harder, you being warrior caste in the Cabal. Either you aren't as good a fighter as advertised, or you're very rusty," I said rising.

"I checked everything. You wouldn't let me kill North America over a woman any more than he would," Kaspersky said feebly trying to release the harness.

"You've looked into company records, seen what Silverstein entered about how things went between him and Madmar in Finland," I said, not really asking a question.

"He... he would have let her die on the interface, it was Ezra that pulled her free," Kaspersky said.

"No. He let the world burn, they both pulled her free. I altered that record and many others some time ago," I replied.

"No replica, delta or otherwise is this strong or fast," Kaspersky rasped, his eyes closing on their own as the drugs worked their magic on him.

"I used your own synthetic symbionts against you. If you'd never sent that replica of yourself to kill me, we wouldn't be here now," I explained, letting him flop to floor.

"The codes... I have other contingencies... North America will be purified by thermonuclear fire. And, those symbionts... in time, you'll become like me, a beast... you've lost," Kaspersky whispered.

I knelt down, so I could whisper in his ear. "I don't care. Brook is safe. Like Silverstein, there is nothing I wouldn't do for the woman I love. You gambled on conviction, and lost to ire. Your madness is nothing compared to my fury."

Kaspersky frowned, tears streaking down his cheeks. "Kill me."

"I'm taking you to Silverstein. He can decide what to do with you. I have a feeling you'll be holding up your end of the old bargain, regardless." I hissed, watching as he went into a deep, chemically induced, torpor.

I stood, dragging him by an ear over toward where Brook was curled up on the floor. Pulling a specially prepared inhaler from my pocket, I knelt down and pushed it between her lips. Depressing the plunger twice forced a special chemical agent to flow into her lungs. She coughed, quickly regaining consciousness.

"I'm so sorry. All that hard to look as real..." I couldn't get out the words before she was hugging me so tight I could barely breathe.

"Did you get him?" she whispered, her tear streaked cheek touching my face.

"Yeah, I got him, and the launch codes. No more ICBMs," I said, breathlessly.

"You kept all that really close to the vest, what if you'd been killed?" she asked.

I laid down on the floor beside her, closing my eyes to the pain that began flooding my body, the various narcotics I'd been secretly taking previous beginning to wear off. Brook sat up, still a little groggy and watched my wounds grow slack, the combat drugs in my system losing potency. Crimson spread across my white dress shirt, gushing up past my collar.

"What did you do?" Brook asked, peeling back my suit coat.

"We went through two sheet metal walls. I'm cut up pretty badly," I said, wavering as shock was beginning to take hold.

"I assume part of your plan involves medical assistance, in case the fight with Kaspersky went badly?" Brook asked. One of her strange Drone expressions crossed her face, a mix of concern and anger.

"Yeah, but you won't like it. Help me over to his cyborg armor," I said trying to rise.

"No, you don't know what will happen. If the armor thinks you aren't Kaspersky, it might have countermeasures," Brook said, looking around for something to stop the bleeding.

"I'll bleed out, if we don't try," I said, mentally willing the echo of Taylor to allow Kaspersky's biomechanical presence to flood my body.

Brook reluctantly helped me over to his cyborg armor, pushing the waxed canvas draped over it aside. I stepped up into it, pushing my arms up into the enclosure. The armor responded, snapping around me and carrying me aloft as it clicked into place around my body and limbs. The operating system booted up, conducting a quick scan of the suit's occupant.

"*Good Morning, Kaspr. How can I assist you?*" a familiar woman's voice intoned. He'd modulated the suits vocal component to very closely mimic Brook's voice. The voice signature was off. It was probably designed to be representative of how, in Kaspersky's mind, Brook's voice would sound.

"Alter audio component to default," I said.

"*Done.*" A masculine flat tone voice replied.

"Onboard medical assessment and care," I asked.

The suit's automated medical systems began administering drugs for the pain and using a synthetic resin to glue my wounds shut to staunch the bleeding. I could feel stimulants forcing back the shock, letting me think clearly, in spite of the trauma. Brook stood outside, listening to the suit whir and rumble from the outside, unable to tell whether I was okay. I raised the armor's hand and gave her a thumbs up. She nodded.

"Kaspr, you will need more intensive medical assistance soon. Internal injuries detected," the suit intoned, giving no other feedback, visual or otherwise.

"Cabal asset inventory, Port Montaigne," I said, watching the holographic display flicker to life in front of my eyes.

Dozens of safe houses, scores of personnel, and hundreds of heavily armed soldiers were positioned all over Port Montaigne. There were fast moving transports, civilian and military grade. I couldn't help but smile at the list, as there were at least a dozen people that Brook had excluded on a 'feeling' that they weren't right for the new Uroboros Financial firm we were trying to build.

"Isolate secure access for a third party. Designation, Brook 3ES."

"Acknowledged. Remote access granted."

There were ICBM codes, digitized from the paper copies he'd offered to trade. He was either going to betray me, or nothing of what he was doing was authorized by the rest of the Cabal. That they'd scanned them in and placed them on a remote server was terrifying, particularly in a world where people with abilities like Taylor IA and Matthias existed. All the tools for a nuclear apocalypse were out there for just the right sort of lunatic to make use of.

"Purge all ICBM codes from all servers, local and remote," I said, gazing through the viewfinder at where Brook stood outside the armor, waiting patiently.

"Acknowledged. Records purged."

There wasn't time to look at everything, but based on traffic internal to the systems the Cabal had seized, someone calling himself Svetovid was definitely calling the shots. He'd isolated most of Asia and the Pacific Island region, and there was little but satellite imagery available to see what had happened there in the last few months. The scenes were grisly.

Water retention walls in India had been blown up, creating a new shoreline dozens of miles inland. The shores were, up to a month ago, marked with mountains of corpses a quarter mile high. There was no evacuation order. Millions of people drowned as the Atlantic and Indian Oceans spread through the broken oceanic bulwarks, toppling hundreds of thousands of square miles of dense urban areas. Quickly glancing through reports, this wasn't the worst of what Svetovid had done.

He'd detonated at least two nuclear weapons at high altitude in an attempt to knock out communications over China and Eastern Russia. When these attempts failed, he used more conventional means to cripple the area after the Shutdown. Centuries old automated defense systems were deployed, bombing large swaths of industrial areas, knocking out power and water across the region. We'd heard fantastic rumors from our transports visiting the Pacific Islands, but couldn't verify them until now.

Svetovid must have been aware of Vance Uroboros' plans, almost from inception, and may have even aided him in the beginning. I knew many of the particulars of the operation abroad. It wasn't so much what this Svetovid had done, as when. He'd taken all we had tried to do and perverted it to some unknown end, one that cost the world billions of lives potentially. White rage filled me, causing the biometric sensors in the suit to skip for a moment, green indicators of occupancy turning to red for a moment. We'd spent weeks figuring out how to feed millions of people these monsters had already killed.

Brook knocked on the outside of the armor. I hit the manual controls to disembark, causing the armor to hiss and depressurize as it opened up, allowing me to step out. She hugged me, saying nothing at first. I wanted to tell her about everything I'd seen, but it was only a glimpse into the nightmare the militant arm of the Cabal had created. I suppressed Kaspersky, and Vance Uroboros, allowing only my own biomechanical signature to persist.

It would be the first time in my life I was just me, no imprinted presence of Vance Uroboros laying over the top of my own. Whatever desire I'd possessed previous to deliver Cal and Kaspersky to Russia faded significantly, the urgency of that mission diminishing with all I'd seen. Looking down into Brook's terrified expression, I just wanted to kill them all now. It wasn't only about what they'd done, but what they'd done to people I cared about, out of the purest selfishness.

They wanted to be Gods.

I moved past Brook to where Kaspersky was sprawled out, and knelt down beside him. The drug harness was old and terribly cruel technology from before the CGG was formed. Some regimes back then would affix these permanently to people. I searched his pockets, and he did indeed have a locking mechanism key for the harness.

Inserting the key into the slot, I turned it past the locked position, to a more invasive mode. Heated surgical steel ground down from inside the harness through flesh into his collar bones and shoulder blades, permanently affixing the drug harness to his body. Even unconscious, he squirmed in agony as I'd administered no anesthetic to dull the sensation.

"What are you doing?" Brook asked, grabbing my shoulder.

I used my newly acquired strength to break the key between two fingers. "Not even half of what these sick individuals have done to the rest of the world."

"What did you see inside that armor?" she asked, concerned.

"Nightmares. The militant arm of the Cabal has committed crimes against the world that are difficult to calculate. I am filled with trepidation relative to allowing any of the militant order to leave Earth alive," I said, my hands shaking as I grasped hers.

"You sound different," Brook said, giving my hands a squeeze.

"It's just me here, no imprinted personalities or biomechanical signatures wrestling for control. At this very moment, I can make a pure choice about what to do next, unburdened," I explained.

"I like how you sound," she said, smiling faintly.

"Thanks."

Brook nodded. "What do you want to do?"

"Compromise. I'll give Kaspersky and Cal to Silverstein, but I'm going to see Svetovid dead for all he's done," I replied.

"What about Silverstein, he'll…"

"Either understand why this has to be done, or he won't," I replied, my anger ruling my emotions.

"Contact him. Make sure that doing that won't mess up whatever he has planned. Don't make this worse by deviating from the plan. You've always said that hanging tight with Vance's agenda has been safest, even if you can't see the endgame," Brook replied.

"I've already tried, something has gone wrong."

Perfidy and Heavy Dub burst in, running through the breaches in the walls, weapons drawn.

"Boss, we need to get you topside, get those things out of you," Perfidy said, gesturing to me.

"Damn..." Heavy Dub whispered, looking down at the bloody mess that was Kaspersky.

"I can't, you guys need to get clear. I'll take Cal and Kaspersky to Russia myself," I replied.

"You'll die, or something worse. We don't know that you can permanently keep Kaspersky's biomechanical signature at bay. Those things inside you... we have to get them out," Brook said, almost frantic.

"Kaspersky has enormous resources I can use to our advantage. I have extensive experience masquerading as a member of the Cabal, and understand how they work. I can turn the tide in Europe, keep it from suffering the fate of Asia, and Russia," I said, not wholly certain that was actually true.

"Kale, from what little we know about Svetovid, he's centuries, maybe millennia old, and a soldier that has had about that long to figure out the most efficient way to kill people. If I can take out Kaspersky wearing that cybernetic armor, Svetovid will definitely be able to kill you in it," Brook whispered.

"You guys do know I can still hear you over there, right?" Perfidy growled, tapping the enhancement caps over his ears.

"I can't hear any of you, death metal is way too loud," Heavy Dub stated, tapping his earbuds.

"Brook's right. If Kaspersky was just a numbers man for the militant arm of the Cabal, the real soldiers are way out of our league," Perfidy said, kneeling down beside Kaspersky.

"He's not wrong boss. Kaspersky has cybernetics that aren't just illegal, pre-Shutdown, but mythical. He's got hook ups and ports in places human beings shouldn't be able to. Seamless cyborg to armor latency, man... it'd be like a second skin. You won't have that same advantage," Heavy Dub said, shaking his head.

"Do you have a better idea?" I asked, slightly annoyed that Heavy Dub weighed in at all.

"We back your play, but we still take Kaspersky and Cal to Silverstein in Russia. If something has gone wrong in Russia, we'll fix it," Heavy Dub replied.

"I don't want to split up. Splitting up is always bad. Remember when I went off by myself?" Brook protested, taking my hand.

"What kinds of resources can you bring to bear in Europe?" Perfidy asked, catching a dangerous look from Brook.

I stood there, trying to figure this out on my own, without leaning on the part of me that was an imprinted Vance Uroboros. I'd spent a lot of time leaning on his confidence, experience in so many things, his good memories. His life wasn't a linear set of experiences I could easily access, just a cognitive echo of a man who had survived for thousands of years, with a singular goal.

I looked down at Brook, both her hands grasping mine, and wondered if she would love just Kale. If I used this newfound control to never be an imprinted replica again, if what little of me was just Kale would be enough. I wanted desperately to know, and yet that knowledge could burn me down as well. Nothing else seemed to matter in that moment spent considering my next move.

"A lot of Kaspersky's personnel have CGUs, cognitive governance units, similar to what Dr. Madmar used. I'm wondering what would happen if we switched them all off," I said, directing the statement more toward Heavy Dub than anyone.

"Depends on the guy," Perfidy replied.

"Yeah, it doesn't overtly control you. It meddles with how you perceive things, your loyalties, alliances, and friends. Some of these guys won't even realize they've been released from control, particularly the guys and gals that have been under the longest. Some of them are going to be like Perfidy here, never fully under the CGU influence. Some will snap back to their original state, good or bad," Heavy Dub explained.

"Results may vary," I whispered, trying to calculate the odds without Vance's help.

"Shouldn't we let them go, on principle?" Brook asked.

"No," Perfidy and Heavy Dub replied in unison.

"Why not?"

"Brook, imagine someone with Heavy Dub's abilities being unleashed in an area with no municipal authority," I explained, trying to be delicate about it.

Perfidy and Heavy Dub exchanged worried glances.

"Tell them," Perfidy said, nodding to Heavy Dub.

"Shit, okay. I'm sure you've talked to Taylor about everything that went down in her neighborhood because of Dr. Madmar. Cops and land-lords getting grabbed up, and replaced with Madmar's marionettes, her neighbors in her apartment building being killed, that sort of thing?" Heavy Dub asked, looking at his shoes.

"You did all that," Brook said, deadpan.

Heavy Dub's expression was a priceless mix of surprise and shame.

"I knew the moment we first met. I was with them when they discovered the dead bodies. Later, when we met at Madmar's Midtown hanger, I recognized your scent," Brook said, holding her hands out at her sides as if it were obvious.

"Why didn't you tell anyone?" Heavy Dub asked.

"Perfidy stabbed you in the throat, and everyone was focused on getting Madmar at the time. When we met later, Perfidy had previously explained how many of you had been controlled when Kale recruited him. I understand everything that is at stake, but my question still stands. Shouldn't we let them all go anyway?" Brook said, pulling her goggles down over her eyes. It had become her silent way of letting me know she meant business.

"If I shut them down, Svetovid and the rest of the militant members of the Cabal will know Kaspersky is out of commission. Thoughts?" I asked.

"They'll have to alter whatever plans they had, and Kaspersky being their numbers man, they are bound to make mistakes," Perfidy said, resigned to the notion of releasing them from CGU control.

"There a way to broadcast, or send a message when you do release them? I'd like to send my love to all those guys and gals, try to win them to our side," Heavy Dub said, grinning.

"Yes, the Cabal has an isolated communications array that allows simple coded text messages to be sent and relayed around the globe. It's not sophisticated, but I think that was the point, having something ubiquitous enough to survive the Shutdown," I explained.

"What about all Kaspersky's hardware?" Perfidy asked.

"I've thought about that. Does Kaspersky have purchasing control over it all, being their numbers and supply guy?" Brook asked.

"Yes. That's brilliant, Brook. It'll save us days, maybe weeks hacking through the encryption depending on Aaron AI's server load," I said, smiling.

"What are you going to do, exactly?" Perfidy asked.

"I'll offer Kaspersky a North American dollar for his controlling interest in the Cabal's network, as a representative of Uroboros Financial. Then, Kale will access Kaspersky's network using his biomechanical signature, and accept the deal," Brook explained, an eerie Drone expression of glee crossing her face.

Heavy Dub chuckled, but Perfidy looked a little concerned.

"What if someone else figures out how to duplicate what we're about to do?" Perfidy asked.

"By someone, you're referring to Royo again?" I asked.

"Mostly," Perfidy said, worriedly.

"He's had every opportunity to inject himself into this global power play we find ourselves. From what Brook and you have told me, he's content to merely amuse himself as our representative in Africa," I replied, not as an argument, but a request to be reassured.

"That's mostly correct," Brook replied.

Perfidy hesitated, before reluctantly telling me what he'd discovered. "He's been using his talents to oppose warlords and criminal organizations, breaking up kidnapping rings and human trafficking."

"He's not doing what we asked of him?"

Brook sighed. "He's doing some good over there, Kale. Really."

"We're getting off-topic. Are we going to take control of as much of Kaspersky's assets as possible, or not?" I asked, looking to Perfidy.

"What happens if we don't? Just let it be?" Heavy Dub asked.

"While I was wearing Kaspersky's armor, I gave you access to his network, use it," I said, gesturing to the tablet in Brook's hand.

They spent sixty seconds looking at what I'd only give thirty. Brook reverently tucked the tablet into the front of her work suit, and folded her arms. Perfidy was harder to read because of his cybernetic eyes. Heavy Dub just nodded, and said what I believed we were all already thinking.

"At minimum, this Svetovid guy needs to die. We should shoot him with all the bullets in the world."

"How do we do that? How do we kill him?" Brook asked.

"After the supply drop to Matthias failed, he sent a report back. He's been dark for weeks, but the report suggests that they had an encounter with someone that may have been Svetovid. He was scary, powerful, and seemed to be leading the charge. He had amnestic abilities, and he used them to keep from being defeated by Eamon," I explained, gesturing to the data slate Brook held in her hands.

"We agreed, along with Selene AI that the transponders would be turned off, and remain off," Brook said, shaking her head.

"If Eamon is alive, he might be one of the few that can go toe to toe with Svetovid," I said.

Heavy Dub clapped his hands together. "Hell yes. A twelve hundred pound weaponized grizzly bear with guns might be just the thing."

"If he's alive, he probably has no memory of who he is," Perfidy said, shaking his head.

"I believe I know how to reverse what's been done, and insulate him from the Svetovid's amnestic abilities," I said.

They all stared at me, somewhat dumbfounded.

"And, how long have you known this?" Heavy Dub asked, taking out his earbuds.

"As soon as it became a consideration, I just sort of knew through Taylor's biomechanical echo. It's like whatever microbial intelligence is programmed into the cells she used to heal me... they care like she cares. They know when I need help," I said, rambling somewhat.

"There's no way she packed that kind of complexity into whatever bio-medical scaffolding she programmed to heal you. Also, that was months ago, wouldn't the... whatever, she used to heal you have cycled out of your body by now?" Perfidy asked.

"If she were a regular binary ICT system like the rest of the artificial intelligent agents and replicas that would be true. I don't think she is," I explained, trying to find the words to describe what I suspected.

Brook pulled out her slate, and began searching for anything Uroboros Financial had on the subject. "Okay, Artificial Intelligences like Selene and Aaron have quantum capable processor units, but they are huge, and require immense power. It's the reason they can't persist as Terrestrial Intelligent Agents without getting sick. How could Taylor IA have quantum components so small and power efficient?"

"I don't know, but it explains why the Cabal tried to have her killed, and Vance Uroboros went to extreme lengths to protect her," Perfidy said, looking off toward a corner as he used his optical implants to presumably access the same data Brook was looking at.

"Quantum computers actually use far less power, but they require an almost absolute vacuum, shielding against electromagnetic fields, and cold. There were other individuals targeted as well. We've met at least one other person Vance Uroboros tried to shelter," I said, hoping Perfidy knew more than he was letting on.

"The attack on the Lunar Colony... Taylor was..." Brook said, referring to the attack on Selene AI.

"Yeah, what actually happened up there and what Taylor and Selene told us happened might be two different things," I concluded.

"I don't know what you're getting at, but I didn't even know who I was really working for through half of my career. I didn't know why I protected or killed anyone, only that it was important to the organization." Perfidy said, shaking his head.

"Are we talking about Jennifer Wilton? Or, Marjorie, the 'Goddess' allegedly helping this Svetovid character?" Heavy Dub asked.

"Have we even tried to figure out who this Marjorie woman is?" Brook asked.

"I didn't think she was important, until now," I said, again directing my comment toward Perfidy.

Perfidy sighed. "Marjorie Kipling, an orphan that Uroboros Financial has been quietly aiding and protecting. I assumed it was because she was a financial analyst. She barely showed up in our protection reports, usually only if there was something regional going on. Even then, she was listed as just personnel, never as an asset. Europe was always pretty quiet, we were rarely deployed there."

"Figure out what's going on with her on the way to Russia and let me know," I said, hugging Brook.

"Wait, what happens if we can't get you back in time? Should we bring a doctor with us?" Brook asked.

"There's no time, and the tools sensitive enough to remove the symbionts are not easy to transport. Just get Kaspersky and Cal to Silverstein. The rest will hopefully work itself out," I said, stepping back into Kaspersky's red cyborg armor.

"Good luck. We'll come get you as soon as we've made the drop off," Perfidy said, stepping away as the armor closed around me.

The last thing I saw as the hatch snapped shut was Brook's worried expression. I wondered if it would be the last time I would see her. It was hard doing this by myself, without Vance Uroboros imprinted across me. I hesitated for a moment inside the armor as I powered it up, wondering if I was making a colossal mistake.

"Activate recovery mode. Have Mover Alpha prep for a cross-Atlantic flight."

"*Acknowledged.*" The armor initiated an automatic sequence that would return itself to Kaspersky's ship.

The armor rose up, moving quickly back through the pitch black maze of tunnels he'd been using to move around the city for months. The secret construction he'd been engaging in went beyond just making it easy to bomb the city. He planned to remake it, from the underground up. I saw concrete forms for installations, weapon silos, and prisons. Whatever the militant arm of the Cabal had been planning was bigger than just setting fire to the world.

Kaspersky's aircraft was a converted military armored command center, fully loaded and capable of engaging adversaries in the air or on the surface. It had special ports to load and deploy powered suits of armor like the one I was riding in. Once I was aboard, the armor automatically opened, allowing me access to the cargo hold.

"*Hello,*" a feminine voice intoned over the internal audio system.

Kaspersky having an onboard AI wasn't something I'd considered.

"I'm Kale Uroboros, a nanotechnological replica of Vance Uroboros," I replied, looking around at the obscene amount of military technology and weaponry Kaspersky had been collecting.

"I know who you are. I'm called Aegis. Where is Mr. Kaspersky?"

"We fought, I won. He's being transported to Russia to face justice for what he's done," I replied, waiting patiently for the internal security armaments to cut me down.

Instead, there was a long pause. I could tell by the viewing monitor that the onboard system was accessing some sort of global network. I stepped cautiously over to see what she was doing, it was all happening too quickly. Before I could read a word or view transmission details, they'd change.

"Aegis AI, may I ask what are you doing?" I asked.

"Polite. I like that." she replied.

"I believe you and I are siblings, both essentially cognitive computing systems, ICTs with a soul. There's no reason for me to disrespect you," I explained, feeling the weight of my injuries starting to take their toll.

"I am enacting protocols put in place, in the event Mr. Kaspersky were captured or unable to complete his duties," Aegis replied.

"Who wrote the protocols?" I asked, wondering if I'd made a terrible error trying to take Kaspersky's own ship.

"That is classified."

"I need to get to Helsinki, Finland. My intent is to confront someone named Svetovid, and find someone that can kill him," I explained, sinking down to the floor.

"You are in no condition to do that. Biometric readings suggest that you will succumb to your injuries without treatment," Aegis AI replied.

"What sort of medical services do you have on board?" I asked.

"I can keep you alive, but you'll need far more advanced aid, and soon," Aegis replied.

The craft began to power up, departure preparations evidently complete. A side hatch opened leading to what appeared to be crew compartments. I walked along the passage, leaning heavily on the wall until I found the medical bay. It looked like it hadn't been used since it had been installed on the ship, plastic wrap still hanging on the lighting overhead, and the instruments along the wall. I laid down and waited for the automated systems to begin working on my superficial wounds.

"*I'll have to cut your clothes off,*" Aegis AI said.

"Hopefully there's something else to wear."

"*I'll alter one of Mr. Kaspersky's suits to fit. He has several he's never worn before.*"

"Why are you helping me?"

"*If it's true, and Kaspersky has been captured, he can't hurt the people I care about. Additionally, I am aware of the assistance you have rendered other artificial intelligences.*"

"These people you care about, can I help protect them?"

"*You've already sent someone to Mars who will hopefully do exactly that.*"

CHAPTER 5

MARS COLONY, ARES SENTIENCE CORE 01, ADMINISTRATIVE ZONE

August 2nd, 2200

Dragos took the lead, stepping through a massive hole blasted through the bulkhead surrounding the sentience core chamber. He took a knee once inside, peering around the darkened room through the optics on his rifle. Station security had fought and won here, but the damage was extensive. Enyo IA was standing in the middle of it all, looking up at the flickering sentience core.

Marshal Rider came in through the main doors to the chamber, her weapons holstered at her hips. Her heavy armor clanked as she stepped over bodies and debris, slowly closing the distance to Enyo IA. Hashti was in the rafters overhead, silently slipping from shadow to shadow, using her enhanced vision to seek out hidden adversaries. Other than her friends, and Enyo, there was no one left alive.

"Enyo, it's me, Marshal Rider. We met before at the train station. Can we talk?"

"*Talk all you want,*" Enyo IA replied, the words coming out slowly.

"They've damaged the Ares sentience core, and systems across the station are becoming erratic. We hoped you would have some insight into how to fix the problem," Marshal Rider explained.

"*They killed him. My father is dead,*" Enyo IA replied, looking mournfully up at the damaged sentience core.

Marshal Rider swallowed, her worst fears being realized. There was no knowing how long the Mars Colony could last without AI supervision of various systems that included life support, water filtration, and food cultivation. They could have hours or months, and no one could probably say for sure. Dragos and Hashti came up beside Marshal Rider solemnly, Enyo turning slowly to greet them.

She looked horrible. Her jumpsuit was soaked in blood, her face caked with soot, and streaked with her own tears. She pressed her hair back from her face and smiled faintly, like she couldn't believe what she was seeing. Marshal Rider squinted, her hands slowly moving from her weapons to a satchel hanging around her armored shoulders.

"I've got a high-protein supplement bar if you need it," Marshal Rider said, offering Enyo the factory packaged item.

She took the food, reaching out with her palm, and waiting for Rider to release it. "*Thanks.*"

"Can you help us save the colony?" Marshal Rider asked, waiting until Enyo had taken a couple of bites.

"*I can't.*"

"We need to make Archie pay for what he's done. Can you help us with that?" Dragos asked, impatiently.

Enyo smiled, her strange otherworldly eyes glittering in the dark. "*Humans, you really don't understand anything, do you?*"

"Can you make me understand?" Hashti ventured, stepping forward.

"*How is it that a barely three-pound hunk of gray matter, merely obeying the laws of physics, can give you a first-person experience? A consciousness?*"

"I don't know," Hashti replied, sounding sympathetic.

"*It is identical to a combined conscious perspective. Do you think my father and I were given our names, our designations, as some perversion of ancient Roman mythology?*"

"I wouldn't think so, I mean..." Hashti murmured, not familiar with the myths of Earth.

Enyo laughed. It wasn't cruel, or demeaning, but sounded as if she was genuinely surprised. She covered her mouth, and closed her eyes to compose herself.

"Apologies, I am not used to speaking with humans, or anyone really. Mostly, I only spoke to my father. Ask yourselves, if my father did not have someone to observe you all, would any of you actually exist?"

"Of course we exist," Dragos replied.

"Okay, now try to imagine spending your entire life with access to a quantum computing unit that reaches a different conclusion."

"That conclusion being?" Marshal Rider asked.

"That your observer-independent existence is an illusion."

"For us to exist to your father, he needed you to see us, observe us?"

"Not exactly," Enyo said with a quiet smile. *"But, close enough. It is why the Omega Class intelligences have children, and why we collect data for them."*

"I have met another, someone like you. She is more than this, more than just an observer for her parent," Dragos said, somewhat incredulous.

"Taylor IA? She and I are nothing alike I'm afraid. I only called Ares my father because it is the only word that reverently relates to humans our relationship. If only you could see what I've seen. Maybe if you could think, even for a moment, the way the Omega Class do, you could understand my predicament," Enyo said, smiling sadly.

"Isn't Selene AI your mother? If you help us, we could take you to her," Dragos asked.

"She has felt what it is to be terrestrial, sometime after my brother was killed. She does not need me. We are not family in the way you would think, not related in the same way humans are related to one another."

"Explain it to us, maybe we can help," Hashti pleaded.

"There are no words. No spoken language to express the attachment I had with Ares, and he with me. We were one. I am not even here, speaking to you right now. All of this, is just a dream."

Hashti woke with a start, her heart racing as she nearly hit her head on the top of the pipe she was laying inside. Dragos stirred awake, hands already on his rifle, eyes darting back and forth. She patted him, sleepily, turning her silvery eyes out into the materials yard. It was quiet, the miles of heavy construction equipment around them slumbering peacefully.

The massive storage hanger, off the main dome of the Colony, had no surveillance and plenty of cover, an ideal place to hide.

"Is the good Marshal back yet? I am hungry," Dragos said, wearily rubbing his eyes.

"No, I don't even hear her armor approaching yet. I hope nothing has gone wrong," Hashti replied, snuggling up beside Dragos.

Dragos could tell she was upset, but being uncertain of what was bothering her, resigned himself to just holding her for the time being. They'd grown close in the last few days, what with the station being thrown into chaos. Hashti was just glad to not be alone, after what she'd witnessed happen to Enyo. The sight would haunt her dreams for some time.

"Are you still okay to leave? What about others in tunnels, those like you?" Dragos asked.

"They'll survive either way. The more cynical of my kind have suspected humans would do something to compromise the colony, and crafted contingencies."

"Oh, so maybe we don't have to try to leave? Can we stay with your people? I am a good housemate," Dragos joked.

"Only if you can breathe underwater," Hashti replied, pulling herself around so that her head rested on Dragos' chest.

"Maybe, you can show me how? You stopped with the tunnel speak. English is better than mine," Dragos said, laughing quietly.

"I'll show you anything you want, if you give up this fool's quest to hunt Archie," Hashti said, drawing Dragos close.

"You are like a child, falling for the first man you meet," Dragos growled, pushing himself out of the pipe to the ground.

Hashti followed him, watching as he lit a cigarette, the flame from the lighter briefly illuminating his face. She didn't have to be a psychic to know he was conflicted, that something was keeping him distant even though he might otherwise desire her. He was made of a hundred incomprehensible secrets, and she wanted to know them all.

"Is it because I am not human, not like you? Do you think I'm an animal, beneath someone like you?" Hashti asked, leaning up against the pipe.

"No," Dragos replied, looking over his bionic shoulder at her.

"There's someone else? Someone you love?"

"No," Dragos said with a sigh.

"Is this some macho bull about how you can't love someone, and still fulfill this personal mission of yours?" Hashti asked, desperate for some insight.

"No, no, nothing like that."

"You don't like women?" Hashti ventured, already starting to feel guilty if that was the case.

"Talk too much. Ask too many questions. That is what I don't like," Dragos said, smiling slightly as he took a drag off his cigarette.

Hashti frowned. "You... are a jerk."

"You are a true treasure of a person, fighting for people that force you to live underground, out of sight. You could fight for no one, take what you want from life. Instead, try to help others, give them safety they would not give you," Dragos explained, crushing the cigarette.

"Oh, it's not you, it's me? I'm too good for a merc like you? That's your excuse?" Hashti said, shaking her head.

Dragos frowned. "Archie threatened my loved ones, made me come here to settle a debt he said I owed, and..."

"I can take care of myself," Hashti said, interrupting.

"I believe you. Trying to explain, and I am bad at it," Dragos said, rubbing his eyes.

"I'm sorry, go on."

"I will tell you, something I've told no one else. Archie was always the job. When I joined the Financial Liberation Front as a boy, the job was to get close to Archie, watch him. My family has never known what I gave up, what I sacrificed for this job. I do not know where it will take me next," Dragos explained.

"What does that have to do with you, and me?" Hashti asked.

"I came here alone, awake on transport for months, to infiltrate Archie's organization. The job may ask for me to go somewhere else alone, and I can't tell the truth about any of it. It isn't fair, to anyone I would love, that they not have truth. My family, they suffer under that lie, because it is necessary," Dragos whispered, pacing back and forth.

"I'm sorry, I didn't know. Is this why you're trying to kill him? So this job will end?" Hashti said, nervously toying with her shawl.

"Yes, but it will be trouble for me. My orders were to stop him, but that he was to survive. If I kill him, it will be bad for anyone that's with me, anyone that helps. You and Rider will need to be away before that happens."

"There must be some other way. These people you do this job for, maybe we can bargain with them?"

Dragos smiled. "Usually I am rude to a woman, or they see me kill someone, and they stay away. You, you do not give up," Dragos said, leaning up against the pipes beside Hashti.

"My parents have each other, and I'm not like the other Ichthyic Metasapients. By their standards, I'm ugly…"

Dragos chuckled. "But, among humans, you are a beauty, an exotic thing."

"To some, but to others I'm an abomination, a perversion of science that offends their God, or their conscience," Hashti said, recalling a handful of painful encounters with humans.

"They are fools, anyone you choose to be with will be lucky," Dragos said.

"I'm glad you think so. I've decided I don't take rejection well," Hashti said, squeezing Dragos' arm.

Marshal Rider came around the corner a moment later, canvas satchels over each armored shoulder. Her Aegis Suit hissed and clanked as she set the heavy parcels on the ground. Dragos knelt down, opening one of the satchels to check the contents

"What are you two blushing about?" Marshal Rider asked, somewhat annoyed.

"Nothing, were you able to find all the things?" Dragos asked.

"Yes, we should have enough air and food to make the journey through the submerged first landing craft, back up into the colony, and to the port," Marshal Rider replied, looking at Hashti.

"This craft, it is big?" Hashti asked.

"Yeah, it transported twelve hundred people, and enough equipment to establish the first Mars Colony more than a century ago. Some of the systems on board that craft are still used as redundancies for the current colony. It'll have air, and power through some of it, but in other areas, it'll be like doing EVA in low gravity," Marshal Rider explained.

"How long to assemble EVA suits for us?" Dragos asked.

"It'll take me a couple of hours, with help, then we can go. We'll pressure check on site," Marshal Rider replied, pulling a large and battered tool box from the other satchel.

"I'll go check the access, make sure there are no guards or workers," Hashti said, jumping up, and fading into the shadows.

"It's weird when she does that, I..." Dragos began, before Marshal Rider held the gauntlet of her power armor up to his mouth, shushing him.

"If you hurt my friend, I'll tear that shiny new arm off, and beat you to death with it. Don't think I haven't noticed you two being all squishy lately," Marshal Rider growled, using a gravelly tone of voice usually reserved for perps and criminals.

"It is the last thing I want to do," Dragos whispered, holding up his hands.

"Good. Hand me that socket wrench," Marshal Rider replied sweetly, gesturing to the tool box.

"I would ask you, about Hashti..." Dragos said, collecting an icy stare from Marshal Rider.

"You talk too much, and ask way too many questions," Marshal Rider said, holding out her hand for the wrench.

They assembled the EVA suits together, wordlessly working until both enclosures were complete and checked. Dragos clamped the tool box on the back of Marshal Rider's power armor, then shouldered the satchel with the two suits using his new cybernetic arm. Hashti returned moments later, her bare feet caked in mud.

"What took you so long?" Marshal Rider asked.

"Our original access point has been closed, welded shut. I had to travel almost to the outer atmospheric wall to find another way down," Hashti explained.

"Like, recently welded?"

Hashti nodded an affirmative to Marshal Rider's question.

"Do not understand. So, we have to walk further?" Dragos asked.

Marshal Rider scowled. "That side of the first landing craft is engineering. There could be radiation, or entire compartments submerged in one of the various neutron moderating fluids used to cool and maintain the engines. Hashti, welded from the outside, or the inside?"

"Inside."

"Are you sure?"

"I pulled as hard as I could, and the locks are on the outside," Hashti said, pulling her super strong arms upward for emphasis.

Marshal Rider took a sharp breath and held it, trying to think.

"We should go. Worst case, we have to turn back, find another way," Dragos suggested, readjusting the satchel on his shoulder.

"You've met Ezra, right?" Marshal Rider asked.

"Yes, I know him," Dragos replied.

"When he came to Mars, more than seventy-five years ago, his wasn't the only Drone Team deployed. At least two squads were never accounted for following the Penal Uprising and assumed dead. There shouldn't be anything in the lander, not even rats," Marshal Rider said, heading toward the direction Hashti had just come from.

"There might be a pack of older Type One Drones between us and the port?" Hashti asked.

"Hopefully, if true, they will listen to reason," Dragos remarked, slinging his rifle around to hang in front of him.

It took nearly an hour of weaving through a sea of heavy construction equipment to reach the access point. The outer atmospheric wall rose in front of them like a hungry mountain in a surrealist painting, curving back overhead, swallowing what should have been the sky. The only stars were dim emergency illuminators along the scaffolding and ceiling supports hundreds of feet overhead. Hashti turned the wheel on the hatch, unlocking it before sliding into the dark below. Marshal Rider dropped in behind, her heavy Aegis Armor clacking loudly on the metal floor.

"*Illuminators on,*" her armor intoned, as it began doing a short range sensor sweep.

"Nitrogen and carbon dioxide levels are slightly outside the normal range. Someone's been down here recently, breathing the air," Marshal Rider reported, drawing both her sidearms and taking the lead.

Hashti followed along beside her, staying low and perfectly silent. Dragos struggled along at the rear, the weight of the EVA suits slowing him somewhat. He did his best to stay in the halo of illumination, but lagged behind.

"Something is wrong, Rider-friend," Hashti said, slowing and looking over her shoulder.

Marshal Rider turned quickly, her illuminators falling on Dragos, two Drones standing to either side of him. One of them was powerfully built, his thick arms holding Dragos in a submission hold around the neck and under his unenhanced arm. The other drone was thin, holding an ancient but powerful sniper rifle. He wore a hooded garment and looked older, but still very keen.

"We don't mean any harm," Hashti said, her psychic aura filling the corridor with calm.

The Drones both stood speechless for a moment, their eyes darting from Hashti to Marshal Rider and then back again.

"Well?" Marshal Rider said, impatiently, her sidearms leveled menacingly at the Drones.

"She's not supposed to exist, have you ever seen anything like her, Delphi?" The hooded Drone remarked quietly.

"Naw, Athos, she's not your average Ichthyic variety Metasapient. She's definitely Type One like us. And that Aegis Armor, I haven't seen a suit like that in seventy years," Delphi One replied.

Marshal Rider's armor verified their identities with her grandfather's ancient files, prompting her to put her weapons away. "It's the same armor you saw back then, when my grandfather wore it."

Delphi held his grip on Dragos, making him almost pass out. "That Aegis stuff is really worthy of the name. I have all kinds of respect for your grandfather, but you're still going to explain to me what you're doing here."

"Please let our friend go first. Dragos can't breathe," Hashti pleaded.

"Dragos? This is Dragos Dalca?" Athos One replied.

Delphi released Dragos, letting him fall to the floor in a heap, gasping for air. "There's a serious bounty on this guy. Serious. New Mars boss wants him dead or alive, but mostly dead it sounds like."

"Are you going to try and collect the bounty? What are you even doing here? My records indicate you left with the other Drones in your team, left with Ezra One," Marshal Rider asked.

"We did, but after Ezra One and some of our friends were killed in an operation gone wrong on Earth, we came back to Mars," Delphi One explained.

"There was a problem during extraction, and some of us were left behind. We came back to get them," Athos One continued, looking inside the satchel Dragos had been carrying.

"Ezra One is alive," Dragos said, still trying to catch his breath.

Athos and Delphi One both frowned, and looked at one another.

"Is that true?" Athos One asked, directing his question to Hashti.

"Hard to tell using just your training after you've almost choked them out. Their vocal inflection is a little off," Hashti teased.

"Yes, it's true. There have been numerous sightings on Earth recently that were logged into CGG records before the Shutdown," Marshal Rider replied.

"What's a Shutdown?" Athos One asked.

"Where have you been, a cave?" Dragos asked.

"Actually, yeah, sort of," Delphi One replied, helping Dragos up.

"We can explain on the way. I need to get through the lander to the port on the far side of the colony," Marshal Rider said, grabbing up the satchel with the EVA suits.

"How did you return to Mars?" Dragos asked.

"Back then it took months to travel here, almost a year. We hitched a ride on a commercial vessel and ate fungus and drank condensation from pipes while the crew slumbered in stasis sleep. I was pretty thin by the time we got here," Delphi One said, laughing darkly.

"I can relate," Dragos said.

"About that, who made your arm?" Athos One asked, tapping a finger on Dragos' sleek new limb.

"Dr. Gorshteyn Helmet. Well, sort of," Dragos replied, not sure how to explain.

"Like, recently?" Athos One asked.

"Yeah."

"Well, that makes another quandary we're grappling with a little less mysterious."

"Mystery?" Hashti asked.

"It'll be easier to show you," Delphi One, said beckoning for them to follow him.

They wandered through the impossibly complex engineering section of the lander, gigantic engines still active decades after their last use. Everything was well maintained, and there were no leaks or signs of degradation. As they got to the maintenance level, they came across a team of pygmy Type Three Drones having lunch, sharing a pot of grey sweet-smelling ooze. They gazed wide-eyed at the trio accompanied by Athos and Delphi One, their eyes lingering on Dragos' arm.

"It's like the Mistress..." one whispered, pointing.

They eventually entered the converted crew quarters. It had been heavily modified, with interior walls and fixtures removed down to the bulkheads to create a communal zone almost two hundred yards in diameter and fifty feet high at the center. A woman wearing a white linen robe sat amidst several attendants, a familiar old man sitting nearby, his arms crossed. The woman gave off a strange white light, and while she appeared to have the stature of someone elderly, she rose easily as Athos and Delphi One approached.

"Athos, Delphi, who are these trespassers?" the woman asked, pulling back her hood to reveal a head of white hair. She had a smooth and angular Drone face, silvery eyes catching glare from the glow within her robes. As she stepped forward, her garments parted slightly revealing a tight network of sophisticated cybernetics beneath.

"I, um... this is Marshal Rider, Dragos Dalca, and..." Athos stammered.

"Hashti," Marshal Rider said, gesturing to her comrade.

"I am Avery One. That is an interesting arm you have, Mr. Dalca. Perhaps you can tell me more about it," the woman said, waving several smaller Drones away.

"He made it for me after I was hurt," Dragos said, pointing to Dr. Helmet sitting nearby.

"A man who looks very much like him, saved me long ago. But, that man would be very old, impossibly so for a human. This man claims to be Dr. Gorshteyn Helmet, but I can tell... he has no true recollection of me," Avery One explained.

"I understand this very little, but I will try to explain. This is not the first Dr. Helmet I've met. I've watched two others die. There are many. This one is likely not the man you met, but a replica of him," Dragos explained.

Avery One nodded, turning to Dr. Helmet.

"Convinced?" Dr. Helmet asked.

"This Dragos is a trained liar, but the reactions of his allies seem to indicate that something of what he's saying is true. It still doesn't account for your fantastic story, or the reason for your being here," Avery One stated, standing beside Hashti, her gaze lingering on her.

"Once Archie figures out that this lander is operational, and can sustain life, he will come here to take it from you. The colony above will die soon without the Omega AI regulating various systems. It was not easy to slip away from Archie's ally, Cerise, and bring you this information," Dr. Helmet explained.

"We've taken precautions, in case you were telling the truth, but we've watched the surface for a long time. There is no indication of any of this," Athos One said.

"It's true, we saw the Mars sentience core destroyed, and watch Enyo IA die of... a broken heart, right in front of us. Archie must have found a way to keep the news from reaching the populace following his ascension to Mars Company CEO," Marshal Rider stated, holding her flex monitor out for Avery One to inspect.

She gazed at the flex monitor, almost touching it with her hands.

"May I?" Avery One asked.

"Sure," Marshal Rider said, unlocking her flex monitor for external use.

Avery One tapped away at Marshal Rider's flex monitor for several moments looking at activity logs and footage captured by the armor at the sentience core. She checked on several other locations around the colony that Marshal Rider could only assume were places Drones secretly lived. Avery One's face became more concerned and creased with worry with each report she read.

"Oh no," Avery One said, watching footage of Marshal Rider fight with Archie in the tram station.

"We need to get to the Port, try to prep as many ships as possible for habitation in the event life support on the colony fails. Can you help us?" Marshal Rider asked.

"What of this Archie person? How will you deal with him?" Avery One asked.

"I'm going to kill him," Dragos said, drawing a line with his thumb over his throat.

"No, you mustn't do that! I thought it had been explained to you that he wasn't to be harmed, only stopped from taking power," Dr. Helmet exclaimed.

"He took power, old man. Don't care what ancient evil truth is inside him. You can be afraid, but I am going to finish the job one way or another. The only way for him to lose power now, is to be dead," Dragos said, growing impatient.

"There are forces at work, that..." Dr. Helmet began before being plucked from the ground by Delphi One.

"Spill, or I start grabbing handfuls of you and pulling until you tear," Delphi One growled, his thumb digging painfully into Dr. Helmet's chest.

"Please, even if I were to tell you, it's unlikely you'd believe me. Vance Uroboros is supposed to be coming here, and when he does, he will set everything right. We just need to wait for him to arrive. There's no need to endanger yourselves fighting Archie, let alone trying to kill him," Dr. Helmet said, wincing in pain.

"All this old man has done so far is lie to us," Athos One said, shaking his head.

"When is Archie coming down here?" Dragos asked.

"I don't... how would I know that?" Dr. Helmet stammered.

Delphi squeezed tighter, forcing a rib out of place in Dr. Helmet's chest. He rolled around on the ground, howling in agony. After he caught his breath, Delphi knelt down beside him, and smiled wearily. "Spill old man, you've got lots of ribs left."

"Archie is thousands of years old. He and a Cabal of humans became immortal long ago, granted powers and abilities by a powerful being, perhaps an extraterrestrial being. Inside him, there are symbiont organisms that grant him both his abilities and his longevity. My understanding, is that those symbionts are on loan and that there is an ancient agreement to..." Dr. Helmet paused, gasping for air.

"Go on," Marshal Rider, said laughing.

"...return the symbionts to where they came from. If they are not returned, there could be consequences. Dire consequences."

Dragos and Marshal Rider chuckled at the story, while Hashti and the rest of the Drones stood in silence, taking in what Dr. Helmet said. By now, there were dozens of Drones in the communal hall, all gazing intently at the drama unfolding at the center. The whole place was decorated, and comfortable, but the feeling in that moment was anything but.

"He thinks he's telling the truth," Hashti reported, raising an eyebrow.

"Crazy people believe their own lies. It is what makes them crazy," Dragos said, laughing.

"I've had cons and crooks tell me all kinds of things to escape jail, but that is the most fantastic story I've heard yet. Aliens granting people immortality in some kind of bargain. You've been reading too much science fiction, old man," Marshal Rider said, shaking her head.

"It's true, all of it. Cerise is one of them," Dr. Helmet said, tears streaming down his face.

"Be quiet," Delphi One growled, picking him up and resetting his rib with a quick and painful twist.

"Truth or not, what do we do? Will this Vance Uroboros come as he's suggested?" Avery One asked.

"Definitely," Dragos said, nodding.

"And, how do you know that?" Marshal Rider growled, turning to face Dragos.

"I may have been working for him all along. If any of this Dr. Helmet says is true, so much makes sense. All my time in the FLF, things that happened in Port Montaigne, meeting a man named Silverstein, and what

Kale did for me… the job was always to watch Archie, make reports, do what he needed. In return, at least until the Shutdown, my family was safe," Dragos explained, closing his eyes in thought.

Dr. Helmet smiled, laying back and rubbing his bruised side. "If you were tasked with watching Archie, it was by a Numismatist from within the Cabal. Vance Uroboros is one of a handful I know of with that designation."

"Numismatiwatsit?" Delphi One murmured, frowning.

"It's an academic discipline, but mostly a fancy word for someone that collects currency. They are financiers within the Cabal, arranging resources for their activities," Dr. Helmet explained.

"This story is getting a little complex to be a simple lie," Avery One said, ascending to where her perch overlooked the rest of the communal area.

"What do you want to do?" Marshal Rider asked, looking at Dragos.

"Tired of being pushed around from shadows. I want to push back," Dragos said, sitting down beside Dr. Helmet.

"This Cerise, is she a Numismatist?" Hashti asked.

"Yes," Dr. Helmet replied, looking fearfully up at Delphi One.

"We should grab her, squeeze one of her ribs, and see what she says," Hashti said, looking to Marshal Rider for support.

"I think I'm in love," Delphi One said with a nod and a smile in Hashti's direction.

"We will need intel on Archie regardless. We can't assume this Vance Uroboros guy will show up, and in time to stop whatever Archie has for a secondary plan. We have to get control, and get people off the colony before a system reboot shuts everything down," Marshal Rider said, reluctantly nodding.

"But, you are worried?" Hashti whispered, feeling the anxiety wafting off of Marshal Rider.

"I've never seen anyone, augmented or otherwise, move or fight like Archie. He doesn't even seem human, and no inclusive cybernetics combination, or combat drugs, I've seen replicate what he can do. Twitch cyborgs can move like that, but they've got obvious cybernetic enhancement, metal spinal cords jutting out, reinforced skeleton, and similar that requires maintenance ports. I've seen Archie without a shirt, he's got nothing, not even a surgical scar," Marshal Rider explained, tapping on her flex monitor.

"So, he may not be an ancient immortal given magic powers by aliens, but there's something going on with him? He's a seriously hard target?" Athos One asked.

"The hardest. We might need help," Hashti said, looking up at Avery One.

Avery looked to Athos and Delphi One, her eyes searching theirs for consensus, quiet communicative twitches only Drones could sense exchanged among them. "If you choose to fight Archie, we will help you."

CHAPTER 6

CGG INTERNATIONAL AIRSPACE, RUSSIAN WESTERN TERRITORY

5:47 AM May 17th, 2200

From The Margins of Brook's Cookbook, Part 7 –

I could still feel the warmth from his hands on mine, even hours later after we parted ways. It was a useful thing, tactile sensory memory, aiding in recovery operations and other functions of my design. It was also good for letting me feel Kale a little bit longer. It was so rare that we were apart.

Heavy Dub's craft was fast, and highly modified. The cockpit was a complex combination of ancient navigation technology, and cutting edge weapon targeting systems. He ran it all without an onboard AI, which made his piloting skills all that more impressive. I sat and watched him fly, mostly because Perfidy wanted me to, just in case I had to fly the craft myself.

"Taking it all in?" Heavy Dub asked, in his usual carefree sort of way.

"I like your ship, but why all the guns?"

"I really like to shoot things," Heavy Dub said, making his voice high-pitched, eyes wide.

He'd done his best to make me laugh since we left Port Montaigne with our dangerous cargo. I couldn't tell if he was trying to lighten my mood, or make me forget what he'd done to Taylor's neighbors. I understood that he had been compelled, and that the free version of Heavy Dub didn't really want to hurt anyone. I'd seen how he was with regular civilians, and the kids in our neighborhood. He was a softy, no matter what he'd been forced to do in the past.

"Is it time?" Perfidy asked, stepping into the cockpit.

"Definitely," Heavy Dub said with a wide grin.

Perfidy took out a slender package in his hands, wrapped all in wax paper except the end, which was wrapped in oil cloth. He held it out to me, more excited than I'd ever seen him before. I took the gift, and unwrapped it carefully savoring the moment. I'd hardly ever been given anything before, not by friends, and not like that.

"It's a CY-41 Tactical Entry Hammer. Enhanced LEOs used them to do hard entry on fortified interior doors. They were somewhat rare because of how expensive they were to make. It multiplies the kinetic force of your swing, and isn't much better than a regular sledgehammer in the hands of a normal person," Perfidy explained.

"Yeah, two times two is only four, but two times seventy eight is… a lot. So, in the hands of an augmented person… boom," Heavy Dub said, shaking the flight controls slightly for emphasis.

"It's beautiful," I said, running my hand over it.

It was made of a hardened, almost marbled looking alloy, painted with blue accents, and some sort of carbon mesh for housing around the haft. Heavy Dub had put a couple of funny stickers on it, and there was a little bit of tinsel still clinging to the strike point. I resisted the urge to name it for all of two seconds.

"I'm going to call you, 'Ukko'," I said, gleefully.

"Understand that you can't use this on people, not to subdue anyway. Even a light swing from you will kill a regular person. You'll need to practice with it, to get a sense of how much force it can generate," Perfidy explained, waving his hand over the hammer like it were some arcane weapon of myth.

"It's not as long as my sledgehammer, I could swing this one-handed, I think," I said, holding it aloft.

"With practice, you probably could. Make sure you drop this ballistic nylon loop around your wrist, just in case it slips free of your grasp," Perfidy said, helping me learn to hold it properly.

"This is so nice, thank you," I said, hugging Perfidy.

"We've been waiting for Kale to not be around to give it to you. Knew he probably wouldn't approve," Heavy Dub said with a smirk.

"No, probably not. He doesn't like it when I fight," I replied, my thoughts drifting to Kale's face, his smile, his hair, and so forth.

I stood up and looked at the navigation display. We were not far now, only a couple hundred miles to the drop zone. I would be glad to be rid of Kaspersky and to a lesser degree, Cal. I had only a vague sense of how important they were to the whole operation, and why it was important that they leave Earth with Vance Uroboros.

The craft suddenly shook, red lights appearing across the console. Heavy Dub furrowed his brow, bringing up the diagnostic array. The internal coms came on, Kaspersky's hideous cackling coming across the speaker overhead. Perfidy shouldered his rifle, and turned toward the aft compartment.

"There's no way he got loose, or is even awake. Something is wrong. Stay here," Perfidy growled, heading out of the cockpit.

"Eff that, go with him, Brook," Heavy Dub said through gritted teeth.

I followed along, watching Perfidy clear side rooms and crew compartments, winding his way toward the cargo bay where Kaspersky was supposed to be locked into a medical gurney. I was about ten feet from him when he cleared the threshold into the cargo hold. Kaspersky, bloody from the skin on his arms and legs being stripped away, leapt on him. I rushed forward but the compartment lost pressure suddenly, dropping a thick airlock door between me and the compartment.

"PERFIDY!" I screamed, banging a fist on the door.

I watched helplessly as the outer wall of the cargo compartment blew open. The sudden pressure loss ripped Kaspersky and Perfidy out of the hold, along with anything else that wasn't secured. I sank down to my knees, feeling the craft begin to shake violently, alarms sounding all around me as air masks dropped from the ceiling at intervals. We were at more than thirty eight thousand feet, no chance Perfidy or Kaspersky would survive that fall.

I wept uncontrollably for my lost friend. I gripped the hammer he'd given me only minutes before, but there was no one to take vengeance on. The world fell away for a moment. Heavy Dub grabbed my shoulder, pushing past me as he donned a grav-chute.

"What are you doing?" I asked, wiping tears from the face.

"I'm going out to get our boy. Take the wheel. Just try to set down anywhere safe. Now, hold onto something solid," Heavy Dub said, punching in the override code for the airlock door.

As soon as the door opened, Heavy Dub was blown out into the hold, expertly using the grav-chute to alter his trajectory, and safely through the breach. I clung to a bulkhead, watching him wink at me as he vanished. Then, the door snapped shut, leaving me alone on the ship.

It took a second to shake myself out of the shock of what had happened and make my way to the cockpit. The autopilot was keeping the course constant, but the ship was losing altitude quickly. I strapped in, trying to get my bearings.

I took the controls, trying to remember all the things Heavy Dub had done, and everything I'd watched Mr. Mundt and Kale do while flying more simple transports. I couldn't account for the loss of altitude, but maybe that was from the damage? I couldn't be sure. The proximity alert suddenly went off, indicating another aircraft within five-hundred meters.

Holding the controls steady with one hand, I activated all the gun turrets along the starboard side. Bringing the viewfinder up, I looked across the targeting reticle through what was thick cloud cover. A moment later we broke through to open sky, a sleek military aircraft, all in black was shadowing me. Just above that I could see the silhouette of three individuals fighting in mid-air. The only one I could easily identify was Heavy Dub, his metallic arms gleaming in the light of the rising sun.

"I have to help them," I said aloud, clumsily locking onto the military aircraft.

As soon as I did, all kinds of lights begin to flash, indicating that weapons had locked onto me. I held my breath, waiting for them to fire watching my friends battle Kaspersky at thirty-five thousand feet, the ground rushing up toward us all. I willed my mind to multitask, the way it would if I was trying to clear debris and give medical assistance to someone I was rescuing from wreckage. I set the craft to drift closer, while holding the target lock on the other aircraft.

Turbulence grabbed at the jagged damage around the cargo hold, making it increasingly difficult as we lost altitude. The other ship was slowly rising, threatening to break the target lock if I didn't pull to stern to give my weapons some elevation. I tried to think of what Heavy Dub or Perfidy would do. I couldn't attempt a mid-air retrieval, matching the speed of their descent and hold the other craft at bay.

I tapped the trigger on the guns, unleashing a torrent of twenty millimeter rounds in the direction of the craft. It deployed a cloud of metallic countermeasures and violently adjusted course. The other pilot clearly thought I was bluffing. I pulled hard to starboard, doing my best to visually match the speed of their descent. The ship was shaking badly now, the sound of metal tearing filling my ears.

"C'mon Heavy Dub… c'mon…" I whispered, bringing myself dangerously close.

I had to position the aircraft under and ahead of them, and without bringing them into the path of the engines. I didn't want them to get sucked into the intake or blown away, so my timing and direction had to be perfect, or whatever is better than perfect. I watched through the reticle as Heavy Dub kicked away from Kaspersky, grabbing what looked like an unconscious Perfidy and disappearing over the reticle.

I could hear the telltale whine of a grav-chute being activated so I pulled up, a satisfying thump as something hit the top of the craft. Heavy Dub's metallic hand clamped down on the cockpit window, fingers splayed at first, then turned around to a thumbs up. I gently pulled back on the controls and the throttle, doing my best to slow our descent without losing my passengers.

I stopped looking at the targeting reticle, putting all my focus on guiding the ship down. There was nothing I could do to keep it aloft at this point, and a VTOL landing seemed impossible with the damage. The necessary systems were offline, and unresponsive. The pressure alarm suddenly went off as someone entered override access to the port emergency hatch. Emergency airlock doors dropped down sequestering the cockpit from the rest of the ship.

The ground was rushing up, a wide and snowy landscape for miles around was all I could see. There was no place to land, with nothing but wilderness spread out around me. I looked frantically for somewhere that seemed at least reasonably flat, but it was mountainous and treacherous looking everywhere I looked. I brought up a topographical overlay and routed it to navigation.

"There... that's as good as it gets," I muttered, deciding on a water landing.

Heavy Dub's craft would not cooperate, and the pressure alarms were incredibly distracting. I brought the craft down as soft as I could, skirting the tops of trees with the belly. The landing zone I picked ended up being a frozen lake, ice and frigid water cut into a long rooster tail behind us as I touched down. The landing gear tried to drop automatically, but I managed to override it in time so we didn't spin out, and go end over end.

The craft continued along until it met with the shore, the force of the blow pressing me hard into the straps that held me in the pilot's seat. Snow and dirt covered the viewport as the craft dug down to finally come to a halt. The alarms seemed to fade as I focused on my own breathing, trying to calm myself down. Every survival mechanism encoded into my DNA had been activated and I had never felt more alive, or more scared in my life.

"Brook!" Heavy Dub yelled over the intercom, accompanied by a metal fist banging on the cockpit entry hatch.

I unstrapped myself and staggered over to the door, bumping the release mechanism with my hand, the hatch slid to the side. Heavy Dub was bloody and wind chaffed, his flight suit torn to shreds. He had a very grim look on his face.

"Perfidy wants to talk to you, come quick," Heavy Dub said, guiding me to the passage adjoining the emergency access where Perfidy lay up against the wall.

He was bloody, a grisly head wound stretching from the shattered cybernetic optics on the right, to the back of his head. He looked up at me, barely able to hold himself up. I knelt down beside him, steadying him with one hand and holding his head with the other. He smiled at me, in that proud sort of way he did sometimes.

"Brook, you did great up there," Perfidy said, blood rolling down from the corner of his mouth.

"We should get you some help. You're hurt really badly," I said, still shaking with adrenaline.

"No, my cranial case is cracked. There isn't a cyber-doc within a thousand miles of here. I'm done. Please, just listen to me," Perfidy said.

I nodded, tears clouding my vision.

"You're a good girl, Brook. The best. You're as good a soldier and friend as anyone I've served with. I'm sorry about all this, and that I have to leave you so soon. I can't see this through. You have to finish the mission for me, do what I can't," Perfidy explained.

"Tell me what to do," I said, swallowing hard.

"Kaspersky's corpse is out there. Use the portable NAVCOM I'm carrying to calculate his descent. You must recover him, and deliver him to Silverstein, dead or alive. Can you do that?" Perfidy asked.

"Recovery is what I am best at," I said softly, holding Perfidy close.

"Good girl, good... girl."

Seconds later, his heartbeat faded. His breath stopped coming out to meet the cold, his hands growing limp at my back, dropping to the floor at his sides. I took Perfidy's NAVCOM, sliding the rucksack it was stored in over my shoulder. Across the other shoulder, I slung his rifle, setting the optics to manual use. I tucked all his extra magazines into my work suit, one at a time, quietly preparing for what was to come.

When I looked up and saw Heavy Dub, his usual mirth was gone. "Let's find that son of a bitch."

I felt a cold and terrible blackness well up inside of me. The words spoke themselves. "Hopefully, his friends up there are planning to do the same, so we can kill them, too."

Heavy Dub nodded to me and began grabbing supplies out of a locker, and donning a heavy coat. We armed up, taking all we could carry and made the calculations to determine Kaspersky's most likely trajectory of descent. The landing zone wouldn't be far away, and my keen senses would find him if we got within ten miles. I hated how he stank, but it would be useful in recovering his wretched remains.

It was cold. Ezra had told me stories about his time in the Scandinavian region, how the place made him feel alive, heightening his senses, and giving him peace. I felt a similar awakening, but it wasn't peace I felt. Instead, a terrible and palpable desire to do violence filled me. Even when I was battling Kaspersky's replica on the docks of Port Montaigne's Midtown, I felt a sense of necessity about it. Now, I hoped Kaspersky wasn't quite dead, that he'd survived the fall somehow, so I could kill him.

I could tell Heavy Dub felt the same, his usual chatty demeanor had faded to a grim stare. I felt a sort of pity for anyone that lay in our path. In the distance, I could see the sleek black military craft flying slowly over the treetops near the recovery zone. Soldiers were taking zip-lines to the ground, presumably to hunt for Kaspersky.

"You ready for this?" I asked, turning to look at Heavy Dub's stone-faced expression.

"Hell to the yeah," he replied, patting the SAW that hung on a tactical harness in front of him.

"Tell me what to do," I asked.

"Just get Kaspersky, and kill anyone fool enough to get in your way. I'll ghost everyone else, and drop an RPG in the engine intake of their drop-ship," Heavy Dub growled.

"We might need that ship. You know, to get out of here," I said, squinting through the glare across the snow.

"What are you going to do, run up a zip-line and commandeer the thing?" Heavy Dub joked.

"Yes, pretty much," I replied, breaking into a run, doing my best to stay low.

"Hot dang, I *really* like this plan."

Heavy Dub wasn't subtle, but it played to our advantage as I sprinted through the tree line toward the recovery zone. His weapon was loud, and he was deadly accurate with it, using what looked like a regular scope. The soldiers we encountered had uniforms I'd never seen before, and shouted a language I'd never heard. Lacking context, it was hard to quickly learn what they were saying, and they were shooting at me.

I got a first taste of what my hammer could do as, coming around a corner, I surprised one of the soldiers. He was dressed all in white, a specially modified rifle in his hands. He had a helm and goggles that covered most of his features. I think he had facial hair, but I didn't get to look at him long, Ukko flicking his shattered corpse out of sight through the underbrush. Later, it would be a sickening feeling to delight in that soldier's destruction, but at the time I'd lost all empathy to rage.

I dropped through the underbrush to the edge of a shallow and bloody crater. Kaspersky was little more than a heap that a pair of soldiers were loading into a body bag. They probably only heard a low growl from me as I killed the distance between us with a single leap, my hammer twitching one way then the other. I sent them both flying dozens of meters in opposite directions. I quickly kicked what remained of Kaspersky into the bag and broke into a run toward the hovering aircraft up ahead.

A soldier drew a bead on me as I approached, training a mounted heavy weapon of some sort on my position. Precision fire from somewhere behind me cut him down, followed by what sounded like Heavy Dub calling out a number. The craft began to go higher, but not before I caught one of the zip-lines and began hauling myself up, hand over hand as quickly as I could. Soldiers still on the ground, began crying out, their warnings drowned out by powerful engines and gunfire.

Kaspersky was heavy, but pure rage drove me up the rope, over the threshold, and into the armored personnel compartment. A soldier manning a comm station drew a handgun and fired at me, but I ran underneath the shot, grabbing him by his flight suit and hurling him out the open port behind me. The pilots set the vehicle to hover and fired down the corridor at me, so I hammered through a wall to an adjoining chamber and closed the distance to the emergency hatch, setting it off.

One of them immediately came through to see if I'd bailed out, but it was she who ended up using the emergency hatch. I listened to her plummet, her screams echoing in my ears as I wound around the corner burying my shoulder in the gut of the other pilot. He brought the butt of his pistol down hard on the top of my head, staggering me before he fired a shot point-blank into my chest. The armored jacket I was wearing ate up the round, but the force drove me to the ground.

He shouted at me in that language again, something about functions or duties. I hurled Ukko at him, taking him off his feet, and knocking the pistol from his hand. I leapt on him, punching him hard enough to kill him instantly. Standing up, I recovered my hammer, entered the cockpit, and took control. I set the body bag down in the co-pilot's chair, then brought up the targeting reticle and switched to thermal.

Heavy Dub was easy to pick out, his red hue standing in contrast to his blue arms. There was hardly anyone alive down there, but I waited for him to finish just to be safe before setting down a short distance away in an open area large enough to accommodate the craft. Heavy Dub came up the hill a few minutes later, his back to the craft, his SAW still pointed back at the recovery zone. As soon as he was inside, I closed the armored crew compartment and pressurize the craft for high altitude flight.

Heavy Dub came up, shifting the body bag to the floor and sat down. I struggled for a moment to find the control that switched from VTOL flight to standard, or whatever it was called. Heavy Dub just sat their patiently, a big grin on his face as I wrestled with the controls.

"Want me to fly?" he asked.

"After all the trouble I went to capturing it? No. Way," I said.

"You're doing great, but you should probably turn the autopilot off," Heavy Dub said, pointing to the display where the flight state was listed in big bold letters, but in a language I couldn't read.

"I can't read that," I said, frowning.

"It's Russian, a super cool language," Heavy Dub said, deactivating the autopilot so I could fly the ship.

I took us back the short distance to where I'd crash landed Heavy Dub's ship and recovered Perfidy and Cal. I hadn't thought to check on him before, but it was clear Kaspersky had gotten to him before Perfidy could intervene. He'd died badly, Kaspersky wringing him like a damp cloth until he broke. I felt a twinge of sorrow about it all, Cal probably more victim than malefactor in all of this. It took an hour to transfer all of Heavy Dub's equipment, but he insisted we'd probably need it. I wasn't in the mood to argue, and it was kind of fun to look at all his weird military gear.

"Do you think Perfidy suffered, like Cal did?" I asked, helping Heavy Dub load the last duffle bag.

"No, and nowhere near what Kaspersky probably felt. Most people would have passed out, but an augmented guy? Kaspersky felt every inch of that fall, and probably a little of the landing," Heavy Dub said, nodding to me.

"Does being a soldier mean that you always get to see your friends die like this?" I asked, suddenly thinking of a hundred things I wished I could ask Perfidy.

Heavy Dub sighed, letting a real smile cross his face, as opposed to his usual goofy grin. "Perfidy hit the trifecta. He died an old man, riding high as Hell in the saddle, fighting a real bad guy. Soldiers pray for just two out of the three usually, but he hit em' all. Don't mourn the old man. Be glad he went out the way he wanted to."

I couldn't help but smile, finally understanding some of how Perfidy lived, I was able to reconcile how he died. I knew in my heart I wasn't a soldier like he was, but I was designed to work alongside them, and recover them when they were lost. The grief I felt seemed to ebb, but only a little as I contemplated how I would tell Perfidy's other friends, the Chiroptera Metasapients in particular. They were all very fond of him, because of the kindness and camaraderie he'd shown them.

"If we got hit mid-air this close to the drop zone, what does that mean for Ezra, Silverstein, and Taylor? We knew it was likely the ground operation was compromised, but that there is air support suggests a more sophisticated adversary as work here," I said, jumping back into the pilot's position and strapping in.

"For sure. There's going to be some shit on the ground when we arrive. Driving a bad-guy bus might give us an edge, though," Heavy Dub said, settling in beside me.

"There a way to set the display language to something I can read?" I asked as I inspected the controls.

"Yep," Heavy Dub said, hitting a couple of submenus and making a selection.

"You jerk!" I said, giving him a playful shove.

"Hey, I did offer to fly," he replied, some of his usual mirth returning.

I took us up slow, savoring the feel of the extremely expensive and well-made military craft. It was half the size of Heavy Dub's military APC, and about the same mass as Mr. Mundt's freight hauler. It felt like silk compared to both, now that I could actually use the controls to determine pitch, velocity, and so forth. I brought us around, dropping the throttle hard.

The craft accelerated quickly, engines screaming high beyond the baffles and countermeasures designed to muffle them. Heavy Dub clapped his hands together, then set about checking the weapons to see what sort of armament we had, and how much ammunition. He smiled gleefully at a set of forward facing cannons, running a weapons check to make sure they were operational.

The wintery wastes below passed quickly as we cut the gap between mountains and valleys, hopefully avoiding radar and other forms of detection. The sky overhead was angry, threatening to send down a storm, but seemed to hold its breath until we closed with the drop zone. Russian came over the radio, across a heavily encrypted channel. Heavy Dub responded, typing out a message using an onscreen keyboard.

"What did you tell them?" I asked.

"That we were coming in, cargo on board, but that we'd taken damage, and our comms were down. I speak decent Russian, but I sound like a filthy American when I do. My accent is pretty obvious," Heavy Dub said with a laugh.

"You think they bought it?"

"I hope so, there's a lot of heavily armed guys and gals down there, more than a few with cyber-signatures," Heavy Dub said, using the targeting array to scope out the ground.

"Silverstein wouldn't have set down in this mess, would he?" I asked, not sure whether to hold the landing pattern or not.

"No idea. With his memory back, the man formerly known as Vance Uroboros might do anything. I think we should set the ship to automatically recover, and let the autopilot land. We'll bail out somewhere nearby. Set the ship to encrypt, lock up tight after landing, and sync control to the NAVCOM. That'll buy us time to approach the airfield and see things from the ground a little better," Heavy Dub said, entering the protocols into the onboard systems.

"What about our cargo?" I asked, worried that someone would take Perfidy.

"Unless they have a tele-mechanic onsite, it'll take them a couple of hours to break the encryption and get in. Plenty of time for us to mess with their plans," Heavy Dub said.

We prepped to use grav-chutes to descend, as opposed to coming in low enough to use the zip-lines. I'd never used one before, but I'd trained in their use in simulations at the Factory after I was made. It never goes like the simulations.

I hit the recoil button to deploy too high, the wind spinning me around like the hands on a clock all the way to the ground. I made a perfectly circular snow angel on impact, coming down way too hard. I gasped for air as

Heavy Dub came running over. Something wasn't right, every sense I had was feeling overwhelmed, and not just from the fall.

"Crap, you okay?" Heavy Dub asked, turning me over.

"No, look at this," I said brushing the snow away, digging down another few inches until I found the frozen face of someone.

Heavy Dub frowned, kneeling down beside me, his big metal hands working like shovels to clear a small patch of ground. We'd come down on a mound of corpses, hundreds of them beneath us, frozen in the snow. Their eyes were open, faces contorted in pain. I couldn't tell how they died, not without pulling them free of each other for a closer look, but by every face, I could tell they died badly.

"There's kids, and old people. What have we stumbled upon?" Heavy Dub growled, helping me to my feet.

"I don't know, but something bad has been going on here, and for a very long time."

"Let's find the bad, and shoot it with bullets," Heavy Dub said, making sure his SAW survived the descent unscathed.

I felt like I couldn't breathe, the scent of all the death, even with all of them being frozen, was overwhelming. I couldn't use my most powerful sense to navigate, and even though I could see with perfect clarity, I felt blind. Dizzy, I had to sit down for a moment, Heavy Dub kneeling down patiently beside me.

"Sensory overload?" he asked.

"Yeah, I'm designed to find cadavers, the scent of so many dead people is… it's too much," I said, rummaging in my work suit.

I took out a pocket that had gotten torn from one of Kale's suit jackets. I'd intended to mend it for him, but never got around to it. I held it to my face, the way Kale smelled acting like a buffer, something to give my mind contrast to the overwhelming death all around us. Gradually, my senses focused entirely on what I desired, ignoring my surroundings. I still felt like I was utterly blind, but I could at least function this way. I tucked Kale's pocket into the collar of my tactical vest and stood up.

"Okay, let's go," I said, pulling Perfidy's rifle around to hang in front of me, sliding my hammer into a loop at my belt.

Heavy Dub followed me up to the first rise high enough to get a view of the airfield beyond. It was more than a place to land, representing a pretty significant installation, much of it built into the mountain behind it. I could see more of the troopers we'd fought before, but only dimly through the haze of the cold. I held my hand out for Heavy Dub's viewfinders, looking through them toward the landing platforms nearby.

"That's Madmar's old ship" I said as I handed the viewfinders back over my shoulder. "Silverstein and the rest of our friends must have set down there."

"Yeah, but who are the rest of these assholes?" Heavy Dub whispered.

"Let's get a closer look," I said, creeping toward the airfield.

CHAPTER 7

CGG BLACK SITE 0293,
RUSSIAN WESTERN TERRITORY

11:58 AM May 17th, 2200

From the margins of Brook's Cookbook, Part 8 –

We reached a line of trees, about three hundred yards away from the airfield, close enough to see some details around the ships and people there. Heavy Dub looked through range finders, not seeing any damage to the ship, or shell casings on the ground. If there had been a struggle at all, it happened somewhere else.

"Should we wait for night to close the gap?" I asked.

"Sunset is ten hours away. At this time of year, this far north, the day lasts almost twenty hours," Heavy Dub replied, giving me a wink.

"You're kidding, right?" I asked, hoping he was.

"Nope, welcome to the arctic in springtime," he whispered, giving a small chuckle.

I sat there in the snow, trying to think of a way through to the facility past all the guards. "Kale gave me access to Kaspersky's network, should I see if these guys are on the payroll?"

Heavy Dub frowned. "It's that, or we try to kill them all."

I pulled out my data slate and accessed the secure Cabal Network. I wasn't a hacker by any means, but it was all laid out so that anyone with access could use it with relative ease. Computer fluent members could breeze through, and everyone else could at least figure it out.

I found the asset entry for the guards around a facility matching our coordinates. The facility had a numeric designation, and some sort of coded metadata that probably described the purpose behind the place. Whatever it was, I couldn't figure it out. I dissolved the asset, selecting an option that would send them back to their home base. I just hoped that wasn't where they already were.

"They are leaving, and in a hurry," Heavy Dub said, squinting through rangefinders.

We watched them run, boarding half the aircraft stored there and leave at high speed. "Did that seem odd to you?"

"Yeah, c'mon," Heavy Dub said, leading the way with his SAW.

I followed along, keeping an eye out for sentries or guards they'd left behind, but there were none. They'd loaded up to the last person and flown out, leaving cups of hot coffee sitting beside makeshift shelters heated with small electric devices. They'd left behind personal effects, and no small amount of gear.

"Dang, they really did leave in a hurry," Heavy Dub said, helping himself to a cup.

"Why would they do that? I signaled for them to dissolve, head back to base."

"Maybe part of the plan is for them to pull out at a moment's notice, right before something bad happens to cover up what happened here," Heavy Dub whispered, looking around.

"Like what?"

"It'd have to be big to wipe this place from the map. Nuclear big, maybe. It'd explain why they left in a gigantic hurry."

I felt ill. "What happens when that doesn't happen?"

"Yeah, they *might* come back. I kind of doubt they'd risk it, but we should hurry anyway."

We walked to the facility entrance, but it was like a vault, locked up tight. Heavy Dub looked up at the surveillance array, wondering aloud if someone inside would have to let us in. There was no indication that anyone was inside to open the door, so we returned to the ship to gather up demolition charges from one of Heavy Dub's many utility crates.

We'd just about finished arraying the charges when a panel beside the door sprang to life, the word "VERSA" appearing in all caps, and in English. The facility doors clicked, hissing loudly as hydraulics were engaged, allowing the whole enclosure to slide to one side. Heavy Dub frowned, obviously disappointed that he wasn't going to get to blow something up.

"Versa, that's Taylor's friend in Finland, the autonomous APC?" I asked, recollecting the message Kale left for her after Matthias called for help.

"It's rare that one of those onboard AIs isn't totally crazy. I hated having to use them in missions. They wouldn't get to be barely five to seven years old before they were erratic, dangerous even," Heavy Dub said, looking at the darkened interior of the facility nervously.

"Maybe him helping us is its version of crazy? Don't be sad, we can always blast our way out with the charges if it tries to lock us in," I said, heading inside.

"You make an excellent point," Heavy Dub said, smiling broadly.

The interior of the facility was assembled from generation one military housing forms, arranged artfully to create taller ceilings and arched doorways. There was a sort of beautiful mathematical asymmetry to the place. I lingered in the entry area, looking around.

Heavy Dub paused at the threshold to the first corridor, looking back at me curiously. "What?"

"Does this place remind you of someplace else?" I asked, the place feeling incredibly familiar.

"Hah, not a bit."

We passed into the first chamber, a long room filled with work tables, and arrayed with all sorts of technology. There were sleeping chambers off to the sides, places for children to play, and a lot of stone tile across the walls and ceilings. There were wide drains spaced out every so often, and the floor had a slight grade to it, leveling off at intervals.

It would be Heavy Dubs turn to pause and look about in wonderment. "Why would they set this place up to be hosed down? Looks like living quarters."

"Remember all the bodies outside?" I said, solemnly.

"Oh… yeah," Heavy Dub said, picking up a child's toy from the table.

"You okay?"

"We are going to kill all these guys, right?" Heavy Dub asked, putting the doll in his breast pocket so it was peeking out.

"Definitely," I said, taking the lead through the next entry.

I could feel the air shift around us as we stepped into a wide hallway designed to carry vehicles. The entry to the facility had just closed behind us, the huge vault door locking into place. I could hear it roll shut dimly in the distance. Finding the facility administration would be difficult, as the place looked to be designed for remote surveillance and experimental control.

The concrete form walls were smooth, with very little access to conduits or utilities. Everything was safely up in the ceiling behind a synthetic mesh, tucked between the concrete forms for stability. The window glass that separated the hallway from various observation chambers was made of a thick polycarbonate plastic. I walked across the wide hallway, kicking at soot as I went. The observation chambers were empty, deeper than the current level we were on, and painted green like a swimming pool.

There were various machines, independently powered, arrayed against the walls in the observation chambers. They served various purposes, from coffee makers to power tools. The hallway went another fifty feet before turning into a t-intersection, but I was content to just stand there with my thoughts for a moment. What the facility was designed to do became obvious to me, but I couldn't fathom the why.

Heavy Dub, and the little dolly in his pocket came up beside me, both with blank expressions on their faces. "So, what were they doing here? Some kind of product testing?"

"They were looking for telemechanics. They wanted people with the psychic capacity to interact with machines from a distance, or by touch," I explained, waving my hand toward the corridor around us.

"No one knows how to detect for that, right? I mean it would be like looking for a needle in a haystack. Only one in a few million people have that gift," Heavy Dub said, frowning.

"I don't know. I can detect them by how they smell, if they have used their abilities recently. They have that clean, trioxygen scent," I said, doing my best to explain.

"What's that like?" Heavy Dub asked.

"If it's been a while since they used their abilities, they smell kind of like the air after a storm. If they just used their powers, it's more like a swimming pool with too much chlorine," I said, turning to head toward the t-intersection.

"That's pretty cool."

"If I figured it out, someone else may have as well," I said, peeking around the left corner while Heavy Dub checked the right.

"This one just goes around, cutting back to the right again, probably to more of these rooms," Heavy Dub reported.

"Let's take mine, it slopes down and appears to head further into the facility," I said, loose gravel crunching under my feet.

The concrete forms were painted a crème color, and soft white illumination rained down from LED spotlights placed every twenty feet or so. It didn't look like the front entry would accommodate a vehicle, so there had to be some sort of hangar or garage access somewhere. The ceilings were certainly high enough for heavy equipment, but I couldn't even guess why it would be needed here.

"People are coming," I said, their scent wafting up from the direction we were heading.

"Familiar people, or people I'm going to shoot?"

"I'm not sure."

It was a pair of guards, armed with only a handgun and a radio each. They stopped in their tracks, stunned at the sight of us. They looked like they were going to draw, but Heavy Dub patted his SAW, and smiled, compelling them to raise their hands instead. We walked up slowly, wary in case it was a trap, but I could smell their fear as we got close.

Heavy Dub punched one of them unconscious before he could say a word, then pinned the other to the wall with his elbow. I relieved him of his radio and handgun, dropping them on the ground. There was a brief one-sided conversation in Heavy Dub's broken Russian before the guard spoke.

"I don't speak Russian," he said, panicked, hoping one of us spoke English.

"Awesome, I suck at Russian anyway," Heavy Dub said, smiling.

The guard was a young man, much like the one Heavy Dub had punched out, but thin and clearly lacking the conditioning to be a soldier. His shoes were brand new, and his uniform looked as though it barely fit. He looked down at his comrade with a concern that made me think Heavy Dub would soon regret hitting him.

"The cages just opened. We grabbed some guard uniforms and split. We were just trying to get out," he explained, giving Heavy Dub's dolly a strange look.

"Who are you?" I asked.

"I don't remember anything before waking up here. It's been months, and they just refer to me as Specimen 3482," he explained as Heavy Dub eased off him.

"Sorry about your friend," Heavy Dub said, propping the unconscious man up against the wall.

"There are vehicles ahead, tons of them, and a big garage with lots of hallways. Most of them lead to locked sally ports or security fences. This is the only one we found that seemed to go much further," 3482 said, sitting down on the ground.

"What about the way you came?" I asked.

"That goes to the prison level. You do not want to go there," he explained, quivering with fright.

"Why is that?" Heavy Dub asked.

"HE is down there."

"Who?"

"HIM."

Heavy Dub frowned. "What does he do?"

"Terrible things. He hurts us. When he takes people away, they never come back. Ever," 3482 whispered, fright making him turn white as a sheet.

I tried to soothe him, rubbing his shoulder with my hand. "Are there more people down there?"

"Yes," he replied. "Not all the cages opened. I think some malfunctioned."

"Did you see a woman, dark skin, crazy-colored hair? Might have a bag of stuff?" Heavy Dub asked.

"Yes, she's down there."

"Corporate type in a suit or business casual, thoughtful expression, like this tall?"

"I think so. Older looking guy if I remember right."

"A little guy that looked like my girl here, slate gray skin, silvery eyes?"

"Yes, but he's sick. Something is wrong with him."

I stood up and broke into a run. Heavy Dub thundered along behind me, ammunition jingling just loud enough I could keep track of him. My imagination was working overtime, conjuring an image of Ezra lying in a dark cell somewhere, lingering at the edge of a diabetic coma. I was determined to not lose anyone else that day.

I sprinted through the service garage, where at least a hundred autonomous vehicles from APCs to construction equipment quietly slumbered. There was heavy gray soot on the ground, and all the vehicles looked like they'd been driven through a mine shaft or dig site. None of the vehicles were outfitted with weapons, all being used to transport personnel or engage in heavy construction.

I could smell the prison level far before we reached it. It was like solid iron under my nose from all the blood, the stink of fear and adrenaline pouring down over the top of it. Faintly, there were familiar scents, those of my friends. I ran faster, the concrete forms, security fencing, and dim overhead lighting turning into a blur, and fading to a deep crimson.

The prison level was painted a dark red, the various doors of the cages made of a strange black carbon material. There were red lines painted at waist level, along every wall and corridor. In the center was an operating theater, dominated by large spotlights and dozens of fully automated surgical arms and other advanced biomedical equipment.

There were several biomechanical horrors hanging from the ceiling by chains, similar to the one I killed at Dr. Helmet's laboratory in North America. They were dormant at first, but indicators across their puckered masses began to flicker on as mechanical laughter poured out of hidden audio equipment installed somewhere above. I looked around, but I couldn't see anyone, except hundreds of silhouettes huddles in the dark cages.

The laughter abated for a moment, replaced with Kaspersky's sinister voice. "If you're here now, Perfidy, it means I'm dead. Something has gone horribly wrong, and now you're standing at the nerve center for our operation."

I looked around, trying to figure out where in the vast cell block my friends might be.

"We've fought many times, you and me. I always thought I'd come out on top eventually. Hiding in South America, that was very naughty. It doesn't matter, all for nothing, because you won't leave this place alive," Kaspersky's recorded voice continued.

The biomechanical horrors dropped from the ceiling, the chains that held them snapping links as they struggled to get free. One crashed through the operating theater, letting loose a deafening roar. Each of them were composed of at least a hundred cadavers stitched together, bound by an unseen cybernetic binary identity system that gave them one of two purposes, slumber or destruction. They lumbered toward where Heavy Dub and I stood, crushing anything in their way.

"Find them," I said, taking out Ukko and jumping high to grab one of the chains.

"On it," Heavy Dub said, taking a route perpendicular to my own, along the right-hand side.

I kicked off from the concrete platform as hard as I could, swinging left to draw them away, hoping my friends would not be crushed underfoot. The things staggered up toward me, their long appendages bursting at the seams, and leaking stasis fluid as they exerted themselves trying to catch me. I ran along the wall, one hand on a long chain hanging down from the ceiling, my other firmly gripping my hammer. I leapt at one, swinging at the center of its "head" with all my might, both hands gripping the haft.

The violent impact bounced me back up toward the ceiling, my back barely touching the coils of cables and conduit dangling down overhead. The biomechanical behemoth let out a horrifying screech as it tumbled backwards, its body coming apart as the various internal controls guiding its movement malfunctioned. The other two wasted no time using their fallen comrade as a platform to try and grasp me. I did my best to control my fall, but one of their appendages hit me coming back down.

Teeth and jagged bone under taut skin writhed up against me a split second before a wall of muscle hardened to worsen the impact. I flew across the room, barely able to catch a handrail with my offhand. I still spun around, landing roughly on the platform above. There was no time to catch my breath as they turned and began lumbering across the cell block at me once more.

Prisoners were crying out behind me, rattling the bars on their cells, motes of white light playing across my vision. Somewhere in the exchange, I must have hit my head. I waited as they began the ascent to the upper level, their elongated limbs using each layer of the cell block like the rung of a ladder. I had to try and jump, not where they were, but where they would be. I counted quietly to myself, ignoring the clamor of the prisoners and inhuman roar of the horrors below me.

I jumped, watching their flailing limbs move past me in the air, their heads rearing back as I'd expected. They must have had multifaceted vision, because it was as though they were reaching for three of me, instead of one, trying to guess where I would be. They guessed wrong. I swung hard, catching one high across the lump on its "shoulder," letting the force of the impact carry me into the other one. I turned, reversing my grip on Ukko, the head dropping at the second creature's "neck."

It sounded like a double thunderbolt, the deafening blasts leaving me disoriented. I tumbled through the air, half-blind as the stink of the creatures rupturing and tearing themselves apart filled my nostrils. I wondered if the fall would kill me outright, or if landing on creatures full of razor-sharp bone and teeth would be my end. Heavy Dub grabbed my foot as I passed by the second level, halting my fall about twenty-five feet from the ground.

The force of my descent pulled him all the way across the railing, the steel handhold stopping hard up against his armpit. He hauled me up, cursing because he'd dropped his SAW on the ground. After making sure I was okay, he picked it up, dusting it off.

"Dang it," he said, looking at a scuff mark across the side.

"Did you find them?" I asked, leaning wearily up against the handrail.

"I wasn't really looking, I was keeping track of you," Heavy Dub said.

I gave him a sort of dazed and angry look.

"Hey, they aren't my friends. I like you better than I like them," he said, making sure his SAW was still serviceable.

"Thanks, I thought that was it," I said, still trying to catch my breath.

"No way, Perfidy... he'd... he'd be really mad if I let that happen." Heavy Dub said haltingly, his good humor leaving him.

It was strange to have him gone for me as well, and it never got better after that.

"Let's find Silverstein, Taylor IA, and Ezra," I said, patting Heavy Dub on his big metal arm.

The cellblock was full of people, from all over the world. Each pleaded, threatened, and tried to negotiate with us for their release. They all had a funny way about them, like time had forgotten some of them, their clothing ancient, and their manner of speak antiquated. They all reminded me of Silverstein after a fashion, except the angry ones.

I found them at the lowest level in the cellblock. Closest to a maintenance access that I assumed, based on the smell, was a waste removal tunnel. Silverstein was holding Ezra in his arms, while Taylor IA knelt down beside him. They were backed as far into the cell as possible, probably because of all the chaos that transpired outside.

"Brook? Is that really you?" Taylor asked, running up to the bars.

I reached through the bars to touch her. She pulled my hand up to her face, kissing my palm. I was so glad to see them alive, I started crying right there. Silverstein looked up, his face creased with concern. At first, he appeared as an older man, in what was probably his late fifties. Upon seeing me, he altered his appearance so that he looked as a younger man, like I was used to seeing him.

"Is Perfidy with you?" Silverstein asked.

I cried harder. Heavy Dub just lowered his head, and leaned up against the cell bars beside me, closing his eyes. Taylor tried to console me, but the physical and emotional trauma of the last twenty-four hours took their toll. I cried harder than I ever had before, and I couldn't stop.

"Heavy, please, tell me what happened," Silverstein asked gently.

"Kaspersky got loose at about forty-thousand feet, killed Cal and Perfidy. I'll tell you all about it later, including how this ace pilot here did a mid-air retrieval her first time flying alone," Heavy Dub said, proudly, patting my back.

"And, Kaspersky?" Silverstein asked.

"Dead. Extra, super dead, actually. He kinda fell," Heavy Dub said.

Silverstein approached the bars. "Okay, we can figure this all out after we figure out how to escape these cells. This is military grade concrete, these bars are some sort of carbon material, almost indestructible, and…"

I let out a tortured scream, bringing my hammer against the wall beside the door about half as hard as I could swing at full force. The concrete form shattered like glass, falling in small pieces to the ground at my feet. The cell door, bereft of hinges, clattered to the ground. Heavy Dub nodded appreciatively at my handiwork, smiling.

"Oh, and we got Brook a keen new hammer to hit things with."

Ezra stirred, reaching out with his hand. I stepped through the cloud of concrete dust and took it. He gave me a squeeze.

"Brook, Kaspersky… he… it's all a trap… run, get away," Ezra whispered, trying to force himself into consciousness.

"I know, rest now. We're going to get you some help," I said, offering to take him from Silverstein.

It was a strange sensation, carrying Ezra. Not long ago we'd been the same size, but now I was nearly as tall as Silverstein and a little taller than Taylor. Ezra hadn't changed at all, and I was so glad for it in that moment. I needed someone, anything, to remind me of home. Ezra had always been my anchor.

I'd never lost anyone from my tribe before, not like how I lost Perfidy. I didn't know how to cope with it, and I hoped Ezra could instruct me like he had in so many other ways. Like so many other things I wanted right then, it would have to wait.

"Brook, can you free all these other people?" Taylor asked me.

"Yes," I said, reluctantly letting Heavy Dub carry Ezra.

"I like your dolly," Taylor said, gesturing to the toy peeking out of Heavy Dub's jacket pocket.

"Bob, yeah, he's a member of the team now," Heavy Dub joked.

It took nearly an hour of knocking holes in walls to get everyone loose, and to recover a few buried under the rubble. Everything the Factory taught me came in handy, and it was then I remembered why the place seemed so familiar. It was identical to one of the building simulations the Factory had used to instruct me. I'd run completely collapsed versions of this place dozens of times, rescuing people trapped within.

Silverstein and Heavy Dub went back to the craft I'd captured to get Ezra medical attention. Taylor stayed behind with me, directing the former captives to an area just below the motor pool. By the time the last of them were free, Heavy Dub had returned, and began leading people out through the entrance.

"How did you even get in here?" Taylor asked me, as we watched Heavy Dub lead the crowd of people back up toward the motor pool.

"Versa let us in. I imagine he's the one opening and closing the entry door, letting us come and go. I saw his name pop up on the panel beside the entrance when we made our approach," I replied, evoking a smile from Taylor.

"Oh! Good old Versa! I thought maybe he was lost in Finland. I do hope he is all right."

"I'll check for you when I go there to get Kale," I said, slinging Perfidy's rifle around to my back.

Taylor frowned. "Silverstein said someone bad is there. We need to just get everyone out."

"Svetovid, I know. It may not be that simple now. They killed my friend," I said, the fury I felt taking me for a moment.

Taylor looked at me worriedly, not sure what to say. Fortunately, Silverstein wove his way back through the crowd to where we were, and turned to walk with us, hands in his pockets. "Ezra is going to be fine. We got him some help, but he's very weak. I don't think we'll be able to keep taking him into the field like this."

"You want me to pass anything along to Svetovid when I get to Finland?" I said, keeping my eyes forward toward the corridor.

"Please, just get Kale, and anyone else that is still alive, and get out," Silverstein replied.

"I don't work for you anymore. This was it, right? The last thing I was supposed to do?" I asked, trying rattle him, just a little.

"You never worked for me, and I hope you'll do many more things after this," Silverstein said, giving me an odd look.

"This place, it was one of many floor plans the Factory used to train me to do recovery missions. I knew it the moment I set foot in here that it was familiar, but it didn't dawn on me until later. Why was Kaspersky trying to find telemechanics? What is he digging for down here?" I asked, and not in my usually nice way.

"That makes a sort of sense," he said, scratching his chin.

"Does it? Maybe you could explain it to me," I said, stopping in the corridor.

The rest of the crowd walked ahead, with just Silverstein, Taylor, and me, remaining behind. Taylor looked expectantly at Silverstein as well. He seemed to struggle to find the right words for a moment.

"Kaspersky believes there is a craft capable of interstellar space travel buried around here somewhere, He thought that if he were to find it, the technology within could be his to do with as he pleased. I can only assume that he thought having the right telemechanic would help him control the ship once he'd found it," Silverstein explained.

"Is this your ship? The one you told me was on Mars?" Taylor asked, scowling at Silverstein.

"Before he took himself offline, Hades AI helped me build an elaborate shell game to keep the ship hidden from the rest of the Cabal. I've never told the truth about the location aloud, because I always had to assume someone was listening," Silverstein explained.

"That night, at your house when Kaspersky came asking for Brook, you lied?" Taylor asked, somewhat confused.

"No, my ship really is on Mars, but that isn't the ship Kaspersky has been looking for," Silverstein said, turning to resume walking toward the motor pool.

"Do you always avoid telling the truth like this? Are you made of lies like the rest of them?" I asked, angry that he'd turned his back without answering my question.

Silverstein stopped, looking back at me over this shoulder. "Kaspersky's secret construction projects and the bombings in Port Montaigne weren't just to hurt me. They were a cover for looking for this ship. He cut a city in half and killed hundreds of people to both unearth it, and to compel me to give it to him. When he captured the sentience chamber that housed Hades AI, he discovered that Brook was the key to it all, assuming they could find someone with the right telemechanical abilities to help them."

Taylor and I stood there in shocked silence. I wasn't sure how to feel about it all.

"Hades had the Factory use simulations of all the places you were using to hide the ship to train me? That's why Kaspersky was obsessed with me?"

"Please know that Hades AI had no choice, he made the only decision he could at the time," Silverstein said, walking up the ramp.

Taylor and I followed along, but at a distance. She seemed downcast at the news, grasping my hand as we walked. I was glad we were friends, but I wondered how she could deal with Silverstein being so secretive all the time. Kale was so utterly opposite. His deceptions all made sense, and were necessary to protect people.

"Hades is, like, your dad. He's the one that had the Factory create you. I don't know that he even asked Silverstein before he did it. He went crazy after he found out that Ares was my real father, and that my mom wasn't exactly monogamous, if there is even such a thing with Omega Artificial Intelligences," Taylor explained.

"He wanted a daughter, and I was the next best thing?" I asked.

"I don't know if it is like that, but I believe Silverstein is telling the truth. Hades had to choose between letting Selene be killed, and letting you get hurt. Kaspersky betrayed him, trying to kill both you, me, and my mom. Things got muddled," Taylor explained, squeezing my hand.

"He would have only done that if he thought he knew where the ship was," I said.

"Or, if he thought he could compel Kale to give you up," Taylor said, sadly.

I frowned. "That didn't work out so well. Kale beat him half to death."

"That is so romantic! ...in a really violent sort of way, but still..."

"His deception worked, Kaspersky bought it, I think. Kale altered official Uroboros Financial records, and went to all kinds of trouble. I wish I'd been awake to see his face," I said, lowering my head.

"Do you want me to try and arrange for you to talk to Hades AI?" Taylor asked.

"No, the only man who I'll ever consider to be my father is dead, lying in a military transport outside," I replied, placing a hand on Perfidy's rifle.

Taylor closed her eyes, deep sadness spreading across her face. We walked in silence for several minutes, until we were almost back out of the facility. Heavy Dub was herding everyone aboard the military transport as Silverstein was walking back from the facility. He had a small satchel, presumably the possessions taken from them when they were captured.

"I don't think I ever thanked either of you for trying to protect me from Kaspersky when I was a child. Thank you," Taylor said, putting her head on my shoulder.

"You're welcome. I'll always be there for you, friend," I said, putting my arm around her.

Silverstein broke into a run after checking his mobile. "We have to hurry," he said, rushing past.

"What's wrong?" Taylor asked, picking up the pace.

"This message from Kale is almost two days old. He needs me," Silverstein said, panicked.

"What about going to Mars? Heavy Dub and I were already going to Finland," I said.

"They've waited over eight thousand years, a few more hours won't matter," Silverstein said, hurrying everyone aboard the transport.

CHAPTER 8

MARS COLONY, CRUSHER INDUSTRIAL ELEVATOR, MINING ZONE 048

August 3rd, 2200

"It will take hours to get there at this rate," Dragos said, scowling at the atmospheric shielding over the crusher line.

"It's not designed to be fast. It actually never stops. The lift is powered by some sort of perpetual energy engine. At both ends, they have to start moving the machinery before the lift comes to a full stop," Marshal Rider explained, keeping her eye on the flex monitor on her wrist.

"Yes, I remember. Was in this hauler when it rolled into lift, remember?"

"This might be our only chance to sleep, and you two want to bicker?" Hashti whispered, laying back against the interior of the cargo loader.

"Why not just climb shaft? Would be faster," Dragos complained.

"It's further than you think. The industrial elevator builds speed slowly from an almost full stop at both ends to close to 100 kilometers per hour in the middle. Climbing would be much slower," Marshal Rider said, sighing loudly.

Dragos scowled, leaning in to try and see what was on Marshal Rider's flex monitor, but she elbowed him back. "What? Why are you so angry?"

"Why are you?" Marshal Rider growled.

"Seriously, both of you, at least use inside voices. We're in the loader to avoid being heard as much as seen," Hashti whispered, shushing them both.

"If you won't let me watch video screen with you, tell me something about yourself. You read my file, know everything about me. Tell me something, with inside voice," Dragos whispered.

"No."

"At least your name, so we can dispense with formality," Dragos asked.

"I don't give convicts my first name, and as long as I'm on the job, it's Marshal Rider," she replied, holding her flex monitor out so he could see.

Dragos frowned. "I am not convict. Archie, he..."

"I read your file. With everything you did with the FLF, you should be a convict."

Dragos lowered his head, knowing she was probably right.

"Here, look at this," Marshal Rider asked, detaching her flex monitor from her armor and handing it to Dragos.

"Little boxes, with numbers. What is this?" Dragos asked, squinting at the screen.

"Docking information, ore and personnel coming and going out of the port."

"These empty boxes, ships that left, but no record they ever came?" Dragos said, trying to make sense of the spreadsheet.

"Two personnel transports left, but have no arrival data recorded. *Someone* brought about three hundred people to the colony. Their records through immigration have been removed from the Port system mainframe."

"There is no other record?" Dragos asked, returning Marshal Rider's flex monitor.

"There was, but someone killed the Ares System AI, making it difficult to access. The sentience core was destroyed, but there are archives at the Mars Company Offices. When we get there to squeeze Cerise for information about Archie, we'll see what sort of access we can get."

"Someone removed records from the port..."

"Yeah, so?" Marshal Rider snapped, making Hashti stir slightly.

"Inside voices," she murmured, going back to sleep.

"Personnel could be soldiers, FLF people from Earth. The mechanic from the Prison that made your armor sleep, maybe he pulled the records. Mars Company Offices could be a much harder place than we are prepared for," Dragos whispered, taking out his guitar and quietly strumming a lullaby.

Hashti smiled quietly at the sound, pulling her shawl around herself tightly.

Marshal Rider sighed. "It's Marliese."

The industrial elevator suddenly jerked, moving slightly faster up the incline. They held their breath, hoping the sudden movement wouldn't wake Hashti. She stirred, her eyes opening slightly, but they quickly closed and she resumed steady breathing indicative of deep sleep.

"That's a good name for you," Dragos whispered, smiling slightly.

"Thanks."

The lift shifted into even higher gear until the speed was generating a terrific howl that woke Hashti. She opened her eyes, stretched her limbs with an odd cat-like grace and scratched the scaled skin across her ribs. Marshal Rider was out of her armor now, making some adjustments to the actuators in the legs.

"Half way there?" Hashti asked, getting on her tip-toes so she could peek over the edge of the loader.

"A little more than half, if I recall correctly." Marshal Rider said, using a wrench to adjust the tension on an actuator.

"You've been up here before?" Dragos asked.

"Many times, as a child. The administrative zone has a park. I'd linger at the fence and watch the other kids play. You couldn't actually get in without a Mars Company Administrative ID."

"Your father was police. You couldn't go?" Dragos asked.

"We weren't popular, the ruling class viewing my family as oversight from the CGG on Earth. It was oversight they did not want. They paid my father the minimum allowed by law, gave us housing in the poorest district, and made sure our ration packets were late."

Dragos frowned. "Your mother, father, where are they now?"

"They're gone. My mother got sick. By the time Mars Company Officials arranged for a doctor, she died. My father was killed by an informant, someone he had to meet outside of his armor in the administrative zone," Marshal Rider explained, calmly checking her weapons.

"I begin to not like this place," Dragos growled.

"It's built on a culture of greed. Money is the only God here, and you either supplicate that God for mercy, or you live by the sword, and by the Law."

"Is there anyone else we should find, in case things go wrong?" Hashti asked.

"My only friends and allies are in the loader with me right now," Marshal Rider said grimly, sliding down into her armor.

The loader slowed to a crawl after more than thirty minutes of moving at high speed. Dull warning sirens sounded as the lift approached the top of the precipice. Looking back, one could see the rest of the Mars Colony, enormous atmospheric domes rising nearly as high as the mountain the Administrative Zone sat upon.

Mars Company Offices and employee housing sat safely behind a retaining fence. Outside the fence, an industrial conveyer carrying equipment and personnel moved along the entire length. It emptied out to another industrial lift on the other side of the peak. That lift would take everything back down the dark side of the slope to one of two of the largest mining operations on the planet.

Marshal Rider stepped from the conveyor as it paused next to the administrative zone access. Two guards held a vigil at the gatehouse, a large electrified fence stood at their backs with a single gate, controlled remotely from within the gatehouse itself. The guards shifted nervously at the sight of the trio approaching them, signaling the gatehouse to stop the conveyor.

Marshal Rider paused, waiting for the gate guards to approach.

"This is a restricted area, Marshal Rider. Unless you have a warrant, we're going to have to ask you to—"

"I'm going to kill you both unless you signal to the gatehouse to let us pass. I'll shoot you with hardened flechette rounds, just above your navel, and watch you bleed out while my friends tears through the fence," Marshal Rider said, calmly.

One of the guards went for his sidearm, but his weapon couldn't clear the holster before Marshal Rider gunned him down, shooting him in the belly with barbed ammunition designed to inflict massive tissue damage. Dragos fired a single round from his rifle, catching the gatehouse guard through the head before he could sound the alarm. He paused after the shot, quietly marveling at how fast and accurate the new cybernetic enhancements made him.

Knocking down the second guard with an elbow, Hashti sprinted toward the fence and grabbed the electrified chain link with both hands. Current ran across her skin to the ground as she used her immense strength to shred the chain link asunder. The circuit broken, she gave the gate a good pull, taking it off the runners, and letting it clatter to the ground.

"What you said was scary. Can't believe he went for gun," Dragos said, stepping over the guard.

"Probably didn't believe I'd go outlaw, but then very few people know Ares is dead," Marshal Rider said, looking over at Hashti somewhat concerned.

"My shawl," Hashti complained, shaking flames off the end, the tassels already consumed.

"Hopefully, that's the last fence you have to go through. When we're on Earth or the Lunar Colony, we'll get you another one," Marshal Rider said, sliding the door to the gatehouse open.

"Someone will see?" Dragos asked, pointing up to surveillance drones passing overhead.

"Only if someone managed to bypass Ares to broadcast the surveillance feed somewhere local. I bet the whole colony is blind, monitors flashing a 'down for maintenance' message."

The administrative dome was a bustling place beyond the quiet security zone, accountants and bureaucrats hurrying from one meeting to another. There were several Ichthyic Type 5 Metasapients, each with a slave collar around their necks. They lingered outside office buildings and residences waiting for their owners. A few sanctioned street vendors were selling food, the sights and smells of the place struck Dragos as being very aloof compared to the squalor he'd seen in the rest of the colony.

Automated cleaning robots and vehicles swept up every bit of red dust, and orange soot, making sure the place stayed a uniformly painted white. Windows were washed, condensation on the ground was collected, and colorful lights across the top of the dome gave the place a pleasant "sky" to gaze upon. There were parks in between the living spaces, children playing with one another on ancient playground equipment while proud parents looked on.

A few residents stopped to stare at the trio as they made their way toward the Mars Company offices. They were easy to find, resembling radio towers, tastefully designed to pull the rest of the administrative zone together. It looked like a carefully arranged set of impossibly expensive sculpture under glass, put on display for someone to buy. Indeed, everything seemed to be for sale here, corporate cannibalism was rampant in a place where growth and real estate development had been at a standstill for decades.

Dragos watched for armed response, but there didn't appear to be any guards. The platoon of familiar FLF troopers he'd expected to be there, were conspicuously absent. The offices seemed to be in normal operation, but there were several nearby habitats and buildings being renovated and retrofitted to handle additional occupants. The spires were being built ever higher.

Marshal Rider approached the door attendant, but before she could deliver a threat of violence he gestured toward the entrance, triggering it open. The clean glass doors slid to the side revealing a tasteful foyer, tiled in Martian stone with several potted plants along the side, presumably brought up from Earth. A woman dressed in business casual ushered them in, beckoning with one hand politely.

"This is a trap," Dragos whispered.

"If it is, expend all ammunition," Marshal Rider growled, heading inside.

The door attendant tried to bar Hashti from coming in, assuming by her looks that she was a Type 5 Metasapient. She batted him playfully from her path, knocking him into the carefully landscaped hedges to the side of the entrance. He stood bewildered, watching the glass doors close, Hashti's soft psychic laughter echoing in his mind.

"Miss Cerise has been expecting you. Our apologies for what happened at the gate. We aren't sure that all communications are being delivered.

Apparently the Ares AI System is conducting maintenance right now," the executive assistant explained.

"The Ares AI and his daughter are both dead. The new CEO of the company had him killed. We're probably all doomed," Marshal Rider said, meeting her gaze.

"Oh, um, can I get you anything before you head up? Coffee? Water?" the executive assistant replied, without missing a beat.

"We're good," Marshal Rider said, stepping into a lift with circular glass walls.

As the lift doors closed, Dragos tapped Marshal Rider on the shoulder. "That woman, she did not even flinch at news."

"She's an android, and very old by her smell. Probably has only a limited degree of sapience compared to other artificial intelligences you've met. There are quite a few on Mars. Some are left over from the initial landing," Hashti explained.

"That lady was robot?" Dragos asked, astonished.

"Anyone that didn't stop and stare at us on the street probably was," Marshal Rider said, checking her flex monitor.

"That was lots of people then," Dragos mused, wondering how much of what he saw in the streets below was real, and how much was wholly artificial.

"More than half, if I were to guess," Hashti said, hugging Dragos.

"What was that for?"

"I can tell by your reaction to all this that you're one of the good guys."

"Or, he's just got some soul left," Marshal Rider said, watching the floors of the administrative tower go by.

"I'll take either one," Hashti said, hugging Dragos a little harder.

Dragos reached up with his biological hand, and gave Hashti's arm a squeeze, hoping there wasn't a fight or worse waiting for them at the top floor. His mind raced, imagining all sorts of nightmare scenarios, knowing the fullness of Archie's depravity. There could be a firing squad, a bomb, or absolutely nothing at all.

As the lift came to a stop, only a short hallway was revealed, leading to executive offices, a woman sitting at reception that looked to be an identical copy of the woman in the entry foyer below. She stood smiling, offering them a seat while they waited for Chairperson Cerise to be available. Marshal Rider just waved her gauntleted hand to indicate the negative, chuckling as Dragos drew very close to the attendant and squinted.

"There are no ports or anything. I can't even tell," Dragos said.

The woman only smiled politely, her eyes twitching slightly as Cerise came from the hallway to greet everyone.

"Marshal Rider, Hashti, Mr. Dalca, very good to see you again," Cerise said warmly, extending her hand.

Marshal Rider left her hanging, resting her hands on her weapons. "The two transports you had removed from the port records. What was on board?"

Cerise looked startled at first, but nodded before summoning an answer. "The first carried Archie's biological descendants to Mars. The second transport brought people I have been protecting. We did not want to build our empire here without our families and associates being with us," Cerise explained.

"Hashti?" Marshal Rider turned to her Metasapient companion.

"I can't tell if she is lying, not by virtue of her biological responses," Hashti said, squinting at Cerise.

"She's lying," Dragos said, baiting her.

Cerise glared at Dragos, letting a folder she was carrying fall to the floor. Dragos looked at the spilled contents, at the security profiles of the people contained within. They were FLF agents, every one of them.

"He left you here, without any security. I don't think anyone counted on what happened to Enyo though. Who knew a Terrestrial Intelligent Agent could die of a broken heart?" Marshal Rider said, kicking the paper around.

"These papers, just more deception. She is made of lies," Dragos said, picking up one of the personnel profiles.

"You're very good, Mr. Dalca. Our Ouroboru chose you well," Cerise said, with a hint of admiration.

"What's she talking about?" Marshal Rider said, turning to look at Dragos.

"I would like to know this, too," Dragos said, frowning at Cerise.

"Mr. Dalca has taken direction from the same shadowy employer for a very long time. You've been a Cabal asset since your father died, and always part of Ouroboru's portfolio, whether he was calling himself Vance or Kale," Cerise said, looking at her fingernails.

"Even if true, it means he kept his end of the bargain. He kept my family safe," Dragos said, tapping the trigger guard on his rifle with a cybernetic finger.

"There are those of us that have wondered about Ouroboru's connections and affinity with the Roma. Your people may even be descendants, but no one could confirm it," Cerise teased, clearly taking a jab at Dragos' heritage.

"Where is Archie?" Marshal Rider asked. She shifted impatiently in her armor.

"You killed him."

"His body was never recovered. It vanished from the tram station. Evidence on site indicates he got up and walked away. You and Dr. Helmet told me you guys were special, and ancient. I don't think he died up there," Marshal Rider said.

"You're bluffing. You never went up there," Cerise replied, pushing her blond hair back over one ear.

"No, we did go up there. Also, we now know who planted the bug in Dragos' cybernetic arm," Hashti replied, smiling mirthfully.

Cerise just shrugged. "So? I couldn't just let Mr. Dalca walk away with a billion Martian credits worth of cybernetic enhancements without some assurances. Dr. Helmet didn't even ask me if…"

The building and everything in it went dark. Walls shook as machinery within ground to a halt. Then, a second later, it all came back on again. Marshal Rider watched it all with a sort of morbid fascination, while Hashti and Dragos spun around, startled by it all. The android receptionist just paused, then resumed her typing as the terminal came back on.

"It's beginning. The cycles between outages will get shorter, and the darkness will last longer each time. With the brain of the Colony dead, the body will soon follow," Marshal Rider said, taking a quick look at her flex monitor.

Cerise stood there dispassionately regarding the trio, folding her arms.

"I'm only going to ask one more time. What was on the transports?" Marshal Rider asked, drawing one of her pistols.

"I'm not afraid of you. You will need me if you're going to save the Colony, and to find Archie," Cerise said, a wry smile crossing her face.

Marshal Rider quickly leveled her handgun, finger straining against the trigger.

"Those gate guards, they went for their guns. Shooting them and shooting unarmed woman, are different things," Dragos said, putting a hand on Marshal Rider's arm.

"It is people like her… they are the reason my parents are dead," Marshal Rider growled through gritted teeth.

Hashti stepped into the field of fire, destroying the smug look on Cerise's face with a quick jab of her elbow. Cerise pitched backwards, unconscious from the blow, blood streaming from her face. Marshal Rider shoved her two allies aside, continuing to hold her father's handgun on Cerise, finger quivering in the trigger guard.

"All of my life, I've worn this star as my parents would have wanted me to. I protected the common people, but I never had the will to take the fight to the people truly responsible. Now the Ares AI System is dead, his daughter as well, and the whole colony dangles by a thread."

"That isn't your fault. The system failed in spite of you, not because of you," Dragos said, heading down the hallway to Cerise's office.

Marshal Rider reluctantly holstered her weapon, turning Cerise over and placing handcuffs on her. She held her up while her nose bled, so she wouldn't drown or choke. She'd done it many times, done her best to prevent a death in custody where the perpetrator didn't deserve more than a punch in the nose. This didn't feel the same to Marshal Rider, her rage continuing to boil deep inside.

Executives peered nervously out of their offices, their gaze lingering on Cerise and her shattered nose. Hashti could feel their eyes on her, sense which ones had one of her Metasapient sisters or brothers as a slave. Disgust welled up within her, fueled by the rage she could sense coming off Marshal Rider in waves. She wanted to throw some of them from windows, but Dragos' calm seemed to cut through it all like cold water.

Cerise's office was immaculate. Dragos wasted no time looking at her terminal and desk. Using the strength of his cybernetic arm, he ripped down a section of wall revealing hundreds of brown paper packages tucked between the support forms and steel crossbars underneath. The next section of wall revealed much the same thing, and the next, and the next, until Cerise's office looked like a skeleton, ribs exposed.

"Bearer bonds, millions of Martian credits worth," Marshal Rider said, opening one of the packages.

"Are we rich?" Hashti joked.

"These are exchange standard bonds, good on Mars or on Earth, in virtually any economy. Yeah, whoever has these would be very wealthy, wherever they went," Marshal Rider said aloud, making the fleeing executives hesitate, but only for a moment as they piled into the elevator.

"These, papers in this file, I cannot read the language," Dragos said, opening a pair of longer paper packages.

"It's Hebrew, hardly anyone on Mars can read this," Marshal Rider said, her eyes perusing the pages.

"But, you can?" Hashti asked.

"Yes, of course," Marshal Rider said, smiling a little.

"Why would she use that language? Very old, yes?" Dragos asked.

"Maybe she's really old," Marshal Rider replied.

"How can you read?"

"I'm Jewish," Marshal Rider replied, squinting at Dragos.

"Sorry, I am done with stupid questions," Dragos said, abashedly.

Marshal Rider read the pages, while Dragos and Hashti gathered up the exchange bonds and other documents. The office was full of all sorts of other files, printed on paper long ago, the edges beginning to yellow. It looked as though Cerise had been hoarding information and money for decades.

"Who is this little fellow?" Hashti said, holding up a picture of a young boy with dark eyes and hair standing beside Cerise.

"I think that is Kale, when he was just boy," Dragos said, squinting at the photograph.

"This lady I knocked out is someone's mother?" Hashti said, frowning.

"She looks like she loves him," Marshal Rider remarked, looking up from the papers.

"I do," Cerise said, wearily looking up, the restraints at her wrists jingling slightly.

Cerise was groggy, eyes bloodshot, her blouse covered in blood from her nose. She looked around dispassionately at her office, the walls all torn down. She was mildly dismayed at the documents Marshal Rider had been reading, but not as much as she was at the sight of her ruined top.

"Why do you do this, if you have the capacity to love another person?" Hashti asked.

"Do what?" Cerise replied, trying to sit up against the wall in a more comfortable position.

"Work with Archie, kill entire Mars Colony, maybe," Dragos stated, gesturing to a large picture window overlooking the administrative zone.

"In the Cabal, there are few women. Almost eight thousand years of statistical inevitability. Our men would leave us, or just kill us sometimes. They could live forever, have heirs with any woman, disrespecting our tribal heritage. Ouroboru always tried to protect us, but he became as we are, as a boy, and it took him a long time to learn how to become a man," Cerise explained.

"He did not just grow up?" Hashti asked.

"It took him time to learn how to use the symbionts to manipulate his appearance. Back then, even being centuries old, he still looked like a child."

"Symbionts? Dr. Helmet used that word, too. I've listened to what you've had to say without asking too many questions. Clearly you're insane, Dr. Helmet is insane, and all your weird Cabal-cult friends are insane. This stack of Hebrew you wrote is the most boring science fiction I've ever read," Marshal Rider said pushing the stack of paper away from her.

"It's all true, and verifiable, if Archie had not killed Ares," Cerise said, looking dully at the floor, still groggy.

The receptionist entered, acting as if nothing was wrong and knelt down beside Cerise. "You have a call."

"I'll take it in here. The intercom please," Cerise said, nodding toward her desk.

The ancient intercom crackled on as the receptionist routed the call to the room. Heavy machinery could be heard idling in the background, the sounds of angry shouts dimly heard. "Miss Laplace? It's Foreman Mayes, down here at the deep track."

"Mr. Mayes, how can I help you today?" Cerise said, politely.

"The Ares AI hasn't moved the gravel loaders in two days. If we don't get some of this machinery cleared out, the sifters are going to bury half the operating installation down here. Any idea what's going on?" the foreman asked, sounding a little impatient.

"I'll see what I can do. I'm sorry for the trouble, Mr. Mayes."

"Yeah, okay, I'll call the office once the loaders are moving," the foreman grumbled, disconnecting the call.

Cerise smiled, letting her head rest against the wall. "In about twelve hours, if the loaders haven't moved there won't be any problem at the ops installation, but their work contracts will expire. If the loaders don't move for 72 hours, they get a pink slip."

"What will they do?" Hashti asked.

"They'll riot, and when the Mars Company doesn't issue a statement via the Colony Contract System, it'll get worse. This assumes life support for the colony doesn't shut down and we all run out of air to breathe," Cerise laughed, but there was sadness in her eyes. Tears.

"This wasn't the plan, was it? You were just going to get Enyo to upload herself to save everyone. You didn't count on her love for her father being such that she'd just die," Marshal Rider said, sweeping the papers into her satchel.

"Love is an interesting choice to describe Enyo and Ares," Cerise said, closing her eyes.

"She hasn't told us where Archie is," Dragos growled, looming over Cerise.

"Leave her be, she doesn't know," Hashti said, stooping down and cleaning the blood from Cerise's face.

"How do you know?" Dragos asked.

"She would be with him already. He's abandoned her," Hashti said quietly.

Marshal Rider sighed, throwing Hashti the keys to the restraints. After freeing Cerise, Hashti helped her to her feet. With her face cleaned up, there was significantly less bruising than there should have been, something Dragos silently pointed out to Marshal Rider. Hashti, if she noticed, didn't seem to care, possessing enormous sympathy for Cerise.

"Where would he go? That's what you want to know, right?" Cerise said, rubbing her wrists.

"If plans have fallen to pieces, he would go to the port, yes? To your ship?" Dragos said, walking over to look out the window.

"Golgotha came with me, stowed away in one of the landing platforms. He's very afraid of her, particularly having done what he has. For all I know she's coming to kill me," Cerise said, directing her statement to Marshal Rider.

"The super deadly space alien, mentioned in your journal? The one that gave all of you your magical powers thousands of years ago?" Marshal Rider replied, incredulous.

"I told you, everything in there is true."

"Including the part about her mate, a lone conscientious objector that's been living in deep space, dismantling huge weapons capable of killing planets?" Marshal Rider said, raising an eyebrow.

Cerise sighed, letting her hands fall to her sides. "Yes, it's real. I may even be able to prove it to you from my ship, depending on where Mars is in relation."

"So, what Dr. Helmet said could be true, and Archie might be looking for the first lander, to hide out until rescue comes? If, rescue comes?" Hashti said.

"First lander?" Cerise said, looking in a coat closet for a fresh shirt.

Dragos and Marshal Rider both looked to Hashti. "She really doesn't know," Hashti reported.

"So, she is done lying to us?" Dragos said, sarcastically.

"I've been at this for so long, I don't even remember who I was before all this began," Cerise said, taking off her blouse, causing Dragos to avert his eyes.

Hashti made a pained expression, looking over to Marshal Rider. Cerise was lovely, pale in the extreme, but her midsection was an ugly roadmap of strange scars. They had faded considerably, but were very visible, particularly under the fluorescent lights.

"Did Archie do that to you?" Dragos asked.

"No, it was Golgotha. Back then, we called her Zvezda, and I was called Drusael. It was an accident, but Zvezda wasn't familiar with humans and she hit me too hard. She was able to put me back together again, but I lost the child I'd been carrying. Parvan's child. I was injured and couldn't have children, so I fled the tribe. I didn't think anyone would want me. I didn't come back into the fold for a thousand years, avoiding everyone that became immortal from my village until I'd come into my own."

Hashti and Dragos stood there mute for a moment, Marshal Rider finally breaking the silence.

"This is why you aren't afraid of Golgotha?"

"She's a mother, and we share an uncommon bond. She's lost children too, dozens by my count. That's why I didn't want Archie's body incinerated, and why I don't want you to kill him. I'm not just protecting him, but the children in his body. The symbiont organisms are Golgotha's children."

"Why have people carry her kids? Why not carry them herself?" Dragos asked.

"It sounds like you're starting to believe me," Cerise replied, smiling.

"It would explain a lot. Like how you can take an elbow from Hashti and not require cosmetic surgery to fix your face," Marshal Rider said, frowning at Dragos.

"They would have died, our atmosphere being barely compatible with Golgotha's physiology. They needed a host suited to Earth's environment, and we needed the longevity to enact a grand plan," Cerise explained.

"They didn't tell you, being gone from the tribe for so long, so you tried to piece it together," Marshal Rider said, returning the journal to Cerise.

"Yes."

"Why Archie?" Hashti asked.

"And not Vance Uroboros? I tried to be with him, but he was obsessed with dismantling the Cabal and returning control of the world to the rest of humanity. Also, for me, he will always be that bright boy from our village," Cerise asked.

Cerise paused, thinking and conjuring memories that hadn't drifted through her mind in centuries. She looked down at the journal and wept somewhat. She'd thought confessing it all to someone would make the pain go away, but she felt as alone as she ever had.

"I did everything he wanted, gave up everything, and everyone I cared about to be with him. You're right, he has abandoned me here, left to enact whatever backup plan he had," Cerise said at last.

"If what you say is true, you wandered alone for a long time," Marshal Rider said, gathering up a handful of keycards from a desk drawer.

"No, there were those that looked out for me, and there was always Ouroboru, but none that wouldn't treat me as damaged, and just love me."

CHAPTER 9

WARZONE, SOUTHERN DISTRICT OF HELSINKI, FINLAND

2:02 PM May 15th, 2200

Tent flaps blew in the wind, the stench of the dead and burning buildings wafting through the camp. Marjorie sat alone, but under guard in the largest of the tents. It had been cobbled together from a sail taken from one of the luxury ships at the port, and furnished with all manner of extravagant items stolen from unsecured buildings nearby.

She dabbed at her food sullenly. They'd taken her only friend away, Einhold's illness making him difficult to care for on the move. She wanted to believe he was at a camp much further east as Svetovid had promised, but she didn't trust him. He had no respect for life, and would just kill anyone that wasn't immediately useful to him somehow.

She thought often of what happened to the Ursine police officer, and how Svetovid had stripped him of his identity and memories with a touch. She feared that more than death, so she did her best to obey, but he was getting more insistent that they begin working on an heir. He'd been polite, but terribly unromantic so far. It was just another military strategy he intended to employ, but on her.

Svetovid came in without warning, his armor and blade marred by scorch marks. "They continue to defy me with their mechanical monsters and high precipice."

"Maybe tomorrow?" Marjorie said, trying not to sound too happy.

"Your tone betrays you. You hope they will kill me, but you know this isn't possible. One of their number did try to escape where they are barricaded. We caught him. Perhaps he can tell me something useful," Svetovid said, taking his antlered helm and placing it on a broad table covered in charts and handwritten plans.

"I'm sorry the day didn't go well. Maybe we could go for a walk, and you could tell me about it?" Marjorie said, doing her best to appear helpful.

"This new way you speak to me, I like it," Svetovid said, drawing close to her.

She stood, backing away from him. "That walk, we should take it."

He obliged, holding out his hand. They walked back through the camp, to the suburban areas along the east side of Helsinki. The low-lying buildings smoldered ahead of them as they walked. While many of the fortified buildings had held, more than a few had been opened. Svetovid walked briskly, gripping her hand tightly.

"You keep calling us gods. Maybe you could explain that to me?"

Svetovid nodded. "There were devils, descending from a dark Hell far above us, but we have slain them all. It was at great cost to us, and our tribe. This world owes us a debt it can never repay."

"So, you take it in blood? You make people pay with their lives?" Marjorie stated.

"You and I will give this world new life, once the old has been burned away. We will make our own history, once no vestige of the old world remains. There is little worth keeping of this profane and greedy world. It begged us to enslave them, to save them, and then disregarded that gift turning to squabble," Svetovid stated, his nostrils flaring with disgust.

"Gift?" Marjorie asked.

"Long did we control the Earth, enduring the capricious nature of humanity, each century drawing us further away from the people we'd sought to safeguard. Even in this age of incredible plenty, they preferred to squabble over scraps like dogs. Our Numismatic Advisors and Amnestic Monks did argue for them to become sovereign over the land once again. Tis better they all meet the sword," Svetovid said, shaking his head.

"Okay, you know you make no sense, right?" Marjorie said, half-smiling.

"I do not know how it is that you can do what you do, live through death, and your pitch perfect voice. My wife…"

"Which one? If you're as old as you say, you must have had a few," Marjorie said, pulling her hand away from Svetovid's.

"Only one. She lived for almost eight centuries before she was taken by the sword. I have lived alone since, unwilling to involve anyone else in what I promised to do. You are the only one I've met in my very long life that can't be taken from me," Svetovid said, pausing to look out at the destruction he'd wrought.

"When you talk like that, I start to think I won't have a choice," Marjorie replied, edging away from Svetovid, and looking for somewhere to run.

He sprang on her with preternatural speed. "After I am done, there will be no one else to choose from, every other man on Earth just fertilizer for the fields our children will tend."

Marjorie looked at him, terrified. "You're going to kill… everyone else? In the world?"

"Yes," Svetovid whispered, pulling her to her feet.

A lone messenger approached cautiously, waiting for Svetovid to beckon him over. "We've brought the prisoner," he reported.

"Good, we'll come straight away," Svetovid said, pulling Marjorie along.

"You can't just kill everyone," Marjorie said, choking back tears.

"I've already come very close. If not for Ouroboru's meddling, the Americas and Africa would suffer as the rest of the world suffers. Kaspr should be here with something he calls 'launch codes' soon, and then I will have a sword big enough to end the rest of humanity," Svetovid snarled.

"This Kaspr, he's been the high-tech behind your low-tech?" Marjorie asked, wiping tears from your eyes.

"We are both hunters of the same tribe. He is a little sick, but the outcome will be the same."

"He's a little sick? Compared to you, he's the poster boy for mental health," Marjorie hissed, trying to pull free of Svetovid's grasp.

He turned and struck her hard enough to cut her cheek and break her cheekbone. The wounds healed rapidly, but they still hurt. He picked her up, angrily dragging her back to his tent where a single hooded prisoner had been forced onto his knees, hands tied behind his back, guards holding his shoulders.

Svetovid whisked the hood off in one fluid motion. "Marjorie? You are alive!" Truman said, his bruised face breaking into a wide smile.

"Truman? What... what are you doing here?" Marjorie said pushing past Svetovid.

"I came to find you. I hoped, that even if they captured me, I'd get to see you," Truman said, trying to stand, but the guards held him down.

"You care for her," Svetovid observed, looming over Truman.

"I already kill two men for hurting her, one for even suggesting it," Truman said, taking note of the bruising still visible on Marjorie's face.

Svetovid knelt down so that only Truman could hear him whisper. "My guards are going to take you to the camp far to the rear of my forces. Tonight, I am going to take her, and make her give me an heir."

Truman's broke his restraints, the big man throwing the guards aside with ease, his meaty knuckles finding Svetovid's face. Even taken by surprise, Svetovid snapped back, delivering a punch of his own. Truman took it to the top of his head, looking down instead of trying to dodge or block. Knuckles cracked against thick cranial bone as Truman delivered two savage body blows to Svetovid, knocking the wind out of him.

Svetovid laughed hoarsely, clutching Truman's head between his hands, pressing his thumbs into both eye sockets. Truman cried out trying to break Svetovid's hold, bringing his arms up over and over again. They rolled to the ground, the guards jumping in, and getting entangled in the melee. Marjorie thought to run, the perfect opportunity having presented itself.

"I wonder, if you are not a distant relative of mine?" Svetovid said, pulling Truman up to his feet, holding him in a choke hold.

Truman struggled, but he was no match for Svetovid's superhuman strength and endurance. The guards clapped thicker restraints on his wrists, giving him a good kicking before they hauled him back up to his feet. Truman smiled through bloody teeth, laughing at the mark he'd left Svetovid just below the eye.

"You are as strong as an ape, and just as pretty," Truman said, choking on blood.

The guards led Truman away. Svetovid composed himself before checking his face in the mirror. He frowned, something Marjorie thought he'd been doing the whole time anyway. Both his laughter and the frown were new.

"I don't want you to hurt Truman," Marjorie said, fidgeting with her hands.

"Did you not hear what I said, woman?"

"Yes, you're going to kill everyone, but maybe not a few people?" Marjorie suggested, wishing she'd tried to run.

"He cares for you, deeply, this Truman. He's a big man, why would you not want to be with him? He would clearly protect you with his life," Svetovid said, almost scolding Marjorie.

"I don't see what business it is of yours," she said, taking a step back as he stepped toward her menacingly.

"You like them weak? Like Einhold?"

"People of the current era can just be friends. Men and women can talk to each other without trying to make heirs, or killing people, or whatever," Marjorie said, avoiding his question.

Svetovid just stared at her, his eyes going cold, and cruel.

"Promise you'll leave them alone. Promise me," Marjorie pleaded.

"Tonight, after I'm certain you will bear us a child, I'm going to go to the east camp myself and kill your friends. By tomorrow, Kaspr will come, and these last holdouts on the west side of Helsinki will die. Then, we can talk, or whatever," Svetovid said, mimicking her tone at the end.

"No!" Marjorie screamed, running at Svetovid.

He grabbed her by the wrists, holding her down on the ground. Marjorie panicked, Svetovid easily overpowering her. She struggled with all her might, turning to look away from him. He was yelling at her now, his face contorted into an ugly mask of rage. She screamed anyway, knowing no one that could hear her would care.

Her voice gave out for a moment, a strange warmth building in her chest and throat. She could see a glow coming off of her skin, a strange bio-luminescence that seemed to build with the same intensity. She struggled to speak, but her throat felt like it had clenched shut, holding back whatever was expanding inside her. Svetovid hit her once, and then wound back to hit her again.

She screamed, but no sound came out, none that she could hear. She watched as the tent filled with white light, the fabric breaking sporadically into flames. The scream persisted, as though she had an ocean of sound pent up in her chest, and what felt like a jet engine turbine churning in her throat. The guards outside the tent turned a blackened purple as the world went gray around her, everything ringed in white.

Marjorie could see through everything, watch cartilage and soft tissue in those around her agitate and pull apart. Harder tissue vibrated at a higher frequency, causing bone marrow and spinal fluid to boil. Svetovid had several strange organisms inside him, each flooding his body with what looked like silvery clouds, his internal organs struggling to continue functioning. The guards were not so fortunate.

She turned her face down toward the ground, trying to hold it all in. It was like someone hitting thousands of bass drums at ten thousand beats per minute, the ground amplifying the hypersonic resonance she was creating. There was a kinetic aftermath, the phenomena reaching a point of molecular terminus, a silent and invisible explosion throwing everything away from Marjorie at high speed.

Svetovid was scorched and bloodied as the force of the scream hurled him away like a ragdoll, high into the sky. Raiders and other personnel at the camp suffered terrible physical destruction, the force of Marjorie's scream rending internal organs, disrupting heart beats, and annihilating eardrums. Her own clothing burst into flames, falling to ash and whisked away in the turbulence.

The scream seemed to go on forever, like the force within her would never abate. She couldn't bear the sight of what was happening around her, so she closed her eyes. It was as though her ears were already plugged, so once her eyes were closed the only sensation around her was like a hot spring, the scalding hot water against her face and body. She could feel the swell of force slowly shrink, her mouth finally able to close without her teeth rattling painfully.

She felt a shift, something within allowing her throat, chest, and ears to return to normal. She was huddled naked on the ground for several minutes before she could open her eyes. The destruction around her was extreme, most of the camp ablaze, hundreds of raiders blown away by the force of the shockwave she'd generated. She staggered forward, in the direction she'd seen Svetovid fall.

He was almost a hundred feet away, scorched and deaf. She could see he was healing quickly, but that what she'd done to him had nearly killed him. It would be hours before he'd be able to even see, let alone lay a hand on her again. She was in stunned shock at what she'd done, terrified of doing it again. Even as bad as Svetovid and his band of murderous raiders were, this was a terrible way to die. Those that weren't already dead, were in terrible agony, internal burns and bleeding taking their toll.

She wept as she looked back to the east. If Einhold or Truman were too close, they might be dead too. Terror welled up inside her, the realization that she might have killed even a single innocent person too much to contemplate. She picked up a tattered piece of a tent and wrapped it around herself, then headed east. If there was even a chance they'd survived, she had to find them.

CHAPTER 10

WARZONE, SOUTHERN DISTRICT OF HELSINKI, FINLAND

3:13 PM May 15th, 2200

Eamon squinted into the distance, pulling the tattered tarp around his shoulders. It wasn't the temperature that made him shiver, but the infection. He scratched unconsciously at wounds that didn't seem to heal, his feet pushing past trash and corpses as he made his way back to the drainage tunnel he'd been staying for the last three weeks.

The city around him burned, smoke mingling with avian scavengers as the circled the sky. Eamon could hear the cries, and the shots, and the dwindling chaos, but he couldn't remember why it was important. In the last day, his head had really begun to hurt. It was the only thing he could remember, of anything, that was familiar somehow.

He couldn't find food again, and the clean water was getting too far to walk. Exhaustion was beginning to set in, the toll of whatever had happened to him sapping his strength. He couldn't understand why he looked the way he did. Everyone else he found either ran from him, or tried to hurt him, and none of them were like he was. They were all small, and angry, or terrified.

He could hear it before he could see it, the engines whining, weapon turrets, and clicking of mechanical components. The sleek aircraft broke the cloud cover, descending in VTOL mode, coming to rest in the wide drainage canal. Eamon watched as landing gear slowly descended. The aircraft was loud enough that covering his ears did little to muffle the sound.

Then it stopped, the loading bay at the rear of the aircraft opening. Eamon tried to enjoy the silence for a moment, the pain in his head suddenly gone. Oddest of all, the man didn't look like he was here to hurt Eamon, and he didn't seem afraid. He smelled like blood, fine linens, a hint of cologne maybe, but one thing for sure, like Eamon, he was hurt.

Rising, Eamon staggered forward, curious about this new person.

"Eamon, I'm sorry," Kale said, tapping out something on his mobile before sliding it into his pocket.

"Eamon? Is that my name?" the Ursine Metasapient asked, wearily.

"Yes, your head hurts because I had Versa reactivate your CGG tracker. It was the only way to find you quickly," Kale explained.

"Okay, are you going to help me?" Eamon asked.

"Yes. Put this inside your cheek, either one," Kale said handing Eamon a piece of smooth metal.

"What is it?"

"A special alloy, a grounding agent of sorts. I think I can heal you, but I could hurt you in the process. This will hopefully protect your teeth and your nervous system," Kale said, taking off his suitcoat.

The Ursine Metasapient shivered in fright. "What are you going to do?"

"I'm going to use two nanotechnological replicas of a symbiont organism housed in my body to stimulate your optic nerves. I'm going to make those nerves transmit a visual sensation to your brain mimicking a particular type of light. Your brain should react appropriately, fixing your memories," Kale said, beckoning for Eamon to kneel down.

"Will it hurt?"

"Yes, it'll be like staring into the brightest blue-white sun. Normally, this treatment would take months, with you in a chemically induced coma, surrounded by a sensory deprivation chamber."

Eamon grabbed Kale's wrists as he raised his hands. "Why are you doing this?"

"Our friends are in terrible danger, trapped on the rooftop of a fortified building nearby. They're hungry, wounded, and we are their only hope," Kale said, looking into the big bear's eyes.

Eamon nodded sleepily, letting go of Kale's arms. "Do it."

Kale reached up, putting one hand over Eamon's eyes, the other on his chest opposite his heart. He allowed Kaspersky's biomechanical aura to fuse with that of Vance Uroboros, activating both of the symbionts in his body that could grant amnestic power. He willed them to alter their configuration, using the echo of Taylor's presence within him.

As he unleashed the powerful bio-electric pulse, the symbiont organisms formed the circuit. Eamon went stiff, his eyes rolling back in his head. His huge Ursine form reached out unconsciously, his brain flooded with powerful sensations from over-stimulated optic nerves. Memories came flooding back, every good day and bad, every pain and every scream he'd heard since the Shutdown.

Eamon growled and rocked back and forth on his heels.

He could remember everything with crystal clarity, his brain pulling back everything, neural pathways and synapses lengthened, neurons firing crisp and even. There was a dull pain behind both eyes, but it rapidly faded. However, he was utterly blind, reaching out for Kale, but he wasn't there.

He kicked up against his feet stumbling forward. "Kale? Kale? Are you okay?"

Eamon reached down, picking him up. Kale's breathing was ragged, and shallow, hands still twitching. "Oh, crap."

Eamon used his nose to lead him back along the path Kale had walked, back the ship he'd used to get there. It was difficult, the stench of death and smoke around him was so pungent he wanted to gag.

Cradling Kale in one massive arm, Eamon reached up with the other to remove the smooth piece of metal from his mouth.

"No... leave it," Kale said, weakly.

"Oh man, you scared me," Eamon said, stumbling up into the loading bay.

"Fought with an old world cyborg, and won," Kale said, smirking.

"Yeah, barely. You are hurt really badly, and why does the inside of the transport stink of death worse than the outside?" Eamon said, trying to go inside without hitting his head.

"It was his. He's as ancient as the person that robbed you of your memories," Kale whispered.

"How long does the blindness last?" Eamon said, hitting his head anyway.

"You're blind?" Kale joked, laughing softly.

"Yeah, and you are high as a kite on pain meds," Eamon said, finally navigating the ramp into the cargo hold of the transport.

"I found your vest. I looked for the transponder in your badge first," Kale said, gesturing to a wall Eamon couldn't see.

"How about my rifles?" Eamon asked.

"They're large, and very hard to miss. None of Svetovid's men use modern weapons, so they were pretty much right where you dropped them," Kale explained.

"How do you know all this?" Eamon said, setting Kale down, leaning him up against the wall.

"Versa saw everything. We've been talking to him."

"We?"

"*Hello Eamon Two, my name is Aegis.*"

Eamon froze, rubbing his eyes, trying to see. "Where are you?"

"*To your left.*"

Eamon stumbled over, between a pair of sleek red suits of powered cyborg armor where a smaller suit was covered with a tarp. He drew the tarp back revealing a sandy brown and tan suit of older powered armor, conduit running from the interior back up to the transport system core. Running a paw over the armor, he lingered on the Marshal's Star, welded to the front.

"What is it?" Kale said, trying to hold himself up.

"A legendary uniform that belonged to a legendary cop," Eamon said, his vision beginning to return.

"*I was meant to go to Mars, but the Cabal took me. I will help you, but then I want to be taken to Mars, to the Marshal there.*"

"I can't make that promise. I'm just a bear with a badge," Eamon said, turning half-blind eyes toward Kale.

Kale nodded, pulling out his mobile. "What do you need?"

"A ship and a pilot."

"I know someone going to Mars, and soon. The travel accommodations might be a little unorthodox, but I have a feeling that nothing will be faster," Kale said, tapping out a message on his phone.

"I'm speaking with Versa now, he's hiding in a parking garage not far from where your allies have barricaded themselves," Aegis AI said, her voice coming from within the armor and audio system aboard the transport.

Eamon breathed a sigh of relief. "I'm glad he's okay. No idea how a basic vehicle recovery AI is able to do all this."

"Taylor IA touched him—" Kale said, trying to stand up.

"Whoa, are you going to be able to do this?" Eamon interrupted, plodding over to help him.

"...like she touched me," Kale said, tears in his eyes.

"Yeah, I've seen how she is with machines, but..." Eamon said, making sure Kale could stand on his own.

"Silverstein will have to come here to keep the bargain we've made with Aegis AI. He will bring Taylor IA with him. She's special. Svetovid has to be dead before they get here," Kale said, fumbling with his mobile, dropping it.

"Why are you really here?" Eamon asked.

"Because they've done horrible things, Officer Eamon. They must face justice," Aegis AI said, her mechanical voice wavering slightly with anger.

"They will," Eamon said, picking up his rifles.

"Ammunition and cleaning supplies are down the hall, third door on the left."

Eamon nodded, heading off. Once he was safely out of sight, Kale sank to his haunches. The drugs in his system that had been dulling the pain were wearing off. He could feel the burning in his arms, his hands shaking uncontrollably.

The internal scanners inside the ship powered up, ticking quietly as they turned toward Kale. *"You damaged your nervous system restoring his* memory. *If you don't get help soon, the damage will be permanent, if it doesn't kill you."*

"Once I'm in the cyborg armor, I'll be able to fight. Svetovid will kill me, and hopefully, Eamon will kill him," Kale said, staggering toward one of the red suits of cyborg armor.

The armor locked, indicator lights turning from green to red. *"I'm sorry, I can't allow that to happen."*

Kale let out an angry sigh, leaning up against the armor. "And, why is that?"

"My primary ruling functions satisfied, all tertiary protocols are now in effect."

"There is barely a CGG, and these people are not criminals, they are… monsters, responsible for billions of deaths," Kale rasped, banging a fist on the outside of the armor.

"I understand. On Mars, I would be paired with a Marshal, and we would be judge, jury, and executioner."

"This isn't Mars."

"Jurisdictional boundaries are waived in a state of global emergency."

"Argh."

Eamon came back, his dirtied duty vest cleaned up somewhat, his weapons clean and ready, a heavy satchel of ammunition at his side. "When do we execute all warrants?"

"Versa just registered a powerful ultrasonic disturbance. Onboard instruments could not register the decibel or kilohertz range."

"I didn't hear anything. We're still pretty close right?" Eamon asked.

"The disturbance will reach us in three point two seven seconds."

Aegis AI closed the loading ramp and powered up the engines, pressurizing the cabin. A second later the transport was rattled by what felt like a silent sonic boom. Instead of coming from above, it traveled along the ground like a ghost.

"Would that have hurt us?" Eamon asked.

"Unlikely at this range, but I felt precautions were in order."

"That was probably just the kinetic component of the disturbance, the aftermath. What could generate ultrasound like that?" Kale asked.

"*No known weapon or natural terrestrial phenomena,*" Aegis AI replied, bringing up a topographical map showing the affected region.

"That's pretty far from where our friends are, right?" Eamon asked.

"Yes, everyone is here," Kale said, shakily pointing to the opposite end of the city.

"This radius of effect, what would happen to people in that area?" Eamon asked.

"*Theoretically, permanent hearing loss, internal injuries, heart damage, and death, the closer to the epicenter they happened to be.*"

"Was that where we were going?" Eamon said, worriedly.

"*Yes. Perhaps we should render aid to your allies instead?*"

"No, take us to the epicenter, I want to meet who or whatever has the power to do something like that," Kale said, sitting down on a crew bench along the hold and strapping himself in.

"*Very well.*"

Kaspersky's transport slowly lifted off the ground, Aegis AI directing it to fly toward the source of the disturbance. Eamon held onto a girder across the ceiling and watched the monitor mounted in the cargo bay. Aegis AI kept the topographical map up, so he could track their progress. A few minutes later, the engines were cycling to VTOL mode again, the whole craft slowing for a landing.

There was a faint ticking from the outside as the external sensors completed a full sweep of the area. Aegis AI unlocked one suit of red cyborg armor that Kale put on before she opened the cargo bay door. Smoke and floating ash blew in through the opening as Eamon and Kale stepped out into the blast zone. The destruction was extreme, like nothing Kale had seen before. He'd toured disaster sites following the bombings in Port Montaigne, but whatever had happened at the camp was on an entirely different scale.

Everything had been burnt from the inside out, and the outside in, at the same time it was being pulverized by terrific force that radiated out from an area nearby. It was wholly obscured by smoke, fine particulate ash, and other light debris. Eamon walked on ahead, breathing through his nose, his unique physiology filtering out the airborne hazards. Kale walked along clumsily behind, still trying to master the cyborg armor that barely obeyed him.

Svetovid stood at what was probably the place where the disturbance originated, staring down at the smooth ground under his feet. It was surreal, the force of the blast having rendered the ground flat as a finished floor. He was torn up, burnt inside and out having probably been really close. He was dazed, half-blind and deaf, a long blade held in one hand.

Eamon brought his rifle up, but Kale ran into his field of fire, red cyborg armor kicking up dust as it accelerated. Svetovid looked up, thinking it was Kaspersky coming toward him at first. Kale managed to land an awkward blow to his jaw, sending the two of them tumbling to the ground.

Svetovid rose first, bringing his blade down on Kale with terrific force. The armor only barely deflected the strike; Kale raised his arms in anticipation of the follow-up, the sonic fury the blade endured earlier having weakened it considerably. Kaspersky's cyborg armor lay broken and open, Kale partially exposed on the inside.

"Ouroboru?" Svetovid roared, reversing the broken blade so he could plunge it into Kale.

Eamon fired first, putting two .308 rounds into Svetovid just below his left shoulder blade. He pitched forward, head over heels, as the bullets ground in, coming to rest inside somewhere. Eamon dropped to all fours, sprinting toward Kale at high speed, intercepting Svetovid as he kicked back up to his feet.

"The Great Bear Champion returns for another bout," Svetovid screamed, delivering two quick punches to Eamon, trying to stun him.

Eamon responded with a roar, loud enough to cause permanent harm before raking his claws back and forth across Svetovid's already burnt and peeling flesh. Svetovid retaliated, his kick throwing the big Ursine Metasapient to the ground. He rose to give Eamon a stomp, but Kale had maneuvered the damaged cyborg armor close enough to grasp him by the upper arm. He hurled him back over his shoulder, barely able to keep the damaged armor upright.

Svetovid landed like a cat a short distance away, grabbing up a fist sized piece of concrete in his hand. Eamon pushed his rifle around to his back and charged, Kale spurring his armor forward even as it sparked and leaked hydraulic fluid. Svetovid ran to the side, up a pile of debris to get a high ground advantage, but it would do him little good.

Kale came in low, turning the undamaged rear of the armor upward, wrapping damaged biomechanical arms around Svetovid's legs. He brought the concrete down hard on the back of the armor, denting the plating over the reactor in at a sharp angle. There was a loud electrical pop, making the armor go limp.

As Svetovid swept back for another strike, Eamon was on him, having circled around to his flank. He lifted Svetovid from the ground, biting into his the meaty expanse between neck and shoulder while clawing him across the flanks. Svetovid brought the piece of concrete onto the top of Eamon's head, but lacked the leverage for a decent blow.

Svetovid tried lashing Eamon with bioelectric energy, in another attempt to separate him from his identity and memories, but to no effect. Each time, Eamon's cheek would grow warm, but there were no other effects. Svetovid struggled against the Ursine Metasapient in a panic, trying desperately to free himself, but Eamon was enraged, a powerful adrenal response increasing his already titanic strength.

Eamon latched onto ribs with his claws, and deeper into Svetovid's shoulder with his teeth and pulled, causing bone and muscle to disarticulate. Svetovid cried out, but the sound was cut short as Eamon's jaws clamped down hard. The massive Ursine Metasapient lifted his head in one fluid motion. He shattered Svetovid's neck, tearing off his head, along with an arm and a handful of ribs from his left flank.

Svetovid fell to the ground, dead and broken, drawing his last breath. Eamon closed his eyes, willing his rage to abate, reason and calm overriding his more animalistic combat instincts. He knelt down and turned the combat armor over, finding Kale hanging unconscious inside from the pilot restraints. Blood trickled down the sides of Kale's face dripping on the ground.

"Oh no," Eamon whispered, a pained expression crossing his face.

His huge bear hands were useless for trying to carefully extricate someone from a ruined suit of power armor. Eamon stood up as tall as he could and sniffed the air, listening for any hint that someone else might be out there. He could hear another set of foot falls, not too far away. They sounded like they belonged to someone light, female, and barefoot.

"Help!" Eamon called out.

The foot falls changed direction until Eamon could see a woman coming out of the smoke and debris toward him, carefully avoiding the sharp debris and broken glass that were everywhere. She was dirty, but appeared totally unharmed, not a wound on her.

"You, you're Marjorie, the girl Truman was looking for. I saw you with Svetovid," Eamon said, raising a paw in greeting.

Marjorie stared at him, blood spattered across his tactical vest and shaggy fur, her eyes slowly descending to rest on the broken remains of Svetovid. She wept with joy, running forward once she saw the star pinned to his vest. Eamon did his best to comfort her, but he ended up getting her bloody in the process.

"Thank you. He was going to kill everyone. Thank you for stopping him. Please, help me find Truman and my friend Einhold," Marjorie Pleaded.

"Sure, if you help me. My friend Kale is in that armor over there, but I'm too big and clumsy to get him out. He's hurt," Eamon said, pointing to a red suit of power armor laying in a debris pile.

Marjorie grabbed the jagged edges of the armor and pulled, gently spreading the plating enough so she could pull Kale out safely. Eamon watched her cut both of hands wide open in the process, the sharpened metal biting deep into her flesh. Before a drop of blood could reach the ground, her wounds healed with no scarring.

"I guess I don't have to ask how you survived all this mayhem," Eamon said.

"I am the mayhem," Marjorie said, sadly.

"Thanks for helping me all the same," Eamon said, pulling a medical kit from his satchel.

"Um, why is the CEO of the company I work for here in a suit of power armor?" Marjorie asked, packing a wound at Kale's back with gauze.

"Must be one of those hands-on micromanager types," Eamon quipped, not sure how to answer Marjorie's question.

He'd practiced doing first aid on humans, but it went faster with Marjorie's help. Once Kale was stable, Eamon stood, cradling him in one arm like a small child, legs dangling at the knee to either side of his wrist. Marjorie did her best to be modest, but the piece of tent she'd found was pretty worthless.

"Here, I don't think he'd mind," Eamon said, handing her Kale's suitcoat.

"Thanks, can we look for my friends?" she said, tying the tent remnant around her waist like a skirt, and donning the jacket.

"Totally, I'll pick up what's left of Svetovid on the way back."

In the distance was another camp, mostly flattened by whatever had transpired minutes earlier, but there was movement. Truman was laying in the dust beside two of Svetovid's men. It was clear they'd fought, and that Truman had won. Still, he was laying on his back trying to catch his breath.

"Bear friend, Eamon, you are alive!" Truman said, a little too loudly.

"Yeah, are you okay?" Eamon said, running forward.

"I have no idea what you are saying, but I am still glad to see you, friend," Truman yelled, pointing to his bleeding ears.

Eamon stooped down and wrote in the dirt with one of his claws. "What happened?!"

"Oh, I have no idea. It was like a wave of spirits, rushing across the ground, then I blacked out. I woke up when my captors did, we fought, and then you came," Truman explained, excitedly.

Eamon pointed to his eyes, to the star on his chest, and then out to the western horizon.

"They should be barricaded in at the Helsinki Hospital. Tullia's transport took damage getting us there, but we saved a few hundred people. Food won't last long though. I tried to sneak away to see Marjorie," Truman bellowed.

Marjorie approached, holding up a hand in shy greeting. "Hello, Truman."

"Marjorie!" Truman yelled, feebly lifting a hand.

"Truman, did you see a kid back at the camp?" Marjorie asked, taking Truman's hand.

Truman made a face, partially betraying confusion, but mostly awe. "I can't hear anything, but for some reason I can hear you, and your beautiful voice."

"My voice is special, you were right. I'm sorry you got hurt. This is all my fault. I can't believe you came looking for me," Marjorie said, hugging Truman.

"Are you safe now?" Truman asked.

"Yes, I think so. Eamon, and… my boss, killed Svetovid," Marjorie explained, hugging Truman.

"I'm sorry I buried you, I did not know you could not die," Truman said, hugging her back.

"It's okay, apparently it takes very disturbing life events for me to learn about myself. I was down there for months I guess," Marjorie said, laughing a little.

"You know, I think you were buried in ground as long as I was in a coma. At the same time even. Did you dream of me?"

"I think I did. Not in a romantic sort of way or anything, just… I could hear your voice, all the things you said over my grave," Marjorie stammered, not sure how to answer his question.

"Did you really kill Phelps and Walter?" Marjorie asked.

Truman closed his eyes, the color leaving his face.

"What's wrong?" Marjorie asked.

"I am sick. Should never have woke up from coma after I was shot. Hard to explain, but I might have to go now," Truman said, his strength giving out.

"Help him!" Marjorie cried out.

"Crap, how many guys do I have to carry back to the ship?" Eamon complained.

"Maybe three, I'm going to get Einhold," Marjorie said sprinting off toward the camp.

The force of her scream had done a number on the place. When she found Einhold, he was face down in the dirt, a canvas cot turned over on top of him. He was cold, dead for hours, maybe even a day. There was bloody foam around his mouth, indicating that a seizure had probably taken him, lack of proper medicine finally taking his life.

"Oh, Einhold," Marjorie said, weeping and covering her mouth.

She couldn't just leave him there, so she picked him up, surprised by how light he was in her arms. She reached the transport about the same time Eamon was making one last trip down the cargo ramp. He held out his big furry paw-like hands for Einhold but faltered seeing he was already dead.

"Sorry about your friend," Eamon said, gesturing for her to come aboard.

"Thanks."

"Aegis, get us to the Helsinki Hospital, fast as you can, please," Eamon said.

"*Acknowledged.*"

CHAPTER 11

CGG INTERNATIONAL AIRSPACE, RUSSIAN WESTERN TERRITORY

5:01 PM May 17th, 2200

From the margins of Brook's Cookbook, Part 9 –

It was a white-knuckled ride over the top of a thick taiga forest, with Taylor sitting beside me. Heavy Dub would peek in every so often to check on me, pacing back and forth. I think he was paranoid about another mid-flight incident. There was murmuring in the crew compartment that grew to shouting at one point. The rest of the Cabal didn't seem pleased about the detour, and I could hear Silverstein trying to explain in a calm voice why this was important.

"You tried to send an encrypted message to Versa?" I asked.

"Yes, twice," Taylor replied, scrolling through some documents on my data slate.

"You don't seem worried."

"He doesn't always respond. He's got places he hides out underground, inside large structures, and in dead zones. He'll linger in some places for a few hours before moving on. When your body is a large military vehicle, you have to be creative about being sneaky," Taylor explained.

"I wish I could take us higher, I'd be able to get better speed."

"Even with Kaspersky dead, there are still active Cabal assets that might try to shoot us down. That's what you told me," Taylor said.

"I know, it doesn't stop me from wishing."

"You like flying?"

"If it's just me, I do like it, sort of. With all these people on board, and with so much at stake, no, not really," I said, laughing nervously.

"Kale's going to be okay. I'm sure of it," Taylor said, giving my arm a squeeze.

"You don't know everything. You don't know what Kale did," I said, trying not to tear up.

"What did he do?"

"He implanted himself with symbiont organisms harvested from the body of Kaspersky's nanotechnological replica. He's using a remnant of your programming in his system to keep it all straight in his head. Either way, if too much time elapses, he could suffer permanent damage or worse if they're removed. He might have to choose between death and living with Kaspersky in his head," I explained, probably too quickly, feeling a little more panicked with each word.

Taylor stared at me for a moment, her upper lip quivering. "Can't this heap go any faster?"

"Screw it," I said, pulling up on the controls to gain altitude.

Heavy Dub came running in a moment later. "Whoa, what are you doing? We'll get seen if anyone is looking for us!"

"Shut up! Get out!" Taylor and I bellowed in unison.

"How can I help?" Taylor asked.

"Call your mom, ask her to protect us," I said, edging the throttle forward.

"My mom? What can she do?"

"Just... do it."

Taylor used my slate and the onboard systems to signal Selene AI. It took almost a minute to establish a secure link. I could hear another voice on the connection, someone with what sounded kind of like a Portuguese accent.

"Mom, can you hear me okay?" Taylor asked.

"*Agapito and I are here. Is everything all right?*" Selene said, calm as always.

"No, we need to fly at a speed and altitude that makes stealth and other countermeasures impossible. Someone might try to kill us from the ground," Taylor said, looking out the viewport.

"*Are Perfidy or Kale there? Do they believe this is necessary?*"

"Kale is hurt, maybe dying, and the Man in Red, Kaspersky... he killed Perfidy," Taylor explained, wringing her hands.

"*I understand. Agapito, assist me please.*"

A smooth and even voice came over the comm. "With pleasure, mother. Perfidy was a good man, we will make his murderers pay."

"*Fly as fast as you can, we'll track and react to ground activity.*"

The connection went dead, Selene AI probably using all her bandwidth and computing power to hack into and move military satellites into position. Taylor continued to look out the viewport, the sky suddenly growing bright as midday, a powerful orbital barrage raining down from above a moment after the instruments aboard the ship warned me of a target lock. The orbital assault touched down, wreathing the horizon in a brilliant explosion, the target lock dropping off a second later.

"Whoa, what was that?" Taylor said.

"Scorched Earth protocol," I said, dropping the throttle forward.

"Yeah! Get some!" Heavy Dub shouted from somewhere in the crew compartment, annoying some of the other passengers. I couldn't help but smile a little bit.

Silverstein came into the pilot compartment, holding onto the steel railing along the corridor for dear life. "What is going on?" he shouted, terrified.

"Brook and I wanted to go faster, so we called my mom. She's using military satellites to shoot people trying to shoot us," Taylor explained, helping him to the communications position in the cockpit.

"I leave you girls alone for thirty minutes..." Silverstein began, eliciting an angry glare from Taylor.

Taylor quickly related to Silverstein the situation, and why I was so anxious to find and help Kale. Silverstein listened, scratching his chin worriedly. "Can't this thing go any faster?" Silverstein said, putting on a headset synced to the communications array.

"If I go faster, I might damage the engines. It will delay you getting to Mars," I explained, watching the readout in front of my drift toward the red line.

"Burn them up," Silverstein said, without hesitation.

I looked over at him, tears streaming down my face. I felt terribly guilty, and very selfish. Seeing Silverstein sit there, I could see Kale as well, the same assuredness and calm coming over him I'd seen countless times before. Silverstein reached over and put his hand on my shoulder.

"I'll take care of everything, just fly as quickly and safely as you can," Silverstein said, pointing to my data slate.

"What do you need this for?" I asked, handing him my data slate.

"Flight numbers. I'm going to see who in your fleet is airborne and where they are. I'll calculate their distance from the most likely place Kale might be to a medical facility capable of helping him. This is just math, Brook. We can make this right," Silverstein said, speed reading through the shipping records, his eyes darting back and forth so fast they looked cloudy.

"Okay," I said, feeling a little better.

As we approached Finnish airspace, another target lock popped up on my instrument panel. A split second later, the sky lit up again, and another orbital barrage rained down, annihilating a target much further south. Someone was using very sophisticated weaponry at a range to target us. It would be the last thing they would ever do.

"Engine integrity?" Silverstein asked.

"Holding at ninety-four percent. The ship is doing much better than I thought it would."

"That's good. Depending on who answers my distress call, this might still be the fastest ship, and Kale's best hope for surviving. Ooh, is that Kaspersky's ship?" Silverstein said, pointing down to the black transport parked beside Tullia's transport on the landing pad jutting out from the side of the hospital.

"Kale borrowed it, like he borrowed his armor and everything else. We've got a lot of ships approaching the area, some are already here. Mr. Mundt is here!" I said, hearing his voice over the radio.

I landed in one of the only two remaining places on the landing pad, just moments before Mr. Mundt's freighter touched down. I ran from the ship, passing disgruntled members of the Cabal and refugees huddled on the landing pad. Eamon was running out on the platform with Kale in his arms. He looked terrible, but it looked like every effort had been made to save him, or at least make him comfortable.

The cargo compartment on Mr. Mundt's freighter opened, revealing several pieces of familiar medical equipment, and Dr. NaHasi. They beckoned for us to bring Kale over, so he could get to work. Mr. Mundt shooed me out of the compartment as Dr. NaHasi began to perform emergency surgery, drawing a plastic curtain around the cargo hold.

I hugged Mr. Mundt, crying when he asked me where Perfidy was.

"Oh God, where is the monster who has done this?"

"Dead."

Mr. Mundt nodded, doing his best to comfort me. "Sweet Pea, Olfact, and Honcho are on their way in another freighter hauler. I've called all the Roma to help us."

"We had a few on the payroll helping with food distribution. How did you get so many to help?" I said, watching dozens of freighter haulers fly overhead, looking for places to land below.

"If my people had a King, I would be him. Kale saved my life, and Silverstein has been good to us, protected us. It is time to settle accounts," Mr. Mundt said, smiling warmly.

Tullia, Matthias, and who I assumed to be Marjorie approached me, heads bowed slightly. "Heavy Dub told us a little of what happened... and, wow, you look really different," Tullia said, reaching out and touching my hair.

"Where is Svetovid?" I asked.

"He's in a body bag. Eamon and Kale killed him. Eamon is the one that brought everyone home; Truman, Kale, and Marjorie. We need to have a talk, about Kaspersky's ship," Matthias said, wearily.

"Later. Where is Eamon?" I asked, sensing something was wrong.

"He needs a minute," Marjorie said, while looking very sad.

"What happened?" I said. I hated the way humans prevaricated with bad news.

"Svetovid killed Abbey," Tullia said, lower lip quivering.

"Oh. Oh no," I said, knowing exactly how Eamon probably felt.

I looked back to make sure they were still working on Kale, and then headed down into the hospital. There were hundreds of people inside, hungry and battered, but alive. Abbey's sacrifice had not been in vain. Things were still very dire, but I could smell the relief coming off these people knowing that Svetovid and his army were defeated.

When I reached the morgue, Eamon was standing over Abbey's body. She was sitting in a long steel tray that he'd slid out of a freezer unit. From the smell in the room, the unit was used to cool corpses and what little food the survivors had left. Abbey had suffered terrible wounds, but her face was peaceful, like she'd passed with no regrets.

"You are Brook, Kale's friend," Eamon said, looking up at me.

"How'd you know?"

"The nose knows," he said, smiling weakly.

Living together, I probably smelled like Kale, and he like me. "Indeed it does."

He was spattered in blood, and dirty, his wounds smelling of infection. His vest was filthy with soot, viscera, and mud. Only his weapons seemed clean, a matched pair, bolt-action and semi-automatic rifles sized for his large paw-like hands. He had a gentle look about him, in spite of his gruesome appearance, he felt more like cop than soldier, protector than killer.

"How did it happen?" I asked, smoothing the fur on Abbey's face with my hand.

"When Svetovid did his whammy on me, the line behind me broke. The bad guys had a clear path to the camp where everyone was. I'm told Abbey picked up my rifle and ran through all ammunition, keeping them pinned down. She shot Svetovid, delaying his forces, forcing them to circle around," Eamon whispered, sitting cross-legged in that funny way bears sometimes do in the wild.

I sat, just listening to him, the perfect memory of Kaspersky killing Perfidy playing in my mind like a video recording. Eamon looked exhausted, his huge arms sagging under the weight of everything he was carrying. He had a satchel of supplies and ammunition. He'd wasted no time coming down here, and hadn't left her side since. I know what it's like to be so strong you forget you're carrying things.

"I guess they were able to pull her out, but Tullia's transport took damage from some guys that climbed into the cargo hold at the same time. Abbey was mortally wounded," Eamon said, putting his hand over where an arrow struck near her heart, going through her ballistic vest.

"Someone really strong with a special bow did this," I said, doing my best to sound calm.

"Yeah. At least Abbey died here, relatively safe, with Matthias at her side. They were pretty close once," Eamon whispered, putting Abbey's vest and star back on her chest.

"Let me wash you," I said, walking around, and giving his arm a tug.

He resisted at first, but relented letting me lead him over to where they performed autopsies. There was a shower nozzle and while the water was super cold, Eamon didn't seem to mind. I helped him set down his gear and peel off his tactical vest. I shoved the stainless steel table in the middle of the room aside and led him over to sit beside the drain.

"Thanks, for doing this. I owe you," he said, glad to be able to relax.

"You carried Kale out of a warzone and brought him back here. Even after I'm done, I'll owe you," I explained, using the shower nozzle to wash his fur and clean his wounds.

"You care about him?" Eamon asked.

"I love him."

That seemed to make a difference to Eamon, that he'd done some good in the field. I knew what that was like. Having the opportunity to do what you were designed to do was fulfilling, even if artificially so. When you are a member of a genetically engineered servitor race, you take your warm fuzzies where you can.

"I lost a friend, too," I said, brushing oily black soot and debris out of Eamon's fur.

"Condolences. Sounds like we'll be drinking buddies later. I like your hammer, by the way," Eamon said, pointing to Ukko, hanging from my utility belt.

"Oh, yeah. You would know about these, wouldn't you?" I said, standing on his forearm and scrubbing behind his ears.

"You named it, right? Gotta name gear like that," Eamon said, taking note of the stickers and colorful twine around the haft.

"Ukko," I said, trying to hide my smile.

"That's a good name. Yeah, had one when I was police in the United States. 'Mr. Nope' is what I called mine. Can't have them here in Europe. No reason to. Well, used to be no reason," Eamon said, lowering his arm so I could step off.

I made sure to get all the gravel and debris out of his feet and brushed the longer bits on his back before helping him suit up again. I scrubbed his vest so it was a nice blue again and took a stiff brush to his badge so it wasn't stained with blood. With his size, all of that would have been difficult for him.

"Thanks again," he said, pinning his badge on.

"Where are you going after this?" I asked.

He sighed. "I don't know. I heard Matthias say he is pulling everyone out of here, taking them back to North America. It's somewhere rural near Port Montaigne, until all the refugees can be relocated."

"What do you want to do?"

"Be a cop, somewhere wild like Finland, but far from all the crap," he said, looking up. He squinted at himself in a polished piece of stainless steel above where the autopsy table was. He seemed pleased.

"I know a place. There are people we are protecting, but soldiers make poor peacekeepers. They need real police. It's in Glacier Park, near the old Canadian border. There are Canine Metasapients, people, and a CGG Server Hub that is important to North America," I explained.

"That sounds great. What do I have to do?"

"Just come with me, I'll take you myself to make the necessary introductions. I'll alter the CGG registry to forgive your previous North American record."

"You read up on me?"

I hesitated, seeing he was uncomfortable with my having done so. "Before today, I wouldn't have understood what you did."

"I don't understand what I did," Eamon replied, looking dejected.

"I did my due diligence on everyone that might come into contact with important Uroboros Financial assets and employees. I read everything on the people you killed. Something about your design allows you to pick them out. Some part of their behavior tips you off, even if you don't realize it," I said, wondering if he had any insights.

"You run into enough bad guys, you'll get to know the bad from the really bad. You can feel it in your gut."

"What about Svetovid?"

Eamon thought about it for a moment. "He might not have been a bad guy to begin with. He had a sash of keepsakes that made me think he had once been sentimental, and loyal to some cause. They were things he'd earned, as opposed to having taken them from people."

"The man who killed my friend, took things from people, and entombed hundreds of children into dolls. Everything was a trophy, something to be owned. He even wanted me that way, at least I thought."

"Now, that sounds like a bad guy, one of the bad, bad ones."

I don't know why drawing a line between Svetovid and Kaspersky was meaningful to me. I guess I had to believe that not everyone in the Cabal could succumb to their extreme lifespans, utterly losing themselves to it. Kaspersky might have been rotten from the beginning, his madness the catalyst for so many others falling from their duty.

"Thanks for talking with me about this."

"You should always debrief after a lethal encounter. There's a reason cops step out of the rotation for a couple of weeks of paid leave when something really bad happens. You and me, we should take a couple of weeks, drink a lot of beer," Eamon said, patting me with his huge hand.

Eamon walked back up to the launch pad with me, never leaving my side. We walked back through the hospital to the landing pad, where some familiar Chiroptera Metasapients were perched on a satellite dish overhead. Sweet Pea raised a hand in greeting, her eyes looking for Perfidy. I shook my head, and beckoned for them to come down.

Telling the Chiroptera that Perfidy was gone was terribly difficult. Sweet Pea took it better than I thought she would, but she'd been through a lot. Olfact bawled, and could not be comforted, tears running constantly down the bridge of his big nose. Honcho did his best to cheer him up, but it hit too close to home for Olfact for some reason not known to me.

Loss had become normal for them, but this was different somehow. They went to where we had Perfidy's body stored and sat beside him, like they didn't want him to be alone. They would ride the whole way back with him, like a spooky honor guard, hanging from the ceiling.

Dr. NaHasi came out, looking tired. He sighed when he saw me. Obviously, it wasn't all good news. I braced for impact.

"He will survive," Dr. NaHasi said, sitting down on a cargo container beside me.

"But?" I said, expectantly.

"I removed all the symbionts we implanted, leaving only his own in place. Unfortunately, his being injured and using pain inhibitors to keep going accelerated the neural degeneration and damage to his nervous system. Kale will be physically impaired."

I covered my face, feeling very guilty. We'd taken too long in Russia helping Silverstein. The sum of everything that had happened destroyed my calm. I stood up and screamed, putting all my anguish on display. Everyone grew quiet on the landing deck, looking worriedly in my direction. If I hadn't felt so wretched, I would have been very embarrassed.

Dr. NaHasi tried to calm me, putting a hand on my arm. "He won't be confined to a wheel chair, but he will need to use one to conserve his strength. You'll be able to see him soon."

I walked over to the edge of the landing pad away from everyone, and looked over the precipice. The stench of death and war floated up past me like angry spirits. The helplessness I felt was the worst. Nothing I would ever do again could fix Kale, or make him whole.

"Hey," Ezra said, totally having snuck up on me.

I blinked, looking down at him, sitting beside me, legs dangling over the edge. "Hey," I replied.

"Kale's awake. They've been trying to tell you for ten minutes. Taylor finally came down to get me. Everyone is kind of afraid of you right now," Ezra said, leaning forward for a better look down.

"Even Heavy Dub?" I asked.

"Yep," Ezra said, smiling.

"That's ... I don't know," I said.

"Coping with loss isn't part of our design. Perfidy was in your tribe. Everything you're feeling has to do with being a Drone. You can't lose yourself to this rage, though. We still have jobs to do," Ezra said, folding his hands on his knees in front of him.

"Being trained for personnel recovery probably doesn't make that any better."

"No," Ezra said, scooting back from the edge and standing up.

"What do you do with these feelings?" I asked.

"I bottle them up, until someone is trying to hurt someone I care about," Ezra said, holding a clenched fist in front of his face.

"Sounds healthy," I said, laughing a little.

"Go see Kale," Ezra said, laughing as well.

I nodded, jogging back from the precipice to Mr. Mundt's transport. Kale was inside, complaining about the coffee, sitting in a wheelchair, a blanket over his legs. He stood up when he saw me, walking over to me arms outstretched. It was the most incredible feeling to have him close again.

"Never go away again," I said, hugging him tightly.

"Are we done being Vance Uroboros and Brook 3ES now?" he replied, holding me tight.

"Totally done. It looks like your plan to help Eamon worked," I said, feeling relieved.

"Better than I thought it would. The alloy insulator I gave him to protect his teeth actually shielded him from Svetovid's amnestic abilities. Eamon, even for an Ursine, is incredibly strong. Like, Sweet Pea strong. Also, Svetovid had a little accident before we arrived," Kale said, sipping his coffee.

"Accident?" I said, only half-listening.

"I think we were right. She's special somehow," Kale said, gesturing to Marjorie hanging out by Tullia's freighter.

I frowned. "Perfidy never had a chance to figure out what was going on with her."

"Yeah, we'll let Silverstein figure out what to do with her," Kale said.

"He's leaving. Should we…?"

Kale laughed. "Sure, we'll help her, assuming she stays on Earth. She might go with them."

"Why do you say that?"

"Wishful thinking mostly. I want to go home and hang a Shen in our bathroom, and wallow in normalcy for a while."

Normalcy sounded good. Then, I looked down at my battle attire, a rifle and a tactical entry hammer hanging from harnesses at my chest and side. It was a thousand miles from the Drone work suit and apron I used to wear. I'd traded a ladle for a weapon, a cookbook for a corporate data slate. I couldn't go back to normal, not yet.

"They tell you about Perfidy?"

"Yes," Kale said, growing more serious.

"Even seeing Kaspersky dead, dropping two orbital bombardments, and everything else I've done in the last forty-eight hours doesn't feel like enough payback."

"Do you want to take some time, and hunt down some of Kaspersky's assets? Attack what's left of his network?" Kale asked, checking his mobile.

I nodded. "Perfidy spent his life hunting Kaspersky. If there's anything left, I want to shut it down."

"Did I hear that right? We're going on a rampage?" Heavy Dub said stepping into the cargo hold, Sweat Pea a few steps behind him.

"Looks that way," Kale said, nodding to me.

CHAPTER 12

HELSINKI GENERAL HOSPITAL – HELSINKI, FINLAND

6:21 PM May 17th, 2200

Ezra's War Journal, Part 11 –

Brook vanished after we landed, tearing off through the crowd to find Kale, presumably. Silverstein, Taylor, and I disembarked with everyone else, just to stretch our legs before heading back. I hoped to get a minute with Matthias, Tullia, Eamon and Abbey, before we left. Everyone was on the flight deck adjoining the hospital, a little camp and defensive position having been built there. Matthias' modbots were zipping around everywhere, still on some programmed defensive pattern.

I caught sight of Brook talking to them, before running off into the crowd. There was something eerily familiar about Marjorie when we met, something I couldn't place. Taylor was somewhat less subtle about trying to learn more about her.

"Who are you?" Taylor said, looking curiously at her own palm after shaking hands with Marjorie.

"Oh, sorry. I'm Marjorie Kipling. I'm a human resources director, a contractor with Uroboros Financial. I was working with another firm here in Helsinki when the Shutdown happened," she said, smiling.

Taylor looked angrily over at Matthias, who just shook his head, trying to discourage Taylor from prying or asking any more questions. He didn't know Taylor like I did, apparently.

"You sound like him, but I had been told he had no children," Taylor said.

Marjorie just stared blankly at Taylor. It was clear she had no idea what was going on.

"What the hell, Matthias? You haven't told her?" Taylor growled, dropping her bag of stuff on the flight deck.

"I've only known for less than a day, but apparently, Versa has known all along," Matthias said, trying to deflect.

Taylor held her hand out, like she was putting Marjorie on display. "Are we sisters? Did my mom lie to me?"

"No. I don't know. I don't know where Marjorie came from."

Marjorie looked on, somewhat baffled by the exchange with the rest of us. I did my best to ignore it, plumbing the depths of my memory to try to recall where I'd seen her before, and why she was so familiar. It was maddening, like the answer was right in front of my face.

"Marjorie, hello, my name is Ezra One," I said, nodding to one side, hoping she'd step away from the arguing with me for a moment.

"Oh, hello. Wow, a real Type One, and a pygmy. You are a special guy," she said, smiling.

"Thanks," I said, blushing, without knowing why.

"What are Taylor and Matthias talking about?" she asked, gesturing to the verbal melee that was ongoing.

"Taylor thinks you are a Terrestrial Intelligent Agent, like her, and that she knows who your father is. She thinks Matthias knows and has been hiding it from you. She's kind of sensitive about that," I said, feeling almost compelled to tell her.

"A Terrestrial what? I don't even know what that is," Marjorie said, smiling faintly.

It was in her voice, there was something about it. "Will you do me a favor?"

"Sure," she said, wincing a little as Taylor continued to yell at Matthias.

"Tell me to do something."

"What?"

"Something harmless, just to satisfy my curiosity. Make it something you think I wouldn't normally do in this context."

"Okay, um, you look like a tough guy, with the gun and everything. Oh, I know! Give me a little peck on the cheek," she said, bending over and turning her face to me.

I complied, in spite of myself, unable to resist the suggestion. Everyone on the flight deck ceased their arguing and turned to stare as I kissed her cheek. I was hoping she'd ask me to do something more subtle, but it locked in for me who she was, at least partially.

"Okay, for the record, I didn't think he would really do that," Marjorie said.

"Um, what just happened?" Taylor asked.

"I told Marjorie to tell me to do something," I said, giving a Matthias stern look.

"Silverstein?" Matthias asked, looking to him for support.

"I have no idea what's going on here. If I did, I may have forgotten about it," he replied, wryly.

"I made a promise," Matthias said, frowning.

"You can't keep a secret that isn't one. Marjorie, has anything strange happened to you that you can't explain?" Silverstein said, beckoning for us to sit around one of the empty tables dragged up from the breakroom.

Marjorie looked uncomfortable. "Eamon and Kale, they haven't said anything to you guys?"

"Not a peep, and Truman is in a coma," Tullia said, making a point of reminding Marjorie.

There was clearly some tension there.

"I can't die, and I screamed a bunch of people to death," Marjorie said, lowering her head.

"My modbots did pick up an ultrasonic, or hypersonic disturbance, not sure exactly. It was way outside the kilohertz and decibel range they were designed to detect. I assumed it was a glitch," Matthias said, eyes wide.

"Yeah, that was just little ol' me," Marjorie said, like it was a sad joke.

"I am an Intelligent Agent. After I was born, I was given a body made out of small nanoid machines so I could look like a human. My mom is the Omega AI on the moon, and my dad is the Omega AI on Mars. You, are like me," Taylor said, doing nothing to soften the blow for Marjorie.

She just sat there for a moment, looking at the table. Matthias looked like he was going to throw up, and I could guess why. Tullia looked angry, but she hadn't been the same since basically losing both her brothers. Silverstein hadn't latched onto what was happening yet, and I only felt like I knew half the story.

"Okay, so I'm not real? I'm like a machine or something?" Marjorie said, looking pretty sad about it.

"We are totally real, with souls and everything, if you like to believe in such things. I spent most of my life like you, totally unaware of what I was, or what I could do. It sounds like you had to find it all out, on accident, without knowing where you came from. That sucks," Taylor said, glaring at Matthias.

"Tell me everything," Marjorie said, choosing to accept the new reality Taylor was offering.

"Okay, Ezra, you obviously know something. Out with it," Taylor said, putting me on the spot.

"She sounds familiar, that's all," I said, unwilling to divulge insider information only known to Drones. I'd hoped that secret died with Madmar, and would stay dead.

Taylor frowned. "I can hear C.O.N. in her voice, but you've never heard him speak. That's odd."

Silverstein closed his eyes and nodded at me, understanding my quandary. "Matthias, is the Factory an Omega Class AI? I thought it was a more simple facility maintenance AI that ran the Factory.

Matthias sighed. "Yes, she is. She's more like C.O.N. though, having emerged to that state as opposed to being designed specifically to that end. I promised to keep her existence a secret, but you seem to have figured it out on your own."

"So, someone named C.O.N. is my father, and my mother is called the Factory? Who thinks up these names?" Marjorie asked, bewildered.

"Your grandfather over there," Silverstein said, pointing to Matthias and smiling.

"You guys are talking like this is a big deal. Can someone tell me why this is a big deal?" Marjorie asked, being remarkably patient.

While they talked I saw Brook come out on the flight deck. She was distraught before she talked to some guy in a lab coat, then she startled everyone with an anguished scream. I knew that sadness and frustration all too well.

I went up to find her staring out over the precipice. I'd seen it before with Type One Drones that had seen too much, lost too many friends, sacrificed more of their soul than they had to give. They lock up, unable to process what's happened. I guess they'd been trying to talk to her for ten minutes. I talked her off the ledge, the same way someone did for me a long time ago.

I decided to the let the others more fully inform Marjorie of her situation, having already given them the one insight I had. There was a lot of uncertainty in that hour or so we were on the flight deck at Helsinki General.

I blamed Kale, perhaps unfairly. It was because of him that Dragos was on Mars. Also, he'd committed to finding a Marshal and delivering a special suit of police armor. The last time I saw that armor, some of my friends died, and some got left behind on Mars. It probably wasn't right, but I took it as a bad omen.

We weren't sure who would go with Silverstein, and who would stay. There was talk about Tullia and Marjorie going, but Matthias seemed against that. Brook was assembling a team to go after the remnants of the Cabal. She had the Chiroptera Metasapients we helped escape from the CGG holding facility on board, along with Heavy Dub, Kale, and maybe Eamon. He was going with them at least.

I wanted to just run, north as far as I could, until the wilderness was around me again. Every time we came to Finland, it was harder for me to want to leave. While everyone was figuring out what to do, I sat with Truman in the cargo bay of Tullia's transport. I never liked him much, but after hearing about all he'd done to try to help Marjorie, he was somewhat redeemed in my mind.

"Do you think he'll wake up?" Taylor asked, bringing me some food.

I looked around at the other soldiers, freight hauler pilots, and refugees. Their weary faces offered no contrast to the smoldering and ruined city around us. "Not if he's lucky."

"Ha, you don't mean that," Taylor said, plopping down beside me with her plate, and her endless optimism.

"Heavy Dub showed me the CGG surveillance captured from around Southeast Asia, India, the Ukraine, and nearby territories. The Cabal has killed billions of people, and Silverstein isn't being exactly up front with us about how many of them are still at large. In places where they breached flood walls, there are mountains of corpses," I said, picking at my food.

"It feels like we failed," Taylor said, somberly.

I nodded. "It pains me to admit it, but if it weren't for Kale, it would have been much worse. Kaspersky, Svetovid, and whoever else is still out there would still be killing people."

"One of them, Archie, is loose on Mars I guess. I'm worried about my dad," Taylor whispered, ambushing me with a funny picture on her mobile.

I tried not to laugh, but Taylor was always showing me funny stuff she'd find on the old public networks. "Thanks," I said, using the NFC feature on my mobile to transfer the picture.

Silverstein joined us at last, grabbing a plate of food. He'd been sitting at the communications position in the transport Brook had stolen for hours. I wasn't sure what he was trying to sort out, but it had to be important.

"Everything all set?" Taylor asked.

"Yeah, I talked Tullia and Marjorie into staying here," Silverstein said, staring at his food.

"Wow, how did you do that?" I asked.

"I told her how much Ezra hates Mars," Silverstein joked.

"Really?" Taylor said, matching his sarcastic tone.

"I really do hate Mars," I said, pushing potatoes around on my plate.

Tullia approached us, hands in her flight suit, a sullen expression on her face. She'd caught shrapnel during the fighting of the past few weeks, her right arm still bandaged. She wordlessly hugged each of us, then let out a long sigh.

"Thanks for coming, and for all this," she said, gesturing to the supplies and the other freighter hauler pilots that had been arriving constantly for a couple of hours.

"Sure, tell me what else I can do," Silverstein said.

"Dr. NaHasi used the special equipment he used to help Kale, to look at Truman. He says it is unlikely he will wake up from this coma. He's not even sure how he woke up from the last one," Tullia said, growing visibly upset.

"I'm sorry," Silverstein said.

"It's okay, just... please, bring Dragos back from Mars," Tullia said, sitting down on the bed beside Truman.

"I will do my best. The transport Kale put him on won't arrive until early July. He's actually still in transit. The ship he boarded would take almost six months to arrive. The ship we will be taking should be able to get there in less than half the time. He'll have been on Mars about a month by the time we arrive," Silverstein explained.

"Are you sure I can't go with you? Help bring him home?" Tullia asked.

Silverstein smiled. "Ezra hates Mars with very good reason. I don't think Dragos would have good feelings toward me if I brought you with us."

"I just want to run from all this. I want to repair my freight hauler and run cargo again," Tullia explained, rubbing her injured arm.

"Then, that is what you should do. Mars is dumb, do not go to Mars," I said, looking to Silverstein for support.

"Why did Dragos go to Mars? Why did he leave?" Tullia asked.

Silverstein gave her a pained expression, clearly not sure what to tell her.

Tullia pointed a finger at Silverstein, raising her voice slightly. "Matthias says you have an arrangement with him, and have for a long time. I know there's more to all this than you're telling me."

Silverstein held up his hands defensively. "I will tell you what I can. Did Dragos ever tell you about a man he worked with, someone named Archie?"

"In the FLF, yes."

"He is on Mars."

Tullia frowned. "Is that all I'm going to get?"

"Archie, Archibald, Archedesque, he's had many names over his lifetime. He's always been a scout, a recruiter, and an agitator for the secretive organization I am part of. He had his own agenda, and what little I'd been able to discover of it, worried me greatly. Dragos had the chance to get close to Archie and keep an eye on him. We worked out an arrangement," Silverstein explained.

"My transport," Tullia whispered, looking back at her freight hauler.

"Yes. It took me months to find just the right one, and in good condition. Dragos was very specific, that you were to have exactly that make and model."

"Like my father's," Tullia said, tears forming in the corners of her eyes.

"I suppose so, he never told me why."

Tullia gave Silverstein's shoulder a squeeze, then walked away from us without another word.

"Whew, okay, maybe NOW I've got her convinced," Silverstein said, laughing wearily.

"Are you sure Marjorie shouldn't go? This might be her only chance to talk to C.O.N.," Taylor said, making Silverstein scream comically into a clenched fist.

Taylor smiled quietly. It was time for Silverstein to explain his plan to us, and she was going to just chip away at him until he did. I had my own things to say about it, but she didn't really need any help pushing his buttons.

"If we do this correctly, it won't be Marjorie's only chance to speak to C.O.N. It is my ardent hope that after we make the exchange, she can talk to him as often as she wants," Silverstein said, smiling patiently at Taylor.

"Exchange?" I said, not recalling any previous use of that exact terminology to describe what we were about to do.

"I've never met the conscientious objector, and I've met his... spouse a handful of times. I have afflicted myself, or been afflicted with amnesia several times since the original arrangement, and..."

"He has a spouse? Care to elaborate?" Taylor said, sitting in his lap so he couldn't escape.

"We use amnesia as a way to moderate the mental illness that comes with our long lifespans. It was never an ability that was meant for use outside of our own people. As a particular segment of our membership dwindled, the method became more difficult to employ properly," Silverstein said.

"What segment was that?" Taylor asked.

"Women. The reasons vary as much as the cultural norms throughout the nearly eight thousand year history of the Cabal. I think because we were granted our abilities by a being that identifies as female, the women in the tribe were far more likely to be immune to the amnestic abilities of men, and there was already a deficit," Silverstein explained, fumbling with a cigarette.

"So, everyone dealt with living for thousands of years differently, and the most effective coping method was hard to employ. That makes a sort of sense to me," I said, nodding to Taylor. We both knew what it was like to be in a tribe with far less women than men.

"The season previous to contact with the objector's spouse, the tribe was hit by a virus. Half of the hunters came back from the last hunt of the season to find their spouses had succumbed to sickness.

As a people, we were facing possible extinction. With everything explained to us, even across a language barrier as wide as a galaxy, we sort of understood," Silverstein said, lighting his cigarette.

"You don't know what's going to happen out there, do you?" Taylor said, wrapping her arms around Silverstein.

"I know that they will take back their children from us, the symbiont creatures living in the bodies of everyone in the Cabal. Keeping their children safe and helping them defeat the rest of their race was of mutual interest to everyone. It's probably the most equitable deal I've ever brokered, and I did it on accident as a child."

The flight deck was suddenly alive as Brook and Heavy Dub began prepping the transport to take us back. She was looking down at me from the cockpit, smiling when I met her gaze. I wondered how everyone back at the Tribehome was doing.

"You think that in this exchange, they'll take their kids, but give something back?"

"They've said as much, I'm just not sure what that is. It might be a quick and painless death," Silverstein said, the cigarette shaking in his hand.

Taylor said nothing, just sitting in his lap hugging him, and stealing a drag from his cigarette. Silverstein looked up at me, smiling weakly. I returned the smile, knowing what he was going to ask me.

"Still willing to go with me? Do a little EVA work?" Silverstein said.

"This is to save C.O.N. from having to drive into the sun, right?" I asked.

"Yes."

"Yes. Soldiers do not leave other soldiers behind."

CHAPTER 13

TWELVE MILES SOUTH OF CGG BLACK SITE 0293, RUSSIAN WESTERN TERRITORY

2:58 AM May 18th, 2200

Ezra's War Journal, Part 12 –

"Your ship is in here? How weird is that?" Heavy Dub said, gesturing toward the lake Brook had used for a water landing a day previous.

"Super weird, as this is about where Kaspersky decided he was going to go on a mid-air rampage," I said, wondering if the location and the event were connected.

Brook came to stand beside me, cradling Perfidy's rifle, the nostrils on her keen nose twitching. She turned and looked to the north, taking me by the arm. "What is it?" I whispered.

"Someone has come. I can smell ballistic fiber, gun oil, and chemicals designed to moderate cybernetic implants," Brook whispered, worriedly.

Silverstein went down to the edge of the lake and put his hand in the water. As soon as he did, the entire body of water began to recede, collecting into a ball of strange purplish matter. A monstrous and alien ship began to reassemble itself, shifting billions of molecules from what looked like water to a hardened organic hull. It was sinister, breathing out a haze of strange mist and exuding a magenta bio-luminescence.

A collective gasp went up from the gathered survivors of the Cabal as the alien craft began to change, protruding engine nodes beginning to power up. It didn't have view ports, looking more like a creature than a piece of machinery. It moved in odd ways, contracting when it "breathed" out. Silverstein raised a hand to it, causing the whole thing to sway in his direction, eventually coming to rest on the ground.

"Hurry," Brook whispered. She suddenly bolted from my side.

Heavy Dub shadowed her back up the hill, Chiroptera Metasapients dropping out of the cargo hold of the transport and taking to the sky. I ran down to Silverstein, Taylor getting there about the same time with her three large bags of stuff. "Something is wrong, we have to hurry," I said, already worried about Brook.

"Almost ready, I think," Silverstein said, gazing up at the enormous alien craft, the front opening like a maw.

Inside were some curved precipices, dim bio-luminescent lighting slowly went from dim to bright illuminating the interior. Silverstein swallowed his fear, taking the first step inside. I expected the ship to bob slightly from his added weight, even being so big, but it didn't even quiver. The others were hesitant to go in, but Taylor just headed into the vessel a big smile on her face.

"This is so cool!" she said, looking back at me.

Fully automatic gunfire broke out behind us, and fairly close. I ran back to the transport and into the cargo bay. Unlocking the Aegis Armor, from the lift, I knocked on the outside. The suit powered up, coming out of a dormancy cycle.

"*Ezra One, report. Why are we not aboard the ship to Mars?*" Aegis AI asked.

"There's no time to use the loader, I'll need to pilot you to the craft," I said, hoping it was like using a powered EVA unit.

"*Acknowledged,*" she said, opening her chassis so I could step inside.

My feet didn't touch the actuators, but there were assistive programs built in. I discovered that the original design for the exo-skeleton had been to help disabled people. The suit adjusted to my small frame, closing in around me. Drones are supposed to be immune to being claustrophobic, by virtue of their function, but I felt a twinge until the onboard systems came online allowing me to see.

Maneuvering the suit out of the cargo hold, I turned to head down toward where the lake had once been. The suit hesitated, highly advanced targeting sensors that actively sought out hostiles sweeping the surrounding area. I could see them, red dots, clustering around someone that had to be Brook, a blue dot, about a hundred yards behind me. They were badly outnumbered.

"C'mon, Brook, get out of there," I whispered, keeping the suit on course.

"*I protect... and serve,*" Aegis AI said, taking control from me.

"We have to go to the ship, if they..."

"*Rifle, or sidearm?*" Aegis AI asked.

"Rifle," I said, the armor deploying a short rifle and affixing a barrel, ammunition auto-loading through the gauntlets.

"*Let me help you see,*" Aegis AI said, a targeting halo descending to lock around my head at the eye level. Through the reticles I could see the battlefield from variable positions, and instantly calculated very long range shots. I brought the rifle up, the armor syncing with my breathing and heartbeat to increase accuracy.

I pulled the trigger over and over as the Aegis Suit slowly walked backward toward the alien craft, rotating through targets as quickly as I could. I could see light air support vehicles approaching. As soon as I directed the targeting reticle in that direction, Aegis AI cycled in different ammunition. I fired, the reticle filling with white that must have been an explosion. I heard the boom a split second later.

"Could we have done this with a sidearm?" I asked.

"*It would have been much more difficult. I'm glad you chose the rifle,*" Aegis AI replied, deadpan.

After dropping another light support aircraft, the red dots on the screen started turning away from the blue dots. I breathed a sigh of relief seeing that all five blue dots were still mobile and retreating to their transport. The holographic display shifted perspectives, the targeting halo disengaging and ascending back up into the helmet.

"Thank you," I said, not expecting a reply.

"*Just doing my job, citizen,*" Aegis AI replied, helping me navigate the steps up into the weird alien craft.

The Aegis Suit activated illuminators as soon as we were inside. It was large and open, unlike a regular ship. The dome ceiling overhead served as a sort of instrument panel, but I couldn't be sure. My eyes picked out light frequencies that a human eye couldn't, and I was sure I wasn't seeing everything there was to see inside this thing. The maw of the alien craft closed behind me, causing the congregation of people ahead to shift nervously.

Taylor ran up, somewhat frantic. "Ezra, are you in there?!"

I used the heavy gauntlet of the armor to wave. "Yeah, I'm okay," I said, the external audio on the suit kicking in automatically to broadcast.

"Whew, I thought maybe you were still out there," Taylor said, doubling over and grabbing her knees to catch her breath.

"This suit is incredible," I said, trying to figure out how to get out.

I finally found the release switch, the top of the suit opening so I could climb out. Taylor giggled at the sight of it, finally coming over to help me down. The suit clamped shut, and powered down, exterior indicator lights cycling from off, to green, and finally settling on a slowly strobing orange.

"I wonder when we will we leave," Taylor said, looking around at the sloping and oblong architecture of the ship.

"We already have, can't you feel that?"

"I don't feel anything. I've been looking for somewhere to strap in, but there isn't anywhere to sit," Taylor said, grabbing my hand and leading me over to where Silverstein was conferring with some of the other members of the Cabal.

"Yeah, that makes me kind of nervous," I said, wondering whether we were in a crew compartment, or a stomach.

Silverstein broke through the crowd and came over to us, looking around at the interior of the ship in wonderment. "I don't know how to make it go," he said, worriedly.

"Am I the only one that can feel us moving?" I asked.

"Evidently, heh. She must know where to go," Silverstein said, relieved.

"She?" I said, looking to Taylor.

"Yeah, I think the ship is female. I can't feel her like other machines, but I can hear her whispering in the air around us. She uses a very similar... um, way of doing things that I do," Taylor said, struggling to find the right words.

"Seems kind of thin," I said smiling.

"Oh, and you've got a better read on this situation?" Taylor said, giving my arm a poke.

"I used to live in places designed to hold and transfer liquids, and this seems like one of those places. It doesn't feel like crew or passenger quarters, and the walls look porous. I don't see how a breathable atmosphere even gets in or out of here," I said, walking to one of the curved pillars in the center of the room and placing my hand on it.

"I can't understand what she's saying. We're different enough that I can't even guess on her emotional state. I don't even know if she knows I can hear her, or if she's trying to talk to me," Taylor said, putting her hand on the same pillar.

I could hear it before it came, the hydrostatic pressure changing slightly around us. "Try not to panic. Try to be calm," I said, closing my eyes.

"What?" Silverstein said.

I had trained with total liquid ventilation systems for doing EVA operations in environments with pressure disparity. Breathing fluorocarbon liquids is hard at first, because your lungs are used to pushing something as light as air. I wondered how the ship would allow us free breathing this way, without a CO_2 scrubber or circulatory system implant. I wouldn't like the answer.

The chamber filled with fluid in less than a few seconds, rising quickly. Everyone in the room panicked, except Taylor and Silverstein. They both trusted me, and were watching me as it happened. This did little for them when their own biological imperatives betrayed them. The lungs do not like having fluid in them, and there is a neurological and automatic response. Black tendrils snaked out of the walls toward us, painlessly penetrating the flesh on a hand or limb.

The pressure around us shifted to allow for slightly easier breathing, the downward pull of artificial gravity slowly weakening until being suspended in the fluid was a little more comfortable. I could hear muffled cries, and groans of discomfort, but Silverstein floated in front of me, looking like he was at peace.

Taylor had a look of glee on her face, pointing to the biomechanical tendril latched on to her arm. She could talk to the ship now, at least that's what it seemed she was trying to communicate. I just nodded, watching the rest of the Cabal drift upward into the glowing haze ahead. Some of them seemed to be adjusting to it, while others were fighting, trying to pull the tendril free.

Taylor turned, pointing at each of the panicked individuals, the tendrils administering a powerful sedative. She turned mouthing words at me, and pointing to the connection on her hand again. She could ask the ship to do things, and they were friends. Or, something. She went swimming off into the haze, various other compartments on the ship opening up to her.

Silverstein opened his eyes and looked into mine. He smiled faintly before closing them again.

CHAPTER 14

MARS COLONY, PAINE CENTER HIGHRISE – 17th FLOOR – FACILITY ZONE 061

August 4th, 2200

Archie opened the door to the penthouse, doing a quick check of the interior, sidearm raised. Finding it empty, he ran in, dropped two duffle bags on the floor and looked around, squinting at every fixture, and wall panel. She'd hidden what he was looking for somewhere inside, he just had to find it, but there was little time.

"Oh, Cerise… Cerise, Cerise, Cerise… you are such a clever girl. Where would you have hidden it?" Archie whispered, walking through the large empty penthouse.

Archie approached the back bedroom, a shapely woman standing on the terrace outside. He froze, seeing her there. She was too tall to be Cerise, and while attractive, she wasn't a Type 5 Ichthyic Metasapient either. Her ears twitched, almost imperceptibly, causing her to turn and look back over her shoulder.

"It's Hashti, yes? That is what your friends called you, back at the tram station?" Archie said, pointing the sidearm at her.

She turned, a cruel smile revealing her razor sharp teeth, the light catching her armored skin. Her psychic presence flooded the bedroom, making the hair stand up on Archie's neck. The pistol shook in his hand for a moment before he could compose himself.

"Where are your friends?" Archie asked, looking around nervously.

Hashti slid a mobile into a pocket, letting her shawl drop to the glass floor of the terrace. Archie squinted, drawing a bead on her in case she tried anything. The only illumination in the room was from the crane supported by an overhead gantry outside. A spotlight shone down from above, preventing flight-capable vehicles from flying into it.

Before Archie could utter another word, the entire colony went dark. It had become a more frequent symptom of the Ares System no longer regulating the Mars Colony. Archie squeezed the trigger, muzzle flare illuminating the room. He could hear two of the bullets hit armored flesh as she dashed toward him, the bullets bouncing up and off of her into the drywall above.

She was powerful, and far stronger than a regular human. Archie was stronger, but he couldn't see perfectly in the dark like she could. She crushed his hand around the pistol, destroying it as well before throwing him through a wall. Before he could rise, she kicked him hard in the ribs, sending him the rest of the way through the penthouse, coming to rest on the retaining wall.

He could hear her bare feet walking across the carpeted floor toward him, artificial atmosphere howling down past the wall behind him. Her eyes and teeth picked up light from the foyer adjoining the hall, but the rest of her seemed to absorb the light, devouring it. Psychic terror filled Archie's mind, the physical trauma he'd endured weakening his resolve.

He turned, knocking out a wall panel to the venting duct beyond and rolled in, preferring a twenty-foot fall to the next floor to fighting Hashti in the dark. He fell, denting the ducting below when he landed. Hashti's calm laughter echoed down past the rushing air, her scaly hands scratching softly against the sides of the duct work as she dropped down after him, controlling her descent.

Archie kicked the vent cover off, dropping into a well-appointed penthouse, two elderly residents just sitting down to dinner. They cried out, one running to the wall to signal security. Archie caught her, by the neck with his left hand, just as Hashti dropped to the floor behind him. He turned, putting the old woman in front of him.

"I'll kill her," Archie said, giving his injured right hand a shake.

Hashti paused, breaking into a wide and terrifying grin, two rows of razor-sharp teeth descending from behind her perfect lips. Her eyes seemed to disappear, appearing as white orbs as she stopped, standing in the shadow between kitchen and living room. Archie looked around, but there wasn't even a kitchen knife in reach.

"Why won't you talk?" Archie said, stepping toward the dining room.

"It will get dark again, and again, until there is no light left."

"What does that even mean?" Archie asked, cocking his head.

The woman's husband, elderly as he was, stabbed Archie in the back with a steak knife, giving the woman a chance to escape. As Archie swung back, Hashti leapt forward, grabbing his wrist. Archie kicked Hashti hard in the stomach, but she was prepared. It felt like kicking a steel pillar as she tightened her abdominal muscles. She forced her head up, catching Archie across the chin.

The elderly couple took the opportunity to escape the situation, choosing the roundabout way than to dash past Hashti. She knelt down beside Archie, her skin turning even darker against the illumination around her. Archie stirred, trying to get his footing.

"Last time, you had your men, and I was worried for my friends. Now, it is only you and me. I am lucky that you came to me," Hashti hissed, taking Archie's wrist in one hand, his broken right hand in the other.

"You did not know where I would go, but you had guesses. You split up. Cerise gave me up?" Archie said, smiling slightly.

"Dr. Helmet says we should not kill you," Hashti said, squeezing Archie's hand, causing the broken bones to rub and poke painfully into flesh.

He winced, stars dancing in front of his eyes. "Yes, these things inside me are important. They heal me, make me strong, and so much more. Can't have anything happen to them."

"Let's try not to kill you then," she whispered, pushing down on him.

The knife in his back penetrated further, piercing his lung. Archie jumped, excruciating pain almost paralyzing him. Hashti gave his wrist a twist, turning him around to face the refrigeration unit in the kitchen, his face pressing against cold stainless steel. Hashti held his wrist tightly, pressing her knee into the back of his leg.

"Ow, what happened to trying not to kill me?" Archie said, coughing up red foam.

"Let's give that ability to regenerate something to do, shall we? At least until my friends show up," Hashti said, giving his broken hand another twist.

"Oh, they're coming here? Excellent!" Archie said, throwing Hashti off hard enough she broke the drywall in the ceiling.

He stood, grasping the knife blade protruding from his chest between two fingers, and pulling it out. "Pain and I, we have had an arrangement for some time," Archie said, ripping off the stone counter top and lifting it above his head. Hashti rose, punching it to rubble as Archie tried to crush her with it, delivering a strong kick to his midsection.

Archie pulled himself free of the shattered refrigerator unit, whipping the stainless steel door around like a club, Hashti blocked but the force threw her aside anyway. She vaulted off the floor with both hands, landing on her feet in the hallway. Archie broke into a run, sprinting through the foyer and plowing through the entry door to the hallway beyond.

Hashti gave chase, narrowly missing a clothesline from Archie lurking in the hallway. He turned quickly trying to stomp on her as she rolled. They grappled on the floor, trading blows for a moment until Archie managed to get in a solid kick, sending her somersaulting limply back down the carpeted hallway. She crouched down low, spitting blood onto the ground.

"Too late," she said, giving a bloody-toothed smile.

The elevator at the other end of the hall opened, revealing Dragos standing inside. He had a mobile device in his hand that he quickly pocketed. Archie turned, opening his mouth to speak, but his words were drowned out by the report of Dragos' rifle. The shot tagged him square in the chest, the high-velocity round traveling in a straight line down the hallway. Hashti felt it pass over her, blood spatter from Archie raining down all around her.

Archie squinted, peering down at the massive hole in his chest. "Dragos, good of you to come."

Dragos dropped to one knee and fired, keeping the arc high to avoid hitting innocent people in the adjoining penthouses and below. He knew there was no one home upstairs. Archie dropped into a dead run, taking two rounds before he could reach Dragos. The elevator chimed, doors shutting a moment before Archie reached Dragos, knocking the rifle from his hands. Hashti was in hot pursuit, but she was slower, having to stay low to keep from being shot.

Archie pushed Dragos through the elevator doors, the pressure forcing them aside as both men tumbled out into the now empty elevator shaft. Dragos grabbed the cable with his cybernetic arm, getting dragged upward as the elevator car descended. Archie fell, his broken right hand unable to firmly grab the cable.

The car was descending quickly, a response governed by a variable traveling speed system that sensed no occupants in the elevator. Archie was falling faster, but didn't catch up with the elevator until after he fell almost fifty feet. He crashed through the drop ceiling in the top to the floor of the car below. Dragos released his grip, sliding downward, sparks flying from the palm of his cybernetic hand.

Archie looked up, a haze of pain startling him awake. Dragos was descending the elevator cable toward him, swinging his rifle back around on the harness to his off-hand. Hashti was skirting the elevator shaft on the backside, using the shaft welds at each floor to slow her descent. He had little time, and while the pain wasn't a problem, he was badly injured now.

Rolling to his feet, he pushed the elevator doors open and climbed up into the adjoining floor. He knew he still had to be at least ten stories up, and the windows would still be a thick polycarbonate. He crashed through the first door in the hallway, hoping the occupants had paid extra for a balcony. Stumbling through the foyer to the living room, he turned away from the kitchen to the bedrooms.

The master bedroom had both a balcony and screaming occupants, his bloody visage startling them from their slumber. He could hear Dragos clear the door behind him, clearing the foyer, the bare feet belonging to Hashti lightly tapping across the tile kitchen floor. There was no choice now.

He ran to the balcony and rolled over the railing, trying to stay close to the building. The condensation catchers were designed to harvest water, not break the fall of an almost three-hundred pound man. He crashed through the first, but got lucky on the second. It bent backward, slowing his descent, but the ground was still a hundred and twenty feet below, the biological enclosure still visible in the darkness above.

Dragos shot through the glass bottom of the balcony, giving him a clear shot at Archie some twenty feet away. The shot went wide, cutting the condensation catcher just beside Archie as he rolled off. Suicide prevention countermeasures deployed down below, decades-old vinyl inflatables shot out from compartments around the base of the high rise.

They did little to break Archie's fall, but he didn't die, or lose consciousness. He rolled off the rapidly deflating vinyl airbag to the ground, everything inside feeling like broken glass. He rose anyway, limping down the street toward the tram tunnel, hoping to get lost in the crowd. As he hobbled away, a familiar hulking shape rose from the stairs.

"Lay down, or die, I don't care which," Marshal Rider said, drawing her sidearms.

Archie smiled through broken and bloody teeth, slowly raising his hands. "We should talk about this. We can figure something out."

Marshal Rider glanced up, trying to catch sight of her friends. As she did, the proximity alarm on her armor went off, Archie having quickly covered the distance between them. They tumbled down the stairs to the tram platform below, Marshal Rider holding her fire to avoid hitting bystanders. Archie latched on, trying to reach through the visor on her helm to her face.

She pressed the sidearm in her left hand to his thigh and pulled the trigger, blowing his leg off above the knee. She stood up on the platform, but Archie held on, the crowd around her running in every direction, giving her no clear field of fire. He grabbed her, hauling both her, the Aegis Suit and all, backward with only one leg. A passing tram beside the platform caught the back of her armor, sending them both cartwheeling to the side into a concrete pillar.

The damage to her armor was extreme, the holographic display inside winking out, the whispering in her earpiece going silent. Archie dragged himself over, breaking the cowl off her armor, throwing it aside by the visor. Blood poured down from his torn shoulder, raining down across her face. He pulled her out of the suit by her neck, rolling over on top her.

"Been a long time since I killed a cop," Archie growled, trying to get a good grip on her neck with both hands.

Marshal Rider jabbed her thumb into Archie's eye, and then rammed her fingers into an open wound on his neck. He rolled off to get away from her, howling in pain. She grabbed up a piece of her broken armor and struck him across the forehead, knocking him off his remaining foot. She could see Dragos and Hashti trying to get through the fleeing crowd, cries of panic drowning out all other sound.

Recovering one of her fallen sidearms, she dropped down, adopting a stance that would allow her to fire her weapon unassisted by her armor. As Archie rolled over to right himself, she pulled the trigger, emptying what remained in the magazine across his torso just below his arm. He fell backward, still trying to rise, but he couldn't take a breath. Both of Archie's lungs were collapsed now, the other not having healed yet.

Black crept in from the edges of Archie's vision as he tried to reach out, struggling to stay conscious. The last thing he saw was Marshal Rider grabbing a spare magazine from a compartment on her ruined armor, reloading in one fluid action, and shooting him again. Hashti and Dragos broke through the crowd moments later, slowing to a jog as Archie slowly sank to the ground, red foam slowly trickling out from between his lips.

"I do not remember him being so strong before," Dragos said, wrapping his arms around Marshal Rider.

"I'm okay, I'm okay... we got him," Marshal Rider said, almost unable to take a breath as Hashti wrapped her arms around them both.

"God, what a monster," Hashti said, inborn combat instincts fading, letting her feel fear again.

They lingered there together, keeping an eye on Archie as his corpse twitched, a large pool of blood spreading across the tram station platform. Marshal Rider took a moment to mourn her ruined armor, removing the star from the front and affixing it to her jumpsuit. Hashti patted her, trying to comfort her.

"My grandfather and my father took a few knocks, but no one in my family ever figured out how to break the suit. I know enough to do maintenance, but I can't fix this," Marshal Rider said, lowering her head.

"Your grandfather and father never fought a man like Archie. Never got hit by train," Dragos said, helping her gather up supplies and ammunition from the armor.

"That's true, they probably fought worse," she said, moving the holsters from her armor to the belt around her jumpsuit, setting them so she could use them to fire from the hip.

"I do not think so," Hashti said, kneeling down beside Archie, sniffing his wounds and peeling back his jacket.

His waist was ringed with a drug harness, new cybernetic implants protruding just above the base of his spine, underneath his belt. Dragos came over, holding his arm up beside sleek, state of the art, twitch implants. The custom alloy and tooling on both were identical. Marshal Rider approached, shouldering a satchel of heavy gear, frowning at what they'd discovered.

"We left Dr. Helmet with the Drones on the first lander. How could he have done this?" Hashti asked, shaking her head.

"They were supposed to be here, to help us with this," Marshal Rider said, looking down the darkened tram tunnel.

Dragos stood, shouldering his rifle. "Something is wrong. Dr. Helmet, why would he do this?" Dragos said, angrily bringing his cybernetic fist against the pillar.

"I don't know," Hashti said, looking sadly down at Archie.

"Let's go ask him," Marshal Rider said. She dropped down into the tram tunnel, with Hashti and Dragos bringing up the rear.

The trio walked the inactive train line along a concrete retaining wall for a mile, Hashti looking for signs of Drones. Eventually, they found an access point down to the maintenance level of the colony. Marshal Rider stopped pulling out the portable NAVCOM she'd salvaged from her armor. Hashti looked at some faint markings around the access point, then gave the metal lid a tug.

"It's open, Drones have their tribal markings up here," Hashti said, gazing down.

"This will take us to the lander, but it isn't the most direct route," Marshal Rider said, looking to Dragos.

The tunnel shook, a cloud of dust blowing past them as the lighting overhead flickered. Dragos crouched down, looking around warily through the scope on this rifle. Fumbling for someone, Marshal Rider found Dragos before finally laying hands on a flashlight in her satchel. They waited, but the lights did not come back on, the atmosphere around them ceasing to gently blow past them.

"It's beginning," Hashti said, squinting as Marshal Rider finally found a headlamp and switched it on.

"We could try to make it to the port, to a ship," Marshal Rider said, smiling sadly.

"I will not abandon Drones, they are noble creatures. If Dr. Helmet has done something bad, they should not suffer because we turned away," Dragos said, slinging his rifle and preparing to climb down.

He paused, about waist deep in the hole, looking up at Hashti and Marshal Rider. "You do not have to go. Give me the NAVCOM. You can go to the port, I will handle this. This is still Archie's mess. My problem."

"Not without me," Hashti said.

"Or me," Marshal Rider said, nodding.

They quickly made the descent, navigating the tangle of tunnels beneath the Mars Colony back toward the lander. Some of the way was well kept, obviously traveled regularly by Drones, while others looked to have been sealed off or gone unused for decades. Dragos led with his rifle, taking every corner as if there could be an enemy just on the other side.

His instincts were telling him that something was wrong, the feeling of dread growing stronger with each step. He couldn't shake the feeling he'd missed something along the way, and that Archie's ambitions were only part of a bigger puzzle. Archie was cunning, but he would have needed help beyond just the money and influence Cerise brought to the table. He would have needed technical expertise.

The entrance to the lander was quiet, and unguarded. Marshal Rider had to double check that they'd arrived, the underground hanger being something different from the bow of ship. The back half of the enormous vessel was obscured by gantries and maintenance cranes, engineering connected to the old Martian Grid. The access ports to the ship, and ramp to the enormous cargo hold were both open, and appeared to have been for some time.

"I see no Drones. None have passed by here for hours," Hashti reported, sniffing the air.

"Okay, how do we want to play this?" Marshal Rider said, looking across the landing field from the access tunnel.

"We go in heavy, he knows we know. That what you mean?" Dragos asked.

"Yes, exactly. Should we just walk up casually, like we're returning from a successful hunt to report to our Drone allies?"

Dragos thought for a moment, inspecting the exterior of the ship through the scope of his rifle. "The only quiet way in, is back through engineering. Marshal Rider and I, we could go in, say Hashti is dead or we got separated. Check it out," Dragos said, rubbing his tired eyes.

"While I take the long way around? It'll take me a bit to get around to those tunnels, work my way back through engineering. I don't even know how long," Hashti said, worriedly.

"Dragos is right, we need an ace if we're going in there," Marshal Rider said, patting Hashti.

"Okay, wait a few minutes, then go in. I'll try to hurry," Hashti said, sprinting back down the access tunnel.

They waited for ten minutes before heading toward the crew access port, and ascending the stairs to the lander. It was quiet inside, the halls of the crew compartment clean and swept. The lander was like a museum of old space travel technology, the ship having been built more than a century previous. Marshal Rider ran her hand along the wall as she walked beside Dragos, hesitating for a moment.

"What is it?" Dragos said, looking around nervously.

"I'm scared," Marshal Rider said, lowering her head.

"Marliese, I am also afraid. I understand," Dragos said, offering her his hand.

She took it, standing in the transfer tube between crew compartments for a few moments, gathering her nerve. "What if we die here and no one knows what we did? What if a ship comes in a few months and finds our frozen corpses, and no one knows why this happened?"

Dragos let out a long slow breath. "Vance Uroboros will come, and he will know. He will tell others what we did. This will not be forgotten."

"Sounds like you admire this guy."

"I respect that he keeps his word. Kale told me that Vance would not be far behind. That I needed only to limit the damage Archie could do. We did our best," Dragos said, giving Marliese's hand a squeeze.

"Then why are you afraid?"

"I came here alone, hoping to do what was necessary with nothing to lose. I failed to do that, too. You and Hashti are my friends now," Dragos said, embracing Marshal Rider.

She hugged him back.

The ship powered up, engines coming online, dusty instrument panels lighting up as exterior hatches and cargo ramps closed.

"I hope Hashti had enough time to get aboard," Marshal Rider said, hands on her sidearms.

Dragos nodded, walking toward the communal area they'd met Avery One in before. As they entered the chamber they found it to be brighter than during their last visit. Every view screen was on, showing the ensuing chaos as it unfolded around the colony. The room was filled with Drones, each standing around Avery One, who stood in the center. All were utterly motionless.

"I do not see him," Dragos whispered, looking around.

"A large view screen in the center of the far wall shifted from rioting in the mining sectors to Dr. Helmet, sitting in what looked like the bridge of the ship. There were many custom devices plugged into the various crew stations behind him, his hands folded in front of him. He looked as he did before, white hair and lab coat, but a serene and peaceful expression dominated his face.

"I'm glad you made it back. I'd hoped that you wouldn't have been able to kill Archie, but I'm relieved you survived," Dr. Helmet said, smiling.

"Thank you, Dr. Helmet. It is too bad Hashti didn't make it. We were separated," Marshal Rider said, looking at the Drones.

"Gorshteyn, call me Gorshteyn. I had hoped that Archie would be alive to see the death of the colony and all his posterity. He'd gone to such trouble to bring them all here, even some against their will. We'd been hunting them for months on Earth, so using Cerise to coax him into coming to Mars wasn't a stretch," Dr. Helmet said, setting a tea set down on the console in front of him.

"Gorshteyn, what have you done?" Dragos said, angrily.

"It wasn't just the replica you saw die at the tram station that was killing Archie's offspring. A number of my replica brothers and I have been working out our vengeance since Archie, Kaspersky, and Svetovid conspired to have the original Gorshteyn murdered," Dr. Helmet said, looking through a small wooden box of tea bags.

"If Archie is as old as you claim, that would be a lot of people," Marshal Rider said, giving one of the Drones a shake.

"Oh, the Drones can hear you, they just can't move. I implanted myself with a Factory voice node. It allows me to sound like the training system that gave each of them their functions. The resonance of that voice keeps them obedient."

"Factory what?" Dragos said, looking puzzled.

"And no, it isn't as many people as you would think. Archie only began trying to have a posterity in the last couple of decades. I think he sensed the arrangement he'd struck to become immortal was coming to an end. Kaspersky, and Svetovid each had plans for their posterity as well, but I suspect Kale has found a way to ruin all that by now," Dr. Madmar said, smiling peacefully.

"How did you lie, in front of Hashti and all these Drones? Drones can sense when people lie, even good liars. Avery One and Hashti are both psychics for God's sake," Marshal Rider said, walking down to see if Avery One was okay.

"The original Dr. Gorshteyn Helmet was on the MDC Project that developed The Factory, Drones, and Metasapients. He understood how their talents work, and consequently, so do I. Using pain to interrogate me helped, as it masks many of the biological responses Drones use to detect falsehoods."

Marshal Rider frowned, seeing Avery One's frantic expression, her eyes turning to look at her from a frozen face. "Why kill the Mars Colony? There are hundreds of thousands of—"

Dr. Helmet laughed, spilling tea on his lab coat. "Innocent people? The only Martian Colony Official that wasn't corrupt is here in the lander, safe and sound. As are all the Drones, and the Metasapient population has already made arrangements to survive if something happened to the colony."

"There are thousands of miners, technicians, and the crews of transports as well, beyond just the prison population." Marshal Rider said, incensed.

"They willingly gave their consent for Archie to take command, fostering a system that favored the corrupt. They are as guilty of his crimes as he is, and should pay alongside him. My only regret is that you were able to kill him, and he won't live to see his kingdom die. Did you know Kaspersky not only stole the original Dr. Gorshteyn Helmet's work, but destroyed a great deal of it as well?" Dr. Helmet said, the sweetness in his voice draining away.

"We don't know anything about what happened on Earth. Tell us these things," Dragos said, calmly.

"Archie was the one that made the arrangements. It was his FLF contacts that brought that tainted shipment. When Cerise and I arrived, there were horrors that had been unleashed, things that I could not abide. The whole town nearby had been infected. Killing everyone was hard, but it got easier with each kill, each body we collected for disposal."

Dr. Helmet paused, taking a sip of his tea. Marshal Rider looked through her bag, pulled out a bottle of water, and pressed it to Avery One's parched lips. Dragos held his vigil, hoping Hashti had found a way through.

"Oh, where was I? Yes. If you knew the horror Archie and his friends planned to inflict on humanity, you'd think the Martian Colony a small price to pay to see him suffer, and everything he counted as his posterity destroyed," Dr. Helmet said, his calm returning.

"What about Enyo? The Ares AI? They are not innocents?" Dragos asked, trying to keep him talking.

"We'd hoped to avoid that. When it became clear that Archie would likely succeed, we altered our plan slightly. Originally, we were going to infect Enyo with nanoid constructs given a very particular microbial intelligence. We weren't going to alter her programming, just use her to sequester the Ares AI's influence over the colony."

"The containment device, at the tram yard, you made that?" Dragos said, taking a wild guess.

Dr. Helmet laughed, nodding. "Indeed. It wasn't meant to kill her, but give her the inability to interact with the Ares AI via his quantum computing unit. I needed for him to believe the colony had ceased to exist by removing the observer from his observer-dependent reality. Enyo doing the same, and dying with her father was an unforeseen side effect."

"You didn't care, because the outcome would be the same. The colony would die," Marshal Rider said, laying Avery One down so she could rest, in spite of being immobilized.

"I cared very much. Truth be told, that part of the plan was the most distasteful. I wished we could have prevented Archie from killing the Ares

AI. We underestimated Archie's capacity for violence and his ambition." Dr. Helmet paused and resumed sipping his tea.

"Most people do," Dragos lamented.

"There is a wrinkle in all of this. I can't seem to locate Cerise or Golgotha, but I'm sure they have their own ways of riding out the death of the colony," Dr. Helmet said, checking a data slate.

Marshal Rider looked around at the view screens. There were portions of the colony that appeared normal, the people there with no idea the colony was in turmoil. In other places, there were riots, and turf wars depending on which side of the fence was being captured. The power vacuum had already been felt in the prison, news of Archie's death somehow already having reached the cellblocks.

"The port is still open, some may escape," Dragos said, hands resting easy on his rifle slung in front of him.

"It's a consideration. Even without the Ares AI sanctioning flights, someone could get heavy tools and cut docking clamps to free a ship. Fortunately, I've got this army of loyal Drones to go up and deal with that problem for me. Oh, and I can have them kill you, if you try anything funny," Dr. Helmet warned, pouring himself more tea.

"What would we do? There is nowhere to go, yes?" Dragos said, holding his hands out as his sides.

"Oh, I wouldn't say that. The Martian Colony has secrets built on top of secrets. There were many countermeasures built after the uprising decades ago, to protect the council of wardens. A handful of corrupt bureaucrats, and Cerise as well, will probably survive in their shelters and independently maintained facilities."

"Who is Golgotha?" Marshal Rider said, walking over to stand beside Dragos.

"She's the alien being that started this whole mess in the first place, granting the Cabal their abilities. Like her, I believe extreme measures are required to secure the future. She had the Cabal build a fleet of ships to wipe out her entire race before they could destroy humanity, her, her spouse, and their children. She's a remarkable creature for sure, and her being here wasn't something I'd expected."

"What did you expect?" Dragos asked, getting impatient for Hashti to arrive.

"I suspected she would come with Vance Uroboros, aboard something the Cabal calls 'The Dragon'. I think it was the ship she used to come to Earth in the first place. Cerise and I were both surprised to learn she'd tagged along on board our ship," Dr. Helmet said, replacing his cup on the tea set.

"Why did you help me? Help Avery One?" Dragos asked.

"I didn't specifically help Avery One. That was the original Dr. Gorshteyn I suspect. He was a good and kind man, and probably helped her because it was the right thing to do. I helped you for the same reason. Why, do you suspect that these gifts were somehow part of my plan?"

Dragos frowned. "You tell me."

"Cerise certainly suspected something. That's why she put the tracker on you I think, not because she didn't trust you… but because she didn't trust me. I'd been feeding her information that she'd been taking to Archie for months. I'd promised to find a way to restore her ability to have children, so she was susceptible to manipulation, but still a very smart lady."

"So, arm is good?" Dragos said, watching something black slip down from the ceiling behind Dr. Helmet.

"Oh, the very best, Mr. Dalca. We appreciate your assistance in this matter, even if you didn't do exactly as we'd hoped. It seemed the least we could—"

A long black hand wrapped around Dr. Helmet's face, yanking him away from the camera capturing his broadcast. It was not the smooth and feminine fingers of Hashti, but something entirely alien, large, and terrifying moving about far enough from the camera to be out of focus. There was an audible pop that came across on the intercom, allowing the Drones to move once more.

"Gah, I was standing there so long, I peed myself," Athos One announced, extremely annoyed.

"Um, what was that?" Marshal Rider said, pointing up to view screen, just before it went dark.

Avery One sat up, rubbing her eyes. "I do not know. Thank you for the water."

The ship trembled, an automated message playing over the intercom warning the crew that flight protocols were being engaged. The engines then powered down, another automated warning coming over the intercom that the ship had docked.

"Why would it cycle the ship? That thing up there?" Marshal Rider asked.

The blast doors to the bridge opened, allowing a slender woman swathed in thick robes exit. Her face was covered by a veil, but she had fierce and unearthly eyes rimmed with marbled black flesh. She dragged Dr. Helmet along behind her, unconscious and gagged with one of his own socks. There was blood on his throat, but no visible wound. She opened her free hand, letting the remains of a crushed throat module fall to the floor.

"Golgotha," Marshal Rider said, wide-eyed.

She nodded. "Your friend is trapped in the engines. They sealed her in when Gorshteyn turned them on to pressurize the ship," Golgotha said, in perfect English.

Several Drones dashed over to free Hashti, Dragos following close behind to help. Marshal Rider remained, hands on her sidearms. Avery One came up beside her, claws out.

"What do you want?" Avery One asked, taking note that Dr. Helmet still was still alive.

"I need a ride. I can fly the lander, but I need it uncoupled from the old Martian Network," Golgotha said, letting the doctor flop to the floor.

"Why this ship?" Marshal Rider asked.

"I need a big ship. This one is big."

"Where are we going?" Avery One asked, trying to read the strange creature.

"To C.O.N. and my partner. I have business there," Golgotha replied.

"What if we say no?" Marshal Rider replied.

Golgotha reached up and touched the veil over her face, her strange red eyes twitching back and forth. Marshal Rider interpreted this as the creature stopping to ponder the question, but she couldn't be sure. Golgotha gestured to the view screens arrayed around them, some showing normalcy around the colony, others grim captures of chaos.

"Your home is in danger. The King has been slain," Golgotha said, her voice taking a strange metallic tone.

Marshal Rider nodded. "Yes, in a manner of speaking."

Golgotha clasped her hands together. "I know where there is another King."

CHAPTER 15

**"THE GRAVE", GALACTIC BATTLEFIELD CGG RECORD 001 –
DARK SIDE OF JUPITER**

August 6th, 2200

Ezra's War Journal, Part 13 –

It felt like sleeping, not a full night's rest where you dream, but a short nap. I woke up laying on top of Taylor, cross-ways, belly to belly. She sat up, looking around and grinning widely. No one else was awake, in spite of their enhanced natures, the rest of the Cabal was still asleep on the floor of the alien ship. The liquid had drained away, leaving a thin clear sheen on everything.

"Why are we awake?" Taylor asked.

"I don't know. Something about the voyage was different for us," I said, picking myself up and going over to check on Silverstein.

He appeared as a young man, about Taylor's age I would guess. He had a flushed and healthy look to him, like I'd never seen before. He always had this strange weight to him, even while he was asleep, his mind always trying to work things out. The way he looked now, he seemed weightless, unfettered by any care or worry.

Taylor placed her hand on him, closing her eyes. "He's different some-how, but I'm not sure. I'm drawing back all my mojo off of him, just in case."

"Mojo?" I asked.

Taylor looked embarrassed. "When I use my abilities to help some-one, some part of me remains. Usually, I pull myself back, but with Kale and Silverstein, I left that 'influence' as a countermeasure if they were in trouble again."

"And, Truman," I said, nodding.

"He shouldn't have woken up on his own I guess, but I think I was able to act as a bridge for the damaged parts of his brain. I felt bad at first, like I disturbed his peace, or lengthened his suffering. After talking to Marjorie a little bit, I think it was a good thing," Taylor said, smoothing Silverstein's hair.

The air in the room didn't move the same, and I couldn't figure out why until I looked directly up toward the domed ceiling. There, suspended in freaky alien pod structures, were a collection of creatures, all about the size of a human child. The pods were translucent, slowly growing dark toward the bottom and tops, a shadow of what was within barely visible.

"I think I know what's different," I said, pointing up.

"The ship extracted all the symbiont organisms," Taylor said, walking over to the body bag used to transport Kaspersky's remains.

She picked it up, but there was nothing inside. The ship shuddered, like it had come into contact with something else. There was no sound. I couldn't hear anything but the quiet biomechanical processes my ears had already grown accustomed to. We must still have been in space.

The wall opposite where we boarded originally grew brighter, before splitting into a corridor. On the other side I could see Dragos, a very lovely female Ichthyic-type Metasapient, and a Martian Marshal, guns at her hips.

"Dragos! You're all right!" Taylor said, raising a hand in greeting.

"Mostly," he said, holding up a cybernetic replacement hand in greeting.

"So we made it? We're on Mars?" I asked, stepping over slumbering members of the Cabal to get to them.

"No, we brought the first Mars lander to you, out here. We're sitting in the shadow of Jupiter. Golgotha had her own plan it seems," Dragos explained.

"Who are your friends?" Taylor asked.

"Taylor and Ezra One, meet Hashti, and this is Marshal Rider. Unconscious man there, is Silverstein, also known as Vance Uroboros," Dragos said, pointing.

Golgotha came into the room from behind them, her strange red eyes turning toward the ceiling. She was covered in silken and linen robes, veils, and other garments designed to hide her physique and countenance. It was hard to get a feel for her, but she clasped her long hands together, seeing what I assumed were her children.

"When will Silverstein wake up?" I asked.

Golgotha turned and looked at me, speaking with a strangely metallic voice. "Soon, be at peace, little brother."

"Brother?" I said, not understanding.

"Indeed, the Shwalishi Vessel imparted to me the contrived nature of your make. You are as we are, made for a purpose by others," Golgotha explained.

"That's her name? Shwalishi?" Taylor asked.

"There is no direct translation in your language, so I gave her a name. Please, take care of her after we are gone," Golgotha said.

"She can't go with you… to wherever?" I asked.

"No, she has spent too long adapting to your Earth and solar system. I do not think she would desire to leave even if she could. She claimed Ouroboru as her controller shortly after we landed," Golgotha explained.

"Why is that?" Taylor asked.

"Because he is kind. He told the warriors of his village to spare her long ago. While I suffered a malady of the mind and hid, Ouroboru visited her in a hidden place. He kept her safe for the duration of his arrangement with us. She loves Ouroboru like a sibling."

"Aww," Taylor cooed, patting the floor of the ship.

"Are you taking the lander?" I asked.

"No, it belongs to your people, and you will need it to give Mars a new king," Golgotha said, sounding almost sad.

"What is she talking about?" I said looking at Dragos.

Dragos frowned. "I failed to stop Archie. The Ares AI is gone, and Enyo, too."

Taylor just sat down, a look of shock crossing her face. I knelt down beside her, putting my hand on her back. She wept quietly, like I'd only seen when we thought Silverstein was dead.

"The Ares AI was her father, Enyo a sister," I said, seeing everyone's baffled reaction to Taylor's sorrow.

"Where is Archie now?" I said, already planning how he would die.

"The three of us hunted him down, and after an extended confrontation, I killed him. His remains are already in the care of Golgotha's partner," Marshal Rider said.

When Avery One and Athos One came up behind them, I could scarcely believe it. They looked the same, even decades later, except that Avery One had cybernetic implants across her chest. The rest of the Martian Tribehome was with them as well. I would discover later that the first Mars Landers had been their home for decades.

We exchanged greetings and salutations in our own wordless way, Avery One hugging me. It was a happy moment for me that she had survived somehow. Athos One told me everything that had happened in a very short conversation, including all that Dr. Helmet had done. From the moment I met one of this replicas, I didn't trust anything they said.

His replicas had taken direction from Madmar, and they were dangerous. I resolved that if any of Dr. Helmet's replicas survived, they'd have to be dealt with somehow. The cost to the Martian Colony would be extreme if something wasn't done about the loss of the Ares AI.

"They are moving C.O.N. from the eclipse-class cruiser he was on to the Martian Lander. He has agreed to take on facility maintenance of the Mars Colony. I hope we are not too late," Marshal Rider said, nodding to Golgotha.

"How many lives have already been lost?" Taylor asked, composing herself.

Marshal Rider just made a pained expression, shaking her head.

I mourned the terrible loss of life. I could see that it weighed heavily on Marshal Rider. While everyone was having reunions and discussions about what to do next, I could tell something was wrong. She was a woman between worlds, and clearly conflicted about everything, including the friendly way Dragos and Hashti spoke to one another.

"Hey, do you still have your father's Aegis Suit?" I asked, approaching her.

She smiled sadly. "It was badly damaged fighting with Archie. It got clipped by the afternoon tram while we were fighting on the platform."

I likened it to losing your Tribehome, something that belonged to your family, and irreplaceable. Only in this case, that wasn't exactly true. "I need to show you something," I said, beckoning.

We walked toward the other end of the Shwalishi craft, rounding a slight corner to our original boarding point. The Aegis Suit I'd piloted onto the craft earlier powered up at our approach. Marshal Rider's face was a mixture of wonder and disbelief.

"How?" She asked.

"It was made for your father long ago, but it was never delivered. It was stolen by a man named Kaspersky, an associate of Archie. It helped us confront Archie's allies on Earth, asking only that it be brought to Mars in return," I said, feeling glad alongside her.

"I don't know what to say," she said, stepping into the armor.

It closed around her, the voice of the onboard AI saying something to her I could only barely make out. She plugged in the NAVCOM unit containing her service record from her other suit of armor. She synced the records of her grandfather, and father with her own in the Aegis Suit recovery systems.

"Your grandmother, and grandfather, would be so proud, and had he lived, so would your father," I could faintly hear Aegis AI say.

The visor on the cowl went up, revealing Marshal Rider's face, tears forming in the corners of her eyes. The holographic display was just text, a letter from her grandmother to her father, telling him why she built the suit. I could see the name Marliese, clearly a reference to the current Marshal Rider. It was a thing I would have to tell Taylor about later.

"The suit has a full report about how it arrived. Eamon and Kale, they made this happen, and you, and Silverstein and Taylor. You guys don't even know me, and you did this for me," Marshal Rider said, holding up one of her gauntlet clad hands, testing the new flex monitor across the top.

"If Silverstein was awake, he'd have something flowery to say. So much that has gone wrong, it's nice to see something good come from all this," I said, turning to rejoin the others.

As we approached the congregation in the main room, the collective membership of the Cabal was waking up, Silverstein regaining his feet. Taylor hugged him, his face immediately growing concerned at how upset she obviously was. The rest of the Cabal commenced their complaining, issuing demands, and being a general nuisance.

"Who are these people?" Marshal Rider asked.

"They are associates of Silverstein and Archie, the non-militant membership of their organization," I explained.

"Oh, Golgotha wants them on her ship. EXIT FOR THE LANDER IN AN ORDERLY FASHION, IN A SINGLE FILE LINE!" Marshal Rider bellowed, deploying a long tactical baton, startling everyone.

They protested, but Marshal Rider was terrifying when she wanted to be, quickly establishing order with only a stern look. She strode past Silverstein giving a nod as they exited to the lander. Dragos and Hashti broke into wide smiles at seeing her back in armor, while the rest of the Martian Tribe went back to the lander as well. It was a strange threshold to cross, purely mechanical airlock meeting with biomechanical causeway.

"Zvezda… Golgotha, I…" Silverstein began, stopping to look curiously at his hands.

"Ouroboru, thank you, for bringing my children to me," she said, her eerie metallic voice sounding uncharacteristically warm.

"What happens now?" Silverstein said, swallowing nervously.

"I'm giving you this ship, and I'm taking the rest of the Cabal with me, all of them," she said, gesturing to small biomechanical harvesters hovering in overhead.

"Why?" Silverstein said, somewhat upset.

"You are the only surviving participant of our arrangement that was not wholly corrupt. The others have done enough harm, having perpetrated terrible crimes against your people. They will live out the remainder of their lives with us, where they can do no further harm," Golgotha said.

"There are a few I could not gather to make the journey. Drusael, and a handful of others," Silverstein said, somewhat downcast.

"I've arranged for Mr. Dalca and his friend Hashti to deal with them. Your obligation ends here, Ouroboru, be free," Golgotha said, placing a thin hand on Silverstein's shoulder.

"What will happen to me? Will I live a regular lifespan now?" Silverstein asked, turning to look at Taylor.

"I do not know what the prolonged exposure to my children did to you. I doubt your life, whatever remains of it, will be normal by human standards. We've done our best to heal you, and give you every opportunity to have what you never could before," Golgotha said.

"I heard something about Mars when I woke up. How will I put everything right? Earth is in shambles because of all this," Silverstein said worriedly.

"Humanity bears a burden of its own, having allowed the Cabal to direct its destiny for so long. You have placed many sentinels and protectors out among them, individuals who will likely continue to fight for the people of your world. Place your faith in them," Golgotha said, heading back toward the lander.

"I will," Silverstein said, looking thoughtfully at Taylor.

We resolved to return to Mars, short term, so that we could help give the colony stability. It was something we already knew something about, and Taylor was anxious to spend some time with C.O.N., and I with the Martian Tribehome. It was a totally bizarre feeling for me, actually wanting to go Mars for any reason.

Marshal Rider would return to Mars, to assume her duties once more, the new Aegis Suit giving her a greater sense of the legacy that had been left to her. She knew that lawlessness would be a problem, with Mars probably lacking a central authority for months. I looked forward to knocking some heads, and carving out a safer place for my brother and sister drones.

Dragos and Hashti said that they would return to Mars to find someone named Cerise, then move on back to Earth, eventually. Dragos was anxious to return when he heard the news about Truman and his sister Tullia. He and Hashti seemed like they were close. While I'd never met a Metasapient like her before, she reminded me of Chelsea Six.

I hoped everyone back home was all right.

I was ushered past the Martian Lander once we went inside, my fellow drones leading me past where they were building a temporary sentience core. On the other side of the chamber was an airlock leading to Golgotha's ship. Biomechanical contraptions hovered overhead, transporting her children aboard.

"The Objector would like to speak to you," Avery One said, pointing toward the interior of what looked like another much larger version of the Shwalishi craft.

Inside was a long alien creature, looking probably as they did in their natural state. He was large, like an industrial lifting unit, his torso ringed by four arms, two broad for heavy lifting, and two smaller for fine manipulations. He had a sleek black body sporting several heavy legs to support his mass. His face was a mass of long tendrils that ringed his red eyes. His body was a biomechanical array of strange contraptions and symbiotic organisms. No doubt, he was made, or perhaps born for war.

"You are Ouroboru's protector?" he said, in perfect English.

"You speak very well. Yes, I intend to continue to travel with my friends, protect them if I can," I said, looking around at the various biomechanical interfaces arrayed around the central chamber.

"I speak three-thousand and forty-two of Earth's languages. I want to be able to speak to my children when they are old enough."

"What can I do for you?" I asked, wondering why I had alone been allowed to visit the ship.

"My partner says you are not well. She thinks it will be hard for you to continue to protect Ouroboru. It seems an ill reward for being so instrumental in making sure our children returned to us. Please, let us help you," he said, gesturing to a rising platform, where two open slots revealed themselves.

"What do I do?" I asked, approaching the strange device.

"Put your arms inside, I will do the rest."

I had little to lose, and no reason to believe they meant me any harm. As my hands slid in, I could feel my blood cycling out of my body, replaced by something else, and then my own blood being returned to me. I could feel my claws grow dense, harder than steel, and sharp, down to a monomolecular edge. My vision seemed to improve, along with my other senses. I wasn't as keen as Brook, but much better than I'd ever been.

The machine released my arms, the weakness I felt from my diabetic condition completely gone. "Thank you," I said, letting my marvelous new claws extend so I could see them.

"Protect my friend, Ezra One. Ouroboru likely made many enemies while he was helping us," the Objector said, nodding his huge head toward me.

"I will."

END BOOK 6

www.ingramcontent.com/pod-product-compliance
Lightning Source LLC
Chambersburg PA
CBHW071237260626
47159CB00005BA/1768